He kn[illegible] at they m[illegible]

Esme Laurent is a con artist. An accomplished liar. A world-class thief. And probably the most beautiful and intriguing woman that Tyler Barrett has ever met. Sure, he has to arrest her at their first meeting, and she absolutely hates him, but...well, he has a job to do. And Tyler always gets the job done.

Turns out, she is the new job.

The people in charge want to use Esme to bring down a very dangerous criminal operation. And in order to do that, Esme has to stay in the land of the living. She needs protection, she needs a new identity, and she needs to disappear, immediately. Because Esme has more than a bit of power, she makes her own deal...her protection needs to come in the ever-so-gorgeous, ever-so-dangerous, and ever-so-law-abiding form of U.S. Marshal Tyler Barrett.

They'll disappear into Small Town, USA. And they'll pretend to be newlyweds who just can't keep their hands off each other.

No, absolutely, this cannot be happening. But no matter how much Tyler protests, the new job is, in fact, happening. He's being sent to Asylum, Alabama, with the delectable Esme. He's supposed to be her husband—a role that will give him twenty-four, seven access in order to protect her. He needs that access in order to make sure that Esme doesn't run from the authorities and that she stays alive. But what Tyler doesn't count on is the consuming desire he feels for a woman who should be off-limits.

She'll test every limit that he has...

Esme doesn't expect her attraction to the rule-following Tyler. He's big, he's buttoned-down, and he's absolutely... delicious. She also suspects that he may be carefully controlling a wild side—one that she would love to see erupt. Oh, if only.

When danger comes calling, Tyler is more than ready to handle any threat. Who knew that falling for the good guy could be so tempting? And so very...heart-breaking. Because there was no way a guy like Tyler would want to stay around once they stop pretending. Everyone knows the bad girl never gets to keep the good guy, especially when she's still working a very long con.

Author's Note: Are you in the mood for a strong hero who makes "protecting and defending" his life code? Tyler is big, fierce, and more than ready to step into the line of fire in order to protect his charge. He's also falling fast under the spell of a woman he should not trust. Everything with Esme is just pretend...everything, except the desire they feel for each other. And the very, very real danger that stalks her. A danger that may wind up costing Tyler more than he ever expected. WHEN HE PROTECTS, Tyler gives his all, and when he loves...he will fight like hell for the woman who stole his heart.

When He Protects

A Protector and Defender Romance

Cynthia Eden

HOCUS POCUS PUBLISHING INC

This book is a work of fiction. Any similarities to real people, places, or events are not intentional and are purely the result of coincidence. The characters, places, and events in this story are fictional.

Published by Hocus Pocus Publishing, Inc.

If you have any problems, comments, or questions about this publication, please contact info@hocuspocuspublishing.com.

For all the romance readers out there—thank you. Read hard.
Be happy.

Chapter One

"Sometimes, you meet someone…and you know right away that the person is trouble."

Tyler Barrett stiffened when he heard the low, sultry voice. He'd been doing a security sweep at the overpriced party. No one should have been able to sneak up behind him because he knew to keep his guard up but…

He turned slowly and found a gorgeous brunette beaming up at him. Matching dimples flashed in her cheeks, and her lush lips—painted a deep, tempting and slick red—had curved into a smile. Her dark eyes reflected the smile even as she extended her hand toward him. A sparkling emerald flashed around her index finger and a blood-red ruby gleamed on her ring finger.

"What makes you think I'm trouble?" Tyler heard himself ask even as he automatically took her hand. His much bigger fingers swallowed hers. But he was careful not to use too much strength.

He was playing a role that night. Wearing the expensive tux. Acting like he was drinking the fizzing champagne.

And attempting to fit into the land of the wealthy and privileged as he hunted his prey.

"You have this wonderfully intense vibe happening," the woman told him. When she tilted her head, her hair slid over her shoulder. A body-hugging black dress poured over her curves. A dress with a daring slit that crept up ever-so-high on her right thigh.

Sexy.

Laughter came from her. Teasing and husky. "See something you like?"

And, shit, he'd just been caught staring at her legs. Gorgeous legs. She wore two-inch black heels that made her appear a bit taller, but he figured his mystery lady was probably around five-foot-six without them.

His gaze came back to her face. What a face it was. High cheekbones. Wide, intelligent eyes that somehow seemed extra mysterious. Maybe it was the dark shadow around them. Maybe it was her insanely long lashes. Whatever.

Women like her don't usually approach men like me.

And, if it had been a typical situation, she wouldn't be coming to his side that night. She'd probably be running from him. Despite his current appearance, he did not belong in this world. But this night was different. He was working undercover.

"I'm sure men tell you all the time that they *like* everything about you," Tyler murmured.

Her laughter trickled out again. It was as sexy as the rest of her. Dammit.

Tyler released her hand. He needed to get back to studying the—

"I don't think I've seen you before at the usual round of parties. How do you know Jorlan?"

Their host. Jorlan Rodgers. Explorer extraordinaire. The billionaire spent plenty of time traipsing across the world. And when he came back from those traipses? He always had special trinkets with him. Expensive treasures that he liked to showcase at his private events. And sometimes offer in auctions to the highest bidder.

"We went to boarding school together," Tyler said.

She blinked. "Really?" The woman edged closer to him. "You're really going to tell me that you're some country club, boarding school boy?" A shake of her head. "I would have pegged you for something else entirely."

"And just what would that be?"

Her dark stare swept over him. "Muscles for days," she sighed. "So impressive."

He frowned.

She cleared her throat. "Well, if I had to guess—and this is, of course, purely a guess—because I have no personal knowledge of you. I just walked in, saw your sexy self and thought I'd say hello. Introducing yourself is such a nice, courteous thing to do."

His frown deepened. She hadn't *actually* introduced herself to him. He didn't know the mystery lady's name.

"But guessing, I wouldn't say you were a kid who'd grown up with a trust fund. You don't have that money-to-burn-and-no-shits-to-give vibe about you."

Tyler let his brows rise. "And what vibe do I have?"

Her stare was considering. "A dangerous one. A take-no-prisoners vibe. Like you can't stand for bullshit. Like the people here are boring you out of your mind and you cannot wait to escape them."

He made sure to lock down his expression.

She began to twirl a lock of hair. All casual-like. "You look like you're on the job. Studying everyone you see a little too intently. Marking each person the way you would a suspect."

Sonofa—

"So, instead of saying you're a trust fund baby, when I look at you, I see a cop."

He stared back at her.

"Not a beat cop. I say...maybe a Fed. Not CIA." Very definite. "You're rather a bit too big and bold for that crew. They tend to favor agents who don't stick out too much. And you...you certainly stick out." Her gaze swept him. "In a good way. At least in my humble opinion." A delicate clearing of her throat. "I definitely think you're working undercover."

Okay. So he'd just been made by a bored socialite. Not the highlight of his career. "That's funny." Tyler reached up and tugged on his collar—

Her hand flew out and caught his. Her body brushed against him, and the sweet, tempting scent of vanilla curled around him. "That's one of your giveaways," she quietly informed him. "You can't keep tugging on the tux's collar like you're choking and uncomfortable. Instead, you have to act like you've worn this thing a million times. Don't want to arouse suspicion, do you?"

He could hear the drumming of his heartbeat. The heat of her touch pulsed through his whole body and blasted him with a sudden, shocking wave of lust. Sure, he'd thought she was sexy at first glance. Who the hell wouldn't? But...

The lust that Tyler felt was like an electric charge to his system. Heating and burning and—

"Be careful," she warned him, "or you'll blow your cover. Because you're either a Fed...or maybe you're a bad guy."

The drumming of his heartbeat got even louder. Too loud. "Why would you think I was the bad guy?"

Her long lashes flickered. Then the wide smile of hers flashed again. Disarming dimples. "Surely, you've heard the stories on the news. There have been a string of robberies at high-priced events like this one." She didn't let go of his hand. "Granted, the attendees tried to keep things quiet. Not like the ultra-wealthy want to spread word that they were attacked and basically held hostage and forced to give up their valuables—"

The doors to the ballroom—because, sure, why the hell not? Jorlan had a ballroom in his Miami beachfront mansion—came crashing open before she could finish her sentence. Screams filled the air as six individuals all wearing black burst inside. Masks covered their faces, and their bodies were shielded by bulky black jackets and pants.

"Freeze!" A man's voice. The guy in the front. A guy holding a very large, black gun. "No one make a move, and you won't get hurt!"

A gasp came from the gorgeous woman with Tyler. "In armed robberies," she finished in a whisper as her head jerked toward the masked intruders. "Just like this one."

Tyler automatically grabbed her and shoved her behind his much bigger body.

And that movement caught the eye of the creep who was clearly the leader. "I said *freeze!*" he bellowed. He rushed straight toward Tyler and aimed the gun at his chest. "Guess you just don't hear well, do you, buddy? Will a bullet to the chest teach you how to hear better?"

Tyler didn't really see how it possibly could. Before he could tell the dumbass with the weapon that very thing—

"No!" Tyler's mystery brunette jumped in front of him. "Don't shoot him! He's a Fed!"

Sonofabitch.

First, he didn't need her to protect him. His job was to protect the civilians at the party. And second...

Way to blow my cover to hell and back. Thanks so much for that.

"A Fed?" the man in the mask bit out. "You shitting me?"

"I wouldn't shit a man with a gun pointed at me," she replied with a delicate sniff. "My boyfriend is a Fed."

When in the holy hell had he become her boyfriend?

"And you don't want to shoot a Fed. Robbery is one thing. Killing a federal agent is another beast." She faced off with the gunman. "He won't be trouble. Especially not if you, uh, lock us up somewhere. Just get us out of here." She pointed to the right. Toward a nearby door. The rings on her hand gleamed beneath the light. "Lock us in there, and I'll make sure my boyfriend is kept in check."

Kept in check? He'd never been *kept in check* by anyone a day in his life. The very idea was insulting.

But the man in the mask was nodding even as the other wealthy people in their fancy gowns and tuxes were shuddering with fear.

Bodyguards should have been outside to protect these people. Security had been hired by the host. So what in the hell had gone wrong?

Inside job. Wasn't that what he'd suspected? And there had been one private security agency that had been used in several of the previous attacks. *The same agency that is working the door tonight.* Like that wasn't a screaming red flag of guilt.

But he would deal with that agency soon enough. For the moment, his attention was on the prick with the gun. The prick who bobbed his masked head and proclaimed,

"Yeah, yeah, we'll lock his ass up! His ass and your sexy ass."

A growl broke from Tyler.

"He doesn't like it when people talk about my ass," the woman said with a shrug.

"Too fucking bad." Then the masked man grabbed her hand.

Tyler surged forward.

"It's all right!" she cried.

The prick was prying the rings off her fingers.

"I'm okay." Her head turned, and she stared at Tyler. No flashing grin. No dimples. Tears filled her eyes. "The ruby belonged to my grandmother."

Tyler's chest ached. There was just something about her voice that basically made him want to beat the shit out of every bad guy in the room and then spread their bodies at her high-heeled feet.

"Now it belongs to me," the prick crowed. He dropped the rings into a black bag at his waist. Then he yanked Tyler's mystery brunette with him. The gun was positioned dangerously close to her head. "Come on, boyfriend. I'm betting that you won't make a move if I have her."

Don't be so sure.

"Pat him down!" A bark from the jerk in charge. "Take his gun and any weapons you find!"

And one of his cronies was instantly there to pat down Tyler and to take the gun from his right ankle. Then the knife Tyler had strapped to his left ankle. When Tyler was fully disarmed, the leader grunted in approval. He also dragged the woman toward the room she'd indicated moments before. He looked inside, nodded, and then told Tyler, "Get your ass inside. And if you come at me, I will pull this trigger. Fed or no Fed."

The robbers hadn't killed anyone in their attacks...yet. But there could always be a first time. Dammit. Tyler went into the room. A library. One with massive shelves full of old, hardback books. Probably collector's items.

"Take her!" With that snarl, the woman was thrown at Tyler. The prick in the mask kept her small bag, and, presumably, her phone.

The woman's body collided with Tyler's. His arms automatically rose and curled around her.

And the library door was hauled shut.

He put her to the side and leapt for the door. *Too late*. It was already locked.

"It locks on the outside," she told him. "The key was actually right there—I think Jorlan might have wanted people to stay out of his library and he intended to lock it and forgot, but now..." She rubbed her arms. "I guess we're trapped in here."

He couldn't be trapped in there. He had a job to do. A job that involved taking out those punk bad guys and not letting them lock his ass up like he was some green cop on a first case. A growl vibrated from him. *This shit could not happen*. He turned and scanned the room, searching for another way out.

"No, I'm fine. No need for concern." Her droll voice. "Maybe a few bruises on my arms but nothing to be alarmed about."

Tyler whipped back toward her. "He bruised you?"

Her smile came and went on her face. The smile transformed her from a cold beauty into something absolutely breathtaking. *Way too tempting*. "I bruise easily," she told him. "But don't worry, I heal quickly, too." A little hum. She stepped toward him. "I was happy to save your life. Think nothing of it."

He blinked. "Excuse me?"

She waved her hand. A hand that no longer had rings glinting on it. "When I jumped in front of you and shielded you with my body? I was happy to help. Not like I could have a federal agent getting shot in front of me. How terrible would that have been?"

"Never said I was a federal agent." He whirled away from her. His gaze locked on the balcony doors. *Pay dirt*. He stalked toward those doors.

"You never said you weren't, either." Her steps rushed after him. "And did I just hear a note of Texas in your voice? I'm pretty sure I did."

He spun. They almost collided.

He caught her shoulders. "Stay in this room." Her scent teased him. What was that? Kinda reminded him of sweet vanilla cream. A dessert treat that he wanted to gobble right up.

So the wrong time. And place. He didn't get to gobble up gorgeous women in the middle of robberies.

"Well, we both have to stay here," she pointed out with a blink of her incredibly dark eyes. "We're locked in."

Only for the moment. "My job is to stop those bastards. I can't stop them while I'm locked in here." He let her go and turned back for the balcony doors once more. Double doors. He shoved one open and stepped onto the narrow balcony.

She inched right with him. "Yeah, this isn't going to work for you." She looked to the left and then to the right. Her index finger pointed. "That's like...what? A five-inch-wide ledge near the side of the mansion? You really think you're going to magically fit your giant self on that tiny ledge and make it over to the next room?" A shake of her head. "I doubt it would even hold your weight. Way too flimsy. You try, and you die."

"Not like I have a lot of options." Sitting on his ass wasn't on the agenda.

"Sure, you do. Or at least, you have another option that doesn't involve your immediate death." She curled her fingers around his. "Come with me."

And he did.

She led him back into the library. Stared up at the massive row of shelves and books on the left-hand side and frowned.

The moments ticked past.

She kept staring. And frowning. And he was pretty sure he'd just heard a scream from the other side of the library door. Tyler's shoulders tensed. People needed his *help*. "Dammit, I have to go—"

"I think this is the one." Her delicate fingers reached out and curled around the edge of *Great Expectations* by Charles Dickens. She pulled, and the shelf a few feet away swung open.

What in the hell was that? *A freaking secret passage?*

"Voilà." A shrug of one slim shoulder. "Instant escape hatch. This should take you into the billiard room next door. And if the bad guys aren't looking, you can use your mad, bad skills to take them out." A pause. "I am assuming you do have incredible skills, yes? Don't disappoint me and say no."

"How the hell did you know the passage was there?"

Her long lashes fluttered. "Because, unlike you, I've been to Jorlan's parties before. I know his secrets." She waved toward the open passageway door. "So, are we going or what?"

"Yeah...No." He curled his fingers around her shoulders and gently pushed her back. "You aren't going anywhere."

Her expression tensed. "What?"

"You're staying in this room where it's safe because you are a civilian. You aren't about to run into danger." Knowing her, she'd jump between him and the jerk with the gun again. "You stay here. And I'll fight the bad guys."

"How incredibly brave of you." She fanned herself.

His eyes narrowed. "Who are you?"

"Who are *you*?"

His mouth opened.

"And don't even think about giving me a fake name," she warned. "I want the real you." Very, very serious.

"Tyler." A rumble.

"I'm Esme."

Curses rose from outside.

"Sounds like you have a job to do." Her lips pressed together, and she nodded. "Okay, here's the deal. I don't like staying behind. Not really who I am. But I promise you, I will be in this exact spot when you return. And you *will* return, won't you? Because I find that I don't like the idea of you getting hurt."

She didn't like the *idea* of him getting hurt? What the hell? "You don't know me."

"Yes, I do." Then she surprised the hell out of him. Esme fisted her hand in his tux and hauled him down toward her. Her mouth pressed against his. Her lips parted. Her tongue snaked out to lick against Tyler's and, holy fuck, his whole body seemed to ignite. Lust plunged through his veins as she gave him the hottest kiss he'd ever had in his life. He wanted to grab her, hold tight, and fuck her. Right then and there.

Not him. Not his MO at all.

But...

I want her.

Esme pulled back. "Go save the day, hero."

His breath heaved out.

"I'll be in this exact spot."

A curt nod. And then he rushed through the passageway. Once on the other side, he shoved the shelf back into place. There was probably some switch to make it glide seamlessly into position, but he didn't have time to find that damn thing. So he used brute force, and it worked just fine.

Then he got a good look at the new space. Sure enough, he was in the billiard room. Esme had been right. Eyes narrowing, he headed for the wall and pulled down a wooden cue. He tested the weight. Weapon obtained.

Tyler strode for the door. The unlocked door. He curled his fingers around the knob and slowly pulled the door open. One inch. Two. He peered through that opening and saw some of the rich and glittering guests on the floor. Sobbing. He edged from the billiard room with the cue in his hand.

The wealthy guests had been subdued. Zip ties bound their hands. Their jewelry was missing—it was easy to note that the diamond necklaces were all gone. One woman glanced Tyler's way, and her mouth parted in surprise.

He put his fingers to his lips.

Her eyes flared wider. Right then, one of the bastards in a black mask rounded the corner. He saw Tyler and—

Tyler slammed the cue into the side of his head before the guy could call out a warning. The perp sank like a stone.

One down...about five more to go. His hand tightened on the cue. And Tyler went to work.

* * *

THE HERO HAD GONE off to save the day. Esme Laurent peered down at the carpet. A rather boring, abstract design. She looked back up at the now closed secret passageway. She did need to remember this exact spot, after all. A promise was a promise. She liked to keep her promises. Just good form, that. It would be highly rude to go around making promises that she never intended to keep. Who would ever trust her if she did something like that?

Satisfied that she could, in fact, return to this precise position, Esme gave a decisive nod. She kicked off her shoes. Ran for the balcony doors. Esme threw the doors open and hurried onto the narrow balcony.

She would have to be fast. Faster than she anticipated because she definitely suspected the big, dangerous Tyler would be taking out the robbers in record time.

Esme climbed onto the narrow ledge. *Five inches wide.* She hadn't guessed when she told Tyler that figure. She knew exactly how wide the ledge was because Esme believed in doing her research. Being prepared like the good Girl Scout she'd never been. Moving forward, she extended her hands out to help keep her balance. She absolutely refused to look down. Because, unfortunately, she did have a vague fear of heights. Annoying. Bothersome. But, that was life.

She'd learned long ago that it was best to ignore her fears and to just focus on what was immediately in front of her.

And a long, narrow walk was currently waiting.

Good thing she'd trained as a gymnast until she was fifteen. She'd spent countless hours on balance beams that had been narrower than this ledge. And if she pretended just right, Esme could imagine that she was walking across one of those old balance beams again.

And not walking across a ledge on the second story. A fall probably wouldn't kill her. She knew all about landing techniques that could minimize damage. However, a fall from this height would still hurt like hell. Esme didn't particularly enjoy pain. Not her kink.

But she did enjoy a good dose of revenge every now and then. Some people just deserved what they had coming to them.

A drop of rain hit her cheek. For a moment, she froze. *No, no, no.* Somewhere in the distance, thunder rumbled.

She needed to hurry. *Do not dare rain on me.* She had too much to do. No time to waste.

Esme made it to the end of the ledge and went to work.

It was good that her big, true-blue hero was currently busy with the thugs in the masks. That gave her plenty of time...to do a little thievery of her own.

Some people really are trouble. You should have listened to me, Tyler, when I tried to warn you. I am the worst trouble you will ever meet.

She was also the best thief he'd ever meet, but Tyler wouldn't know that ever-so-important fact about her. Too bad they hadn't been given more time to play.

She'd never tempted one of the good guys before, and Tyler? He had *good* written all over him.

Meanwhile, Esme always excelled at being bad.

Chapter Two

"YOU'RE SUPPOSED TO BE LOCKED UP!" THE MAN IN THE black mask stumbled back when Tyler barreled toward him. *"I put you in the damn room myself!"*

Tyler shrugged. The bastard had a gun up and aimed at him. An annoyance. Why did the prick keep doing that? He should know better than to go around waving a gun. "I don't always like to stay where people *put* me."

"Get the fuck back!" A yell. The gun trembled in his gloved hand. "I will shoot! Don't you test me! I will—"

The double doors behind the man flew open. Four federal agents stormed inside. All wore bulletproof vests and take-no-shit expressions. *"Drop the weapon!"* A roar from the lead agent. *"Drop it now!"*

The masked man shuddered. He also dropped his weapon. And immediately threw his empty hands into the air.

"I took the liberty of calling in a few friends," Tyler revealed. He kicked the weapon to the side. No sense leaving it too close to the perp. "You were so busy stealing jewels from the party guests that you didn't notice I was free and taking out your crew." He still held his broken cue in one hand, but his left lifted a cell phone. "Borrowed this from one of your buddies, after I knocked his ass out."

The perp swore.

The Feds swarmed him. Yanked off his mask.

Ragged, blond hair slid over the lead robber's forehead. His features were twisted in rage as he glared at Tyler. He looked young and mean and...scared. *You should be scared. You're about to be locked away. You pulled a gun on me, asshole. You don't walk away after that.*

Tyler smiled at him. "You're under arrest." A joint task force operation. They'd formed it to take down this crew of high-profile robbers. This crime ring was going *down*.

While the Feds cuffed the perp and started reading him his rights, Tyler tossed the cell onto a nearby table. Champagne still bubbled in the flutes on the table. The guests were gasping and begging to be set free. They also wanted their jewelry back.

"We arrested the bodyguards outside." It was the FBI agent in charge, Grayson Stone. Gray to his friends, and Tyler was one of the very few people that Gray considered a friend. Most people just considered Gray to be an all-around asshole. Because he was. "They tried to stop my team from entering." Gray shook his head. "Dumbass mistake."

It was just as they'd thought. "The security company is compromised."

Gray nodded. "We were suspicious of them. They had too many ties to the other thefts." He surveyed the scene. "That's why I wanted an inside man here." His head cocked as he looked at the wooden cue Tyler held. And the blood on the cue. "Stop to play some games, did you?"

Tyler shrugged. "They took my gun."

"Uh, huh."

"And my knife."

"Sure."

"I had to improvise."

"You are good at that." Gray holstered his gun. He also snagged the black bag that had been tied at the ring leader's waist. He opened the bag. "Well, well..." A whistle. "That is a whole lot of sparkle." His eyes shifted to Tyler. "Nice job. If you hadn't been in here, if you hadn't been able to make contact with me and the other agents, we wouldn't have known the bastards were at play. The bodyguards outside kept signaling that all was fine. Before we ever realized what was up, the robbers would have been in the wind."

"You shouldn't be here!" Spittle flew from the blond jerk's mouth as he glared at Tyler. "You should have been locked up, you big bastard! *You shouldn't be here!*"

Yeah, well, as to that...

Tyler turned away. He headed for the library. The key wasn't in the lock. Tyler glanced back at the now cuffed blond. "Key."

"Fuck yourself!"

Whatever.

Tyler lifted his foot and kicked in the door.

As the wood shattered, a nearby redhead in a shimmery blue dress let out a shriek and collapsed back against her date.

Gray frowned and hurried closer to Tyler. "What in the hell are you doing?"

Tyler pushed open the broken door.

Gray crowded in behind him. "Oh. Sure. Yeah. I might have broken the door in, too, in order to get to her." Low. He waved. "Hi, ma'am."

Esme stood near the bookshelves. Her hands were

behind her back. She appeared to have not moved at all from that spot. Her lashes fluttered. "Is the danger over?"

"Yeah." Tyler dropped the cue.

Her smile spread across her face. Her disarming dimples winked. "You took out the bad guys?"

"Who is she?" Gray whispered. "Other than, you know, the future mother of my children."

Not fucking happening. But he ignored his buddy. It was either ignore him or punch his ass out. "They're in custody," Tyler answered her question. He should move toward her. He should not be drinking her in like a man dying of thirst. And why had he just elbowed Gray? Because the asshole was practically drooling, that was why. "Don't you have people to arrest?" he snapped to the Fed.

"Of course, they are in custody." Esme gave a decisive nod. "Bet you didn't even break a sweat subduing them, did you?" She strolled toward Tyler. All relaxed. Confident. Sexy.

She stopped in front of him.

He looked down at her.

"Can I get my ruby ring back?" Esme asked sweetly. "Sentimental importance, you know. And I *did* help save the day."

"Evidence," Tyler bit out.

Gray nudged him. "Use more words."

"The ring is evidence," Tyler managed to say. "You'll get it back, eventually."

Her jaw angled up. "I suppose I can wait." Her gaze shifted to Gray and dipped from the top of his head down to his black dress shoes. Then up again. She nodded. "Are you some sort of agent, too?"

"She knows?" Gray asked.

"She knew the first minute that she saw me," Tyler told him. Like that didn't set off alarm bells.

"A lucky guess. My mother always did say I led a charmed life." Esme's hand moved to her chest. Pressed lightly to her damn gorgeous breasts. "It's been such an exhausting night. Please, can I get an officer to escort me out of here? To take me home? I just...a man held a gun on me earlier," she revealed as she looked—wide-eyed—at Gray. "I'm shaken."

She hadn't appeared shaken at the time. Tyler's head cocked as he studied her. She *sounded* shaken right then, but there was something about her eyes. Something that said...*I'm not scared of any damn thing.*

"Sure," Gray said, clearly more than happy to help her. "We can get you an escort home. No problem. We'll need to get a statement first. Your contact information."

A sigh slipped from her, and then she was glancing back up at Tyler. "Meeting you was very interesting."

He could not look away from her.

And he could suddenly remember their kiss all too well.

"How many did you take down?" she asked.

"Five." He'd give Gray credit for the leader since Tyler hadn't gotten the chance to knock out the SOB.

"Impressive." A pause. "Was it hard?"

"No."

Gray called out for another agent. Probably the person who would escort Esme away from the scene. They would have questions for her, first, though, as Gray had indicated. Questions needed to be asked. A statement taken. Protocol had to be followed.

She drifted past Tyler. His hand reached out and touched the back of her hair. He could have sworn the darkness felt slightly...damp. Tyler frowned after her.

"Holy shit." Gray soundlessly whistled. "I think she may just be the woman of my dreams."

"No." Very, very definite. "She's not. Get over that shit. Now."

"Bossy."

Yeah. He was. And she was also not for Gray. But he wasn't going to argue the point because he had work to do. Victims who needed to be freed. More statements to be taken. A scene to secure.

Esme looked back.

Tyler realized he should say something to her.

But he had no idea what the hell to say.

She sent him a little wave. "Don't forget me."

Tyler didn't think he could if he tried. There were some people you never forgot.

The young agent that Gray had called forward—Agent Sam Garcia—took Esme's arm and escorted her forward. And that was when Tyler noticed the raindrops on Garcia's back.

* * *

"THEY ARE FUCKING *GONE!*" Jorlan Rodgers erupted out of his bedroom suite. His hands were waving, his tux wrinkled, and a vein near his forehead bulged to an alarming degree. "*Someone stole my diamonds!*"

Tyler and Gray exchanged a long look. Then Gray turned to the angry billionaire and tried to sooth him by saying, "Look, Mr. Rodgers, we have all the jewels that the thieves tried to steal. They're currently being kept as evidence."

And Jorlan had just snatched the big evidence bag from

one of the uniforms on scene. He upended the bag and glittering gems flew across the gleaming, marble floor.

"What in the hell?" Gray exploded. "That's fucking evidence! You don't do that shit!" He motioned to the stunned agents and uniformed cops who leapt into motion.

"My diamonds aren't there!" Jorlan rounded on Gray. "They were stolen from the safe in my bedroom. I want them, *now*. Bad enough that these morons held me at gunpoint. For them to take my diamonds..." He whirled back and glared at the blond thief who was being marched out by two cops. The ring leader. "You will pay," he vowed.

The blond thief blanched.

"You need to calm down," Gray announced. Then, blasting, "*Do not touch those!*" He snapped at two women in red dresses who'd edged closer to the jewels. "What in the hell is this? A circus? *Bag and tag the evidence. I want guards on the jewels.*"

Jorlan's breath heaved in and out. His nostrils flared. "Not just anyone could get in my safe." His gaze swept dismissively over the blond and his young crew that were being cuffed and led away. Jorlan whirled back to face Tyler. "You were supposed to guard my possessions."

That had been part of the deal. They'd suspected a hit would occur that night. And in order for Tyler to get admittance to the party so that he could catch the robbers in the act, Jorlan had needed to extend an invitation to his old boarding school buddy.

"Where the hell were you during the theft?" Jorlan snarled.

Was that snarl supposed to be intimidating? Tyler barely managed to contain an eye roll.

"Locked in the library," Gray answered when Tyler

remained silent. "But he got out via your secret passageway."

Jorlan's eyes narrowed. "How the fuck did you know about that?"

"And then he stopped the bad guys so...yeah, you should *thank* him," Gray instructed.

Jorlan didn't thank him. The vein bulged even more. "Five million dollars' worth of diamonds are missing. Someone got in my bedroom. Got to my safe. No one leaves until I have my diamonds!"

The rich prick didn't get to make demands. Time for him to realize that extremely important fact of life. Time for him to—

Esme isn't here.

Tyler did a double-take. Nope, no gorgeous brunette in a body-hugging black dress. Guests were being questioned, yes, so maybe she was being interviewed in a different room...

Tyler took off and began searching for her.

"Hey, asshole!" Jorlan yelled after him. "I was talking to you!"

Like Tyler cared. His heart was racing, and tension had burned its way through his body. Several of the other agents had wet hair. He'd noticed that a few moments ago. First, he'd seen the slight wetness that darkened the back of Garcia's coat. Then he'd caught the slick hair some of the late arriving agents and uniforms sported. And a few moments before, he'd seen a flash of lightning beyond the picture window on the right.

Why did Esme's hair seem damp?

If she'd been in the library the whole time, why was her hair damp? It shouldn't be damp. Not unless she'd been outside. Like some of the agents. Like some of the uniforms. If she'd been outside and she'd gotten caught in the rain...

Impossible, right? Unless...

He bounded down the circular staircase that led to the first floor, and, sure enough, right next to the mansion's entrance, he saw Esme. An FBI agent in a bulletproof vest waited at her right side. Not Garcia. An agent that Tyler didn't recognize.

"A ride home would be great," Esme was saying to the agent. "And I'll come in tomorrow to answer any follow-up questions. It has just been such a grueling experience. I think I'm about to crash."

Tyler rushed up behind her.

"Having the gun shoved at me, being locked in the library..." She fanned herself. "Oh, my. I feel a little faint just remembering about it all."

"You don't look faint," Tyler informed her.

Her shoulders stiffened. The light from the massive, overhead chandelier poured down on her golden skin. She slowly turned so that she could stare straight up at him.

"Nope," he added. "Not faint at all." Damn gorgeous, though. He reached out and caught a lock of her hair.

"Wh-what are you doing?" Esme breathed in that husky, tempting voice of hers.

He tucked the lock behind her ear. His fingers lingered against her cheek. "Your hair is a little damp."

"I just walked outside with the agent. I wanted to get some air. It was raining, though, so we came back in."

The agent beside her nodded. "We're waiting for the rain to slack up, then I'll be taking her home, Marshal Barrett."

"Marshal?" Her brows rose. "Is that what you are? A

U.S. Marshal?" Then her brows lowered. "What is a marshal doing here?"

"Joint task force." And he'd been doing a favor for a friend.

"Oh." Her tongue swiped along her lower lip. "I thought U.S. Marshals hunted big-time, federal fugitives."

"We do." He kept staring at her. "Esme, I'm afraid that I can't allow you to leave."

She took a step toward him. "Why not?" A blink. "Because you met me, fell in love at first sight, and decided that you just can't live your life without me?" A soft sigh. "That is so beautifully romantic."

Tyler shook his head.

"No? Too bad." Her lips curled down.

Yes, it was too bad. For her. "I need to search you."

"Excuse me?"

"Diamonds are missing from Jorlan's safe."

A slow blink. "And that has what to do with me, exactly?"

"Your hair is wet."

"Yes, I told you that I just went out with the agent."

Good try with a cover story. He might have bought it, if he hadn't touched her hair in the library. "It was damp when I kicked in the library door."

Gray rushed off the staircase and hurried toward them. "What is happening right now? Why did you go barreling off, Tyler?"

Esme didn't spare Gray a glance. Her whole focus seemed to be on Tyler, and she looked fascinated. Not scared or intimidated. Fascinated.

Like that made any sense.

But damn if he didn't feel fascinated by her, too. Almost admiring, Tyler shook his head. "You nearly got away with it, didn't you? Hell, getting locked in the library was a stroke of luck for you, wasn't it? It put you in exactly the spot you wanted to be. And I left you alone, so there were no witnesses to see..." He trailed off.

"To see what?" Gray demanded. "Could you clue me in?"

Sure, he could. "She went out on the library's balcony. She crawled across that five-inch-wide ledge that runs on the side of this freaking mansion." He poked his head outside and looked up at the ledge. Too freaking narrow. And with the rain? *Slick*. He ducked back in and glared at her. "You could have broken your neck," he rumbled, angry. "You shouldn't take risks like that."

"Ah, I hate to point this out, but *you* were the one who wanted to go for a stroll along the ledge," Esme reminded him, voice mild and helpful. "I was the one who showed you the secret passageway. Because I am a great asset to law enforcement that way."

Tyler grunted. "How'd you know about the secret passage?"

She smiled at him.

He almost forgot to breathe. *Mental note, her smile is lethal*. He sucked in a breath. "If I ask Jorlan right now, will he tell me that he showed you that passageway?" *Or did you find it when you scoped out the building, while you were planning your theft?*

She leaned toward him. Conspiratorially, she revealed, "Jorlan isn't really someone you should trust. So, don't go taking his words at face value. The man can lie easier than he breathes."

He took that as a no. Jorlan had *not* shown her the passage. "What about you? Are you someone I should trust?"

Her long lashes fluttered. "Don't I look trustworthy?"

Another mental note, *when she deflects, she lies.*

Gray tapped him on the shoulder. "What exactly is occurring here?"

"Your U.S. Marshal friend isn't letting me leave." A definite forlorn tone trembled in her voice. "After my excruciating night, after the way I bravely put myself between your friend and a gun...did he even tell you about that, ah—I'm sorry, what was your name?"

"Agent Grayson Stone."

"Right. Grayson." A nod. "I stepped between Tyler and a pointed gun, trying to save his life because that is just the kind of person I am—"

A disbelieving snort broke from Tyler.

For the moment, she ignored that oddly adorable snort. "And now, he's turning on me. Accusing me of—of committing some sort of crime here tonight, when all I wanted to do was help law enforcement."

Tyler shook his head. "Don't buy the act, buddy," he advised Gray. "She broke into Jorlan's bedroom. She cracked his safe."

No change of expression showed on Esme's lovely face.

"And then she took his diamonds. She walked back across the ledge that led from his bedroom to the library, and Esme was in place before I could open the library door. Damn." Another shake of his head. "You are good, lady."

"That's a crazy story," she murmured.

"If it hadn't been raining, there would have been nothing to tip me off. But your hair was damp." He looked at her dress. It didn't look damp, but it was so dark that it would be hard to tell if there were wet spots on it. Hard to tell, unless you were touching the dress. *Touching her*.

"Wait. Hold up." Gray's fingers rose to pinch the bridge of his nose. "*She* has the diamonds?"

"I'm going to search you," Tyler told Esme.

"Don't you need permission for something like that?" All innocence, she tipped back her head. The dark curtain of her hair trailed down her shoulders.

He stared back at her and then smiled. *Baby, you just admitted your guilt.* And he could see it in her eyes. She knew it, too.

"Dammit," Esme swore. Then she lifted her hands. "Have at it. What do I have to hide? Frisk away."

"Uh, Tyler..." Gray began.

But Tyler was already searching her. Not the top of her body. The top of the dress was far too damn tight for that. But it billowed at her legs. Especially near that tempting slit of fabric that revealed so much thigh. His hands carefully patted up her left leg. Found nothing.

Then he went to her right and...

Bingo.

He lifted up the silky fabric of her dress—slightly damp fabric—to reveal the small, black bag that was strapped to one supple upper thigh. A supple, gorgeous thigh.

"How on earth did that get there?" Esme wondered.

He unstrapped the bag. Opened it. Diamonds spilled into his palm.

"Holy shit." From Gray.

Still kneeling in front of Esme, Tyler glanced up at her. "You warned me."

"Did I?"

He tucked the diamonds back into the bag. Shoved the diamonds and the bag at Gray. "Cuffs," Tyler snapped.

She frowned at him. "Are you about to get kinky? Now? With all of these people staring at us?"

"I'm about to put you under arrest, baby."

"Baby?" A pleased curl of her lips. "What a fascinating first date."

Cuffs were slapped into his hand. He hooked one around her right wrist. Being extra careful because... because hell if he knew why. He turned her around. With her back to him, he pulled her other wrist toward him and snapped the second cuff in place. "Esme..." Hell, he still didn't know her last name. "You're under arrest."

She looked back over her shoulder at him. All smoldering eyes. All plump, kissable lips. And she smiled. "No, I'm not."

Uh, yes, yes, she was. Thus, the handcuffs. And the next item of business? He was going to read Esme her rights. Going to escort her to a jail cell. Going to lock her sexy self away.

Why did that last thought make his chest ache?

"My handsome U.S. Marshal. Tell me, have you ever heard of these two magic words before?" Esme's husky voice poured over him.

Magic words? What in the hell was she talking about? There were no magic words in his world. There was no magic at all in his life. There was crime and evil and a job to do.

With her hands still cuffed behind her back, Esme turned to face him fully. "Two ever-so-magic words." A delicate pause. "Diplomatic. Immunity." She hummed. Might have bounced. "I have it. My father is the French Ambassador. I'm Esme Laurent, and you..." She rose onto her toes and brought her mouth even closer to him.

He bent nearer to her.

"You...my dear, handsome U.S. Marshal...you are shit out of luck."

Then she kissed him again.

Chapter Three

SOMETIMES, IT PAID TO BE BAD.

Esme Laurent sat on top of the interrogation room table. Her legs swung out in front of her as she waited for the authorities to trickle inside. Hopefully, they'd come with major apologies.

Her gaze darted to the clock on the wall. Nearly six a.m. She'd been in that incredibly boring FBI office for *hours*. She'd cooperated. Somewhat. And she'd been waiting patiently. Again, *somewhat*.

She'd offered her terms to the Fed who'd been milling around the most. Grayson Stone. He seemed to be the man in charge of the investigation that was her life. Though, really, why waste time with her? There were much worse criminals out there and—

The door opened.

Her U.S. Marshal appeared. Esme didn't even try to hide the giant smile that burst across her face. How could she? She was far too happy to see him. "I knew you wouldn't be able to stay away." Her legs swung out again.

He looked down at her feet.

Her high heels had long since fallen off, and her bare toes wiggled at him.

A frown pulled at his features. Such sexy, rugged features. Not necessarily handsome, though she had called him that before. The man had an incredible jaw. Hard and square and currently covered with a bit of stubble that she itched to feel against her palm. His eyes were a steely blue that—when they fixed on you and they were certainly fixed on Esme right then—those eyes of his seemed to see right into her. Dark hair. Cut a little too short. Sharp cheekbones. Strong nose. High forehead and—

He marched toward her. Towered over her.

Ah, yes. Something else that Esme enjoyed about her marshal? He was big. He'd ditched the tux that he'd seemed to hate and now wore a black t-shirt and faded jeans. The t-shirt appeared to be in danger of absolutely ripping at the shoulders. The marshal worked out. A lot.

Good for him.

He took out five guys and didn't even break a sweat. The man showed zero fear when a gun was shoved at him.

And the glare currently on his face? Well, it took his features from sexy to a downright diabolical level of dangerousness.

Be still, my heart.

"We haven't gotten hold of your father."

Oh, the other guy had entered the room. Grayson. He was talking. Tyler was busy staring at her, and she was happy to stare back.

"He's out of the country," Grayson continued.

Her eyes did a little roll. Right. Like she didn't know where her father was.

"But we have verified your identity. You're Esme

Laurent, age twenty-seven, daughter of the French Ambassador and his Italian opera singer wife."

Her mother had died years ago. On the eve of Esme's sixteenth birthday. She hadn't celebrated a birthday since that fateful day. Actually, she hadn't celebrated much at all in her life.

Not information for the Fed and the still glaring Marshal to know.

"We have intelligence that ties you to a string of high-end robberies. Art thefts. Jewel heists. Antique disappearances."

Tyler was staring so intently at her as his friend rambled.

For fun, she winked at Tyler.

His stare became all the more intense. He was a delight.

"You were caught red-handed tonight," Gray added in his no-nonsense tone. "There has never been enough evidence to link you concretely to anything before. Hell, most of your crimes occurred in other countries, so the stories about you—they were all smoke and mirrors. The Feds have spent the last six hours trying to piece all the details together. Half of the intel my team is gathering about you seems to be bullshit."

She shrugged. "What's the saying? You're smart if you believe absolutely nothing that you hear and only about half of what your eyes can see? Or something like that." Her head tilted to the side. Her hair slid over her shoulder. "Don't actually remember who first said those words. Was it Poe? I do love his stories. So twisted and dark." Her index finger tapped her chin. "Maybe it was Franklin. I just can't say for certain." Her index finger tapped again. "Oh, well. I'm sure it will come to me later." Her head turned toward Grayson. "I've been here long enough." She'd been good long enough. "And I haven't been charged with a single crime."

His jaw—almost as hard as Tyler's—clenched. A muscle jerked along his clenched jaw as he closed in on her. "My boss wants me to offer you a deal."

Her eyes widened. "A deal? When I haven't been charged with any crime? How would that work?"

"You had the jewels on you," Tyler said.

Ah, yes, there it was again. That deep, rumbly voice that she adored. Just hearing it made her want to shiver in delight. Not that she was the shivering-in-delight type. At least, not usually. But there was just something about this marshal that made her want to break all of her usual rules.

Rule one? *Never fall for the good guy.* And, yet, well, here she was. Falling. Lusting.

Her focus zeroed in on him. "I bet you have never met a rule that you didn't like."

His blue eyes narrowed on her.

"Let me guess, were you a Marine once upon a time? You do have that vibe about you." Her tongue licked across her lower lip. "Semper Fi?" Her heart drummed hard in her chest. "What does that motto mean again? Would you remind me?"

"Always faithful," he rumbled.

Oh, that rumble. Her toes might have curled. "That's what I thought."

"How did you know he was a Marine?" Grayson asked.

"A lucky guess."

Grayson crossed his arms over his chest. "I don't buy that. I don't think you're the guessing type, lady. I think you're a criminal straight to your beautiful core."

Tyler shot him an annoyed glare.

Grayson ignored the glare. "And I think you're playing

some kind of game with me. With us all. I want answers. I want them now."

"We don't necessarily get what we want in this world." Her gaze raked Tyler. *Always faithful.* It was all she could do not to sigh again. No, in this world, we did not always get what we wanted. But sometimes...*we did.*

"My boss wants to offer you a deal," Grayson repeated, as if she'd missed the words the first time. "He talked to some contact he has at the CIA, and they are both about to shit themselves."

She winced. "I'm sure there is a medicine for that."

Wait, did Tyler's lips *almost* twitch? She thought they had. Good to know that, buried ever so deeply inside her marshal, there was a sense of humor.

"They have this idea that you're some big, fucking player in an international game." Grayson was still prattling on about something. Oh, right. The something in question was her. His prattles focused on her.

"What?" Esme twirled a lock of her hair and strove to appear innocent. "Little old me? A big player? I am flattered." Her feet swung again. Lazily.

"You're also on an international hit list." From Grayson once more.

At his revelation, she stopped swinging her feet. "Say that again?"

But it was Tyler who stepped forward. He stepped so close that his crisp, masculine scent teased her nose. "You don't sound French."

"No?" Her brows shot up. "*Je veux te baiser.*"

Grayson choked.

A faint furrow appeared between Tyler's steely blue eyes.

She rolled one shoulder. "I have lived all over the world.

My father—*mon père,* if that makes me sound more French—has been an ambassador for a very long time. I speak five languages fluently, and I can adopt any accent necessary in order for that language to sound very, very clear. *Mon père* always said that speaking as clearly as possible to your audience is necessary. Very important in diplomacy. Being understood, that is. If you're not understood by the people you're communicating with, then chaos will reign." When she'd been a child, her mother had called her chaos. A special little nickname.

She'd loved her mother.

Grayson slapped his hand down on the table near her.

She frowned at him. Had there been some point in that slap against the wood?

"Could we get back to the international hit list?" Grayson gritted out.

Her heart rate had kicked up even more, but she kept her voice cool as she inquired, "A hit list, you say? On *moi?*"

"Reporters got wind of the robbery last night. Not just the crew that we arrested, but your involvement, too. A picture of you—cuffed and being placed in a patrol car—has made the rounds on the Internet."

She slanted a glance at Tyler. "That was your fault. You are way too into bondage."

Did a faint red stain those incredible cheekbones of his? Adorable.

"The Feds have teams that work the dark web. All of the chatter they're picking up suggests that certain very dangerous parties believe you're the international thief known as the Fox. So named because the thief is supposed to be damn cunning, sly, and exceedingly elusive." Grayson was clearly the chatty one in the friend group.

Meanwhile, her marshal was the tall, dark and

dangerously silent type. That was fine. She could chat enough for the both of them. "I am? *I'm the Fox?*" When you made the words sound like a question, they didn't count as a confession. Fun point.

"You're an international thief," Grayson charged. "A thief who has made certain parties very, very angry. We found a hit on you on the dark web. Five million dollars."

Just five million? That was what her life was going for these days? Should she be insulted?

"And because of the picture and the press and the power of social media, you're going to be hunted now," Grayson continued in his doom-and-gloom voice. "The photo proves to certain nefarious parties that you are the Fox. You know, the parties that you stole items from over the years?"

As if she'd admit any guilt. But...

"A deal," Grayson said again. Third time? Did he think it would be the charm for her? "That's what my boss will offer you. He thinks you have the power to bring down some very powerful individuals. A whole criminal operation that has been working in tangent internationally. He wants you to help us."

She nodded. "He wants my help because I have such a generous, caring nature?" *Do not blow this now, Esme. Stay focused. The goal is within reach. Do not look overly eager.*

"Because he thinks you're embedded in the criminal world up to those lovely, dark eyes of yours—"

Tyler's growl cut through Grayson's words.

Grayson shot him a glance. "What? The woman is gorgeous, but she is a criminal."

"Alleged," Esme corrected him. "*Alleged* criminal."

Tyler put his hand down on the table. Not a hard slap the way Grayson had done. Grayson had been trying to intimidate her with the sudden, loud movement. But Tyler just softly slid a hand down on the wood. He leaned in close to her. Seemed to surround her.

She sucked in a breath.

"Sweetheart..."

Oh, that was promising.

"You had the diamonds strapped to your thigh," Tyler reminded her. As if she needed the reminder. She knew exactly where they'd been. His eyes gleamed at her. "Hard to be *alleged* when you're caught red-handed."

She lifted a hand and put it against his chest. *Yep, the goal had definitely been within reach.* She could feel the warmth of Tyler's body even through his black t-shirt. Esme could also feel all of those fabulous muscles that belonged to him. "Was it good for you?"

He blinked.

"The kiss. Both of them," she amended. "The kisses. Plural. Were they good for you? They must be, if you're calling me 'sweetheart' already. Fine, fine, you don't have to beg. I'll go out with you. Be warned, I expect flowers. Chocolates. And for you to be a perfect gentleman."

Tyler just stared back at her.

"Oh, what? You're going to lie now? Say that the kisses didn't rock what I expect to be the incredibly ordered world in which you live? Fine. Do it. Lie to my face." Her voice dipped low as she rasped, "I dare you."

His pupils seemed to fill the steel blue of his eyes. And it sure looked like that was desire staring back at her. And he wasn't saying the kisses hadn't rocked his world. In fact, he wasn't saying anything. Definitely not the chatty one. But he sure was smoldering. Heat practically rolled off him, and joy of joys, his eyes had just fallen to her mouth.

She could make this easier on him. "They certainly

rocked my world, too." Her hand fisted in his shirt, and she tugged him closer.

He jerked back from her as if she'd scalded the man. How very rude.

She sniffed.

"You are playing games." Tyler shook his head. "Lady, I am not someone you want to fuck with."

Grayson snorted. Or choked. Or something.

Her head angled toward him. "You speak French." Because that choking of his right then and there? Had to be related to the words she'd deliberately uttered to Tyler before. *Je veux te baiser*.

Grayson inclined his head in acknowledgement. "Spent a summer in Paris back when I was attending college. I speak enough to get by."

Good to know. "My recent picture should be scrubbed from the Internet. Specifically, the picture of me, in cuffs. So very unflattering, I'm sure." She continued to sit on the table. To appear relaxed. Appearances were everything in this world.

Believe absolutely nothing that you hear and only about half of what your eyes can see.

"Step one, get rid of the picture." A list would probably be important for the Feds. Both for the Fed in the room and for all of those individuals who were—no doubt—watching from behind the one-way mirror on the right. Did they truly think she was clueless? Like she didn't get how an interrogation room worked? "That terrible picture will cause irreparable damage to my glorious reputation. It needs to vanish, immediately."

"You have a reputation for being a party girl," Tyler stated, voice deep and dark and dead sexy. "You dance every night away, drink until dawn, and spend time with as many millionaires and dukes as you can."

"Been digging into my life, have you?" She wagged her finger at him. "Stalker." *Oh, if you only knew*.

"Do you play with them so that you can steal from them easier? Are they the ones who really get drunk while you stay dead sober and help yourself to their valuables?" Tyler asked. His body was rock hard, as if every muscle had locked down.

Did he truly expect her to confess? He'd have to work much harder in order to learn her secrets. "I'm getting bored. And sleepy. Six a.m. is my bedtime." She needed to move things along. Mostly because the longer she stayed in one location—especially with word spreading about her being the silly Fox character—the more danger she'd be in. She didn't enjoy danger. Adrenaline? Yes. Absolutely. She was an adrenaline junkie. But when her life was actually on the line—nope, not so much fun. "Step one, scrub the picture of me. Scrub every bit of gossip about me being the Fox. Such a silly idea." A wave of her hand toward Grayson. "I've heard the FBI and CIA have incredible tech teams. Should be child's play for them. While your tech gurus are at work, you can get that handsome face of yours in front of the press and tell them all about what a tragic mistake you made. Not like we want to have some sort of international incident." Esme mock shuddered. "Can you imagine? Our countries are such close allies. Why create drama over nothing?"

Silence.

Actually, if she strained a bit, she could swear she heard the faint ticking of the clock on the wall. Tick. Tick. Tick.

"Are you seriously giving orders right now?" Grayson asked her.

Tyler had gone back to just watching her. There was something about that intense stare of his. It made her feel like he was...Wait. Hold on. "Are you undressing me with your eyes?"

Tyler's lips parted.

"*Non? Oui?*" A shrug. "See, there I go again. Using French for you. You don't have to answer. We both know what you were doing." But, enough play. For now. She hopped off the table. Without her shoes, both men were just far too big. So Esme took a moment to put her heels back on. Except the two inches didn't really do much. The men remained big and bold. Swamping her. But she wouldn't show that perhaps she felt the slightest bit intimidated. Instead, she casually smoothed her hands over her dress. The slit still worked to maximum effect and showed off her legs when she shifted ever so slightly. As for the bodice... perfection.

She walked toward the mirror. Grimaced. Her hair was a tangled mess. And she looked far too pale under the abysmal lighting in the interrogation room. "Who do I have to kill in order to get some decent coffee in this place?" The question was directed at the agents behind the mirror. Taking her time, she smoothed back her hair. Esme even pinched her cheeks to try and bring back a bit of color to her face.

"I don't think you understand the situation," Grayson informed her.

She looked at his reflection in the mirror. He was now to her right.

Tyler stood just a few feet away. Both men looked intense and grim. Capable. Dangerous.

"In a fight," she murmured, "who do you think would win between the two of you?"

Grayson frowned at her. He also cast a quick, nervous glance Tyler's way.

Answer received.

"Lady..." Tyler's growling voice. Sadly, he'd gone from calling her "sweetheart" to "lady." Such a disappointment. "What is it that you want?"

So many things. "I believe I outlined my first few steps." She held up her hand and began ticking items off her list even as she kept staring into the mirror. It was best to be clearly understood by everyone. *My gut says Grayson's boss is behind the glass watching.* In her experience, the big players in the game always liked to hide in the shadows. Or hide behind one-way glass where they thought they could be all anonymous and protected. "I want my picture removed. I want all references to me being the Fox scrubbed. I want a statement issued saying there has been a misunderstanding, and I am a tragic, tragic victim." She stared harder into the mirror and let her lower lip tremble.

"Are you *crying?*" Tyler demanded.

She wiped away a tear that had slid down her cheek. She hadn't gotten her mother's singing skills, but an opera singer was both incredible vocally and incredible as a performer. Esme knew all about performing. The acting talent was in her blood.

"Stop crying," Tyler ordered roughly.

She did. "If I'm on a hit list because of your incompetence in letting people believe I am some sort of master thief, then I shall need protection." She peered into the glass. "Protection," Esme emphasized. "On my terms." Esme waited a beat so that her message could be received. Then, satisfied, she nodded and turned back to the two angry men in the interrogation room.

"You are insane." Grayson stared at her as if he thought

she might need a straitjacket at any moment. "We have you dead to rights."

"You have nothing. I have diplomatic immunity."

"You had diamonds strapped to your thigh!" His hands flew into the air, then dropped back near his thighs.

"You're the one who mentioned a deal." Her high heels tapped across the floor. *Tap, tap, tap.* "I've cooperated. Haven't even gotten any attorneys in here. Attorneys who could make your life a living hell." A simple phone call could have arranged for a storm of lawyers. "I told you my terms. Well, most of them. And now you will either agree or I'll walk out of here." She paused near the door for dramatic effect.

"You walk out," Tyler told her, "and you could be dead within the hour."

Do not show fear. "I walk out," she returned, "and your buddy Grayson's boss won't ever be able to take down...oh, what did you call it? Ah, yes, some sort of global criminal organization. He wants my cooperation to take down the bad guys. In order to get that cooperation, I have a list of demands. You just heard the start of my list."

"There's more?" Tyler asked.

Grayson stomped toward her. "Do tell. I want to make sure I get everything down."

Oh, there was certainly more. She turned away from Grayson and focused on the man who mattered. The man who had taken out five bad guys without breaking a sweat. The man who was "always faithful." The man who was her end goal. "I will need a bodyguard. Someone who will stay close to me until the case is closed. What with this unfortunate business of a price being put on my head, I need a serious badass to keep me safe. Someone who isn't afraid when bullets fly." She edged closer to him. *Tap, tap* went her heels. "Someone who doesn't mind getting physical. Sometimes, you just have to fight dirty and hard." She closed the last bit of distance between them. *Tap, tap.* "Someone who will truly take the job of protecting his charge very, very seriously." She gazed happily up at him. "Someone just like you, Tyler."

"Excuse me?"

"I want you." In so many ways. For so many things. "That's a non-negotiable point in any deal that is made. *I want you.* You'll be my bodyguard. My shadow. My hero. My protector. My twenty-four, seven companion until all the danger is well and truly over. It will be you and me. Until the bitter end." Now she did smile at him. "Doesn't that sound amazing?"

Chapter Four

"This is insane," Tyler snapped to Grayson. The words were for his friend, but Tyler's gaze? It was fully locked on the woman who had gone back to sitting on the interrogation room table. Her feet were swinging again. Though this time, she wore her insanely sexy heels as she swayed her feet. And he was pretty sure that she was humming or singing some sort of song.

They'd turned off the volume, so he didn't hear her. The other Feds had filed out before Tyler entered the observation room. Hell, Gray had gone with them for a while. Some big Fed and CIA meeting that had excluded him. Why? Because Tyler didn't have the fucking clearance for whatever bullshit was going on.

But Gray had just returned. Only the two of them were in that room. And... "Insane," Tyler snapped again. No way were the Feds going to agree to her terms. No. Way.

"Uh, Tyler..."

Esme turned her head toward the mirror. Her hand lifted. She *waved* at him.

Damn if Tyler didn't almost want to wave back. Instead, his hand fisted at his side.

"You know that you were recruited to work on the joint task force because you do have a history with Jorlan."

Yeah, he did. The story he'd told Esme about the boarding school? It had been true. Once upon a time—in another life—he'd gone to boarding school with the prick. But he'd broken out of that world. Joined the Marines. Fought in hell. Survived. And he'd become a U.S. Marshal. He did the job because it meant something to him. He wanted to make the world a better place. A safer place.

A place where kids didn't lose their whole damn families and wake up alone. Scared. *Lost.*

The way I fucking was.

"There is a lot at play here that you don't know about," Gray continued grimly. "A lot that *I* didn't know about." He pointed toward the glass. "That woman in there is keeping a whole truckload of secrets."

That he could believe.

"And she's got power. Enough power that my boss wants to consent to every demand she has. If she'll cooperate, he'll give her *everything*."

Tyler got a bad feeling in the pit of his stomach. "No." The denial was for Gray, but, again, his eyes were on Esme.

"We need you, Tyler. My boss has already talked to your boss—hell, you know how that interagency shit goes. You scratch my back, and I'll be in your debt forever. Your boss was way too eager to get the Feds owing him, so he agreed to continue the partnership. You have a new assignment."

"No." He kept staring at Esme.

"It won't be that bad." Gray's voice had turned almost

wheedling. "I mean, look at her. Protecting her? How is that a bad job? The woman is gorgeous."

Her head was dipping back and forth as she hummed. Or sang. Definitely sang.

"She's a criminal," Tyler gritted out.

She stopped singing. Her head swung toward him.

She can't see me. She can't hear me.

"She's a super sexy criminal," Gray corrected.

A growl rumbled in his throat.

"What, exactly, is that about?" Gray edged closer. "Each time I mention that she's hot, you get all weird. Growly."

"You mention it too fucking much." *She is hot.* "You need to be professional. Eyes on the prize, man. Eyes on the prize." Tyler's eyes were still on her.

Her legs weren't swinging any longer.

"Criminal," he said again. He needed to remember that important point about her, and not think about how damn angry he'd gotten when he'd seen tears spill from her beautiful eyes. Tears that she had magically stopped in a blink. *The woman is an actress. A true con artist. She can't be trusted.*

"Yeah, well, she *is* a criminal, and your job is to hunt down runaway criminals. You do that shit all the time. You track the baddest of the bad. You transport them. You secure them. Hell, you also secure key witnesses. You help give them new lives. In this case, you're basically combining your two main mission objectives as a marshal." Gray clapped his hands together. "Two worlds collide, but in a great way. You protect the woman who is both a criminal and a witness—and you help her get a new life."

I want you. Her husky words rolled through Tyler's head again. When she'd spoken those three little words, his whole body had jolted. His dick had gotten instantly hard. Oh, who was he kidding? It had gotten *harder* for her. Because he'd already been semi-aroused. How could he not be? Especially after she mentioned their kisses. Kisses that had ignited a dangerously intense lust within him. Which brought him to an important point. "Not a good idea for me to protect her." He did not need to be in twenty-four, seven contact with a woman who tempted him so badly. Nope. Not a stellar plan.

"You excel at protecting. It's your thing. No bad guys are gonna get past your guard."

"Find someone else."

Her eyelashes flickered.

He leaned forward. She looked sad. Esme had damn well better not cry again. Fake tears or not, he didn't like it when she cried.

"There isn't anyone else. You heard her. You're the woman's non-negotiable part. She wants you."

And I want to do all sorts of bad things with her.

Nope. He was the marshal. The good guy. He would not cross that line.

"She has power, Tyler." Low. Careful. "Pull that I didn't expect, and I'm not just talking about her ambassador father. My boss is about to lose his mind because he thinks she is some major player that can do serious damage to some very bad people."

She didn't look like a major player. She looked fragile. Her shoulders had hunched a little. Esme was so much smaller than he was. Small things were breakable in his world.

"She wants you. That's her sticking point. And, I'm sorry, but your boss has agreed to the terms. Unless you want to have one major battle with him, I think you're going to be pulling protection duty with Esme Laurent for the foreseeable future."

Oh, he could handle a battle with his boss. Any day of the week. And in the end, Tyler would get what he wanted because he had plenty of power, too. But...

"We need her to stay alive," Gray continued grimly. "*Alive.* A five-million-dollar hit doesn't just vanish. Some skilled assassins will be closing in. You really think just *anyone* can handle them? Hell, no. We need someone with experience. With a deadly skill set. We need someone who can stay calm under the most extreme of circumstances—stay calm and still kick ass. In other words, I need you for the job. Come on, buddy. Look at it this way. You do this, and the FBI will owe you. The CIA will owe you. *I* will owe you. Hell, I'll name my first-born son after you, if you want."

He grunted. He didn't care about the Feds and the Spooks owing him. What he did care about...

"She could very well die without you."

Fuck.

"Tell me this..." Gray never stopped talking. "*Did* she really step between you and a gun?"

"Yes." A moment burned in his mind. What in the hell had she been thinking?

"So, don't *you* owe the woman? One good life save deserves another and all that?"

Esme lifted her delicate hand to her mouth. Her fingers pressed to her lips. She blew Tyler a kiss.

His eyes narrowed.

"We, ah, even have a cover story." Gray cleared his throat. "Since the two of you will be staying together in such a close manner, it seemed best that you have a paired new identity."

He wasn't going to like this. Not at all.

Esme hopped off the table. She strolled toward the mirror. Her steps were slow. Graceful. Her heels clicked on the floor. She walked across the grungy floor of the Fed's interrogation room like she was taking a glide across a runway at a fashion show.

"You'll be her husband."

Esme stopped in front of the glass. One small hand lifted. Pressed to the mirror.

"She'll, uh, she'll pretend to be your wife."

Esme's brilliant smile curled her lips.

"Tyler?"

He stared at Esme. His hands remained fisted at his sides. He damn well wasn't gonna do some dumb shit like put his hand on top of hers as it rested on the glass. Why the hell would he do that?

Why the hell do I want to do that?

"I get that you're not the chattiest bastard on even the best of days." Gray inched closer. "But it would be really great if I could get some sort of affirmation from you so I can go talk to my boss and get the wheels moving on this thing. So, how about a grunt? One grunt for yes? Or a nod? A nod would be super helpful."

Esme's fingertips tapped on the glass. Tyler's nostrils flared. If the glass didn't separate them, he'd be close enough to inhale her scent. She'd smelled absolutely delicious at Jorlan's party. "What did she say in there?"

"Ah, is that a yes?"

Not yet, it wasn't. Even though he already knew—hell, he and Gray both knew what he'd do. Not like Tyler was the type to throw a woman to the wolves. "When she spoke French in the interrogation room, what did she say?"

Silence.

Slowly, his head turned away from Esme, and he glanced at his friend. He caught Gray mid-wince.

"What. Did. She. Say?"

"I want to fuck you."

Tyler's eyes widened.

"That's what *she* said, okay? She said she wanted to fuck you. I'm sure that she was messing with you. You'd said that crack about her not sounding French, so she just threw out something that she thought was shocking." Gray yanked a hand through his hair. "Word is that's her style. Shocking. Unconventional."

Like he hadn't already figured that out about her? "She had a bag of stolen diamonds strapped to her thigh. Hard to get more unconventional than that."

"She needs you, man. She might seem cocky and bold, but she's in trouble. And you're the kind of man who never turns away from someone in trouble. That's your kryptonite."

His head turned back toward the mirror. Esme's hand had dropped, but she still stood right in front of the glass.

Impatience flashed on her face.

Then her right hand rose up. Her index finger moved to the side of her nose, and she gave the finger a fast twist out.

What the hell?

She did it again.

A bark of laughter escaped from Gray.

Tyler instantly rounded on him. "What in the hell is so funny?"

"I think she figured out that we turned off the volume to her room. Ahem." He wiped his smile away. "She's using sign language now." He repeated the quick gesture that Esme had made.

"What does it *mean?*" He knew Gray's aunt had been

deaf, and his mother had taught her children sign language so they could always communicate easily with her.

"It means that she's bored." Gray glanced back through the glass. His head tilted as he studied her. "Definitely more than meets the eye with her." He sounded impressed. "You know what, I'll just go and—"

Tyler's hand flew out and locked around his shoulder. "I'm taking her protection detail."

"Of course, you are." Gray bit down on a smile.

Had the bastard just played him? Screw it. "But I have conditions of my own."

Gray nodded. "Sure. Witness protection is more your area than mine, so, of course, I'll bow to your superior judgment."

Damn right, he would. "I pick the place. I control the location. Little Miss Sticky Fingers in there does what I say, when I say it. If she's not cooperating fully with me and following my orders at all times, I'm out."

"Uh, this really sounds like a you and a her problem. How about I go share the good news with my boss and you let Little Miss Sticky Fingers know the good news?" He tugged away from Tyler and hurried for the door. But before he exited, Gray glanced back. "This will be more dangerous than it seems. I'm not exaggerating when I say that the people coming after her are the kind that would give most people nightmares."

"*I'm* the kind that gives nightmares."

Gray nodded. "Yeah, you are." He opened the door. "So, to circle back to that first-born son thing—"

"Go tell your boss that I'm in charge of her protection."

"On it."

Tyler looked back to toward the glass. Esme had put her hand up again. Her small palm rested on the glass. And...

His hand rose and pressed over hers. So much bigger. So much stronger.

Esme seemed to stare at him.

What in the hell am I going to do with her?

But, really, wasn't that answer obvious?

Protect her. Keep her safe at all costs. Eliminate any and every threat that comes her way.

After all, wasn't that what a good husband would do?

* * *

The interrogation room door swung open. Esme gave a little jump even as her hand remained pressed to the glass.

Tyler strolled in. All big and strong and...

"Well, damn." She snatched her hand away from the glass. So much for the idea that he'd been in there, watching her. She'd *felt* like she was having a moment, but clearly, she'd been deluding herself.

Esme turned fully toward him and hoped that she looked suitably confident and assured. Her stomach was in so many knots that she ached, and her throat had gone bone dry as she waited for Tyler to make his decision.

He kicked the door shut behind him.

She searched his expression. Not reassuring. Just still intense. Kinda scary. "I can't tell..." Her head cocked. "Is this going to be a yes or a no?"

"Thought I was your non-negotiable."

She started to inch toward him.

Not necessary.

He immediately closed the distance between them. He stopped right in front of her, trapping her between his body and the mirror behind her. Then he lifted one hand—

Is he going to touch me?

And he shoved it against the mirror so that he was leaning toward her. Leaning over her. Doing the lean that she'd always found so very sexy when a man utilized it just right. And he was doing it right. The position stretched his black t-shirt over the powerful muscles in his upper arm.

She should probably not be looking at his arm. She should be looking at his face. With an effort, Esme did just that. "You are my non-negotiable," she agreed.

"If I refuse the protection detail, you're just going to walk that sweet ass out of here and straight into the line of fire for any hitman who wants to take you out?"

She gasped.

He grimaced. "I—"

"You think I have a sweet ass? Thank you so much for noticing. I work out a lot."

His brow furrowed. "Esme..."

Okay, that was a very real shiver that had just skated down her spine. But the way he'd said her name had been extra rumbly and deep and it had been far, far too easy to imagine him speaking the same way when they were, say, tangled together in sweaty bliss in a big bed.

But, they weren't in bed. They were in an interrogation room. And her life was rather on the line. So she had to focus. Now, what had he said? Ah, yes. "You're not going to walk out and leave me to be the target of dangerous hitmen."

"How the hell do you know that?"

"Well, because you're standing in front of me right now. That means you said yes." She put her hands on his chest. *Wow.* Esme swallowed. *Ignore that hard strength.* "You didn't storm in here to deny my request. I suspect you just came in here all angry because you're mad that you were roped into the situation. I get it. I'd be mad, too."

The furrows in his brow deepened.

"But I wanted the best for my protection." Who would want the worst? The worst would just get a woman killed.

"How do you know *I'm* the best?"

Because I did research on you long before our paths crossed at Jorlan's party. Not like she could tell him that bit of news. Not yet. "You took out five men and you didn't break a sweat. If you're not the best, then who is?"

His brow smoothed.

The silence stretched a wee bit too long for her. But she didn't break it. She'd said her part. It was his turn. She waited. Frankly, Esme was curious to see just what intriguing terms he'd have in order to take the job and—

"You're marrying me."

Chapter Five

HER DEEP, DARK EYES BLINKED AT HIM. A BROWN SO dark that it almost appeared black. But, wait, were those small flecks of gold in her eyes? Yes, if you looked deeply enough, there was gold buried in the darkness. The glaring lights in the interrogation room let him see the gold. It had been too dark at the mansion. All that soft lighting bullshit. But now, he could see clearly.

And he caught the shock that came and went on her face. "You want me to marry you?" Her lush lips pursed. "It's rather sudden, isn't it? I mean, I get it. You met me. You fell instantly in love. You want to run away and live happily ever after with me. It happens."

He shook his head. "No."

"No to which part? The instant love? The running away? The marrying?"

"It's a *fake* marriage."

"Oh." Her hands still pressed to his chest. "Well, that's disappointing."

What?

"But I suppose it makes more sense." She licked her lips.

Shit. Do not focus on her mouth. Do not.

"Will that be our glorious cover? Pretending to be man and wife? A fake marriage will certainly explain why you have to stick so closely to me. And why we just can't keep our hands off each other."

"I'm not touching you."

"Alas. You are not. Buzzkill." Her hands dropped.

And he wished that she was still touching him. Dammit. What was wrong with him? This was not how he operated. Maybe the fact that he hadn't slept in twenty-four hours? Was that impacting his judgment? Wrecking his control? Maybe he needed to crash so he could think clearly and do the job appropriately. And stop lusting after Esme.

He *would* crash, eventually, but now was the time to go over his rules. "*My* non-negotiables."

"*Excusez-moi?*"

"I have a list of non-negotiables. Before I agree to the job, you will agree to my terms."

"Oh." Her shoulders slumped. "I'd rather thought we were already a done deal."

Not even close, sweetheart. "You want me on the job? Then you follow my rules."

A little shiver seemed to dart over her. Tyler immediately frowned. Was it too cold in the room for her? Hell, she didn't have sleeves on her dress. He didn't have a coat to give her. Maybe he could go find one. Take it from some Fed who didn't need the thing.

"You sound all dominating and controlling." Esme cocked her head to the side. "Do you always have to get your way?"

His gaze sharpened on her. "You're the one who wanted me."

"Yes."

He inhaled. Absolutely delicious. Was that perfume? Body lotion? Tyler shook his head. "Rules."

"Right. I am waiting eagerly to hear them." She motioned with one hand as if to say, *bring them on.*

And he was leaning far too close to her. As if he might kiss her. So Tyler jerked back. "You follow my orders. If danger is closing in, I won't have time to explain myself. You'll need to do what I say without any hesitation."

"Done."

Had that been too easy? Her response felt too easy. "I'm picking the location that we will use. While Gray and his team are trying to contain the people after you, I'll hide you. I'll give you a new identity. I'll make sure you keep breathing."

"I do like to breathe. One of my very favorite things."

His jaw clenched. She was screwing with him. Tyler was certain of that fact. "*You* will play the role of my wife. In public, we'll need to touch each other. To act like we're in love."

"Just in public?" A little pout pulled down her lips.

He was not going to let her derail him and his list of rules. "In private, I am your guard. I am the person in charge. You will take no risks that make you vulnerable. You will leave your phone behind. You will not contact any friends or family unless I tell you it is safe to do so. I'm sure the Feds will handle things with your father." He took a step back. "Is there a boyfriend who will cause problems when you suddenly vanish?" And why had his voice just gone harder?

She shook her head. "No one will care when I vanish. You and I can ride off into the sunset right now and no one will miss me."

He doubted that. A woman like Esme would always be

missed. For clarity, though, he stated, "We're not riding off. We're doing a job." And speaking of the job... "You have to cooperate with Gray and his team. You don't hold back with them. You tell the Feds and the CIA what they need to know. Cooperation is the price of my protection."

A small click reached him as she swallowed. "Then, of course, I am only too happy to cooperate. But, my protection detail has to begin first. Protection, then full cooperation. Seeing as how the charming Feds and CIA have leaked my location and proclaimed to some very bad people that I'm the Fox, it stands to reason that I need to get out of this station immediately." Her right foot tapped on the floor. "So, new husband, when does your job begin? When will you be rushing me to safety?"

His hand extended and closed around her wrist. "Right the hell now." Because she was right, and he knew it. The location was compromised. She was compromised. He had to get her the hell out of there.

Before killers came straight to the door.

He turned for the door.

And it flew open.

A man in a crisp, white shirt and a blue suit stood on the threshold. A shining badge was pinned to his hip, and the bulk of his holster was clear to see beneath his left arm. The overhead light hit the lenses of his glasses as the guy lifted his chin. "I'm here for prisoner transport."

"Uh, Tyler?" Esme bumped into him. Tyler still clasped her right hand. Her left rose to press against his back. "What's he talking about? I'm not going to be transported anywhere without you, right? Seeing as how you're my new ride or die buddy?"

He didn't answer her. He was too busy evaluating the

man in front of him. "Who the fuck are you?" Tyler demanded of the guy blocking his path.

"FBI Special Agent Patrick O'Donnell. And I'm here to transport the prisoner." His jaw hardened. "I was told that she was in here alone. Exactly who the hell are *you*?"

Tyler ignored the question. "You're not transporting her anywhere."

"Yes, I am." The man advanced into the interrogation room. "Direct orders." His eyes narrowed on Tyler. "You're no Fed."

Was that a guess? "Is it the t-shirt? Is that what is giving me away?" Tyler shook his head as he raked the other man's attire with a disdainful glance. "Feds always wear such boringly predictable suits."

Patrick's eyes narrowed behind his glasses. "I'm moving the prisoner. Got transport instructions from Grayson Stone. Now get out of the way and let me do my job."

"Tyler?" A nervous squeak from Esme.

"Would a hitman really be such a dumbass as to walk straight into an FBI office?" Tyler wondered. He let go of Esme's hand. Moved his body slightly so that he was fully in front of her. With his build, he could shield her completely.

Patrick swallowed. His hand also inched toward the bulk of his holster. "That's why she's being moved. This location is no longer secure enough for her. Anyone could try to bust in and get her."

Not just anyone. Not in an FBI office. It would take quite the professional to gain entrance and to get say...all the way into the interrogation room with Esme. It would certainly take someone who was very good at faking being an FBI agent. Someone who knew all the right things to say and exactly how to blend in with the Feds. Someone who was skilled at being a chameleon. A real professional. "Gray didn't give you any transport instructions."

"Look, I get that you're probably on the task force, but what we've discovered about the woman behind you? That puts her *way* above your pay grade." A trickle of sweat slid down Patrick's cheek. "Get out of the way and let me have the woman."

"No, no." From Esme. "Do not let him have me."

He'll have you over my dead body.

"*Out* of the way," Patrick snapped. "That's an order."

Tyler could feel Esme twisting the back of his t-shirt with her grip. "Make me."

Patrick's eyes bulged. "What?"

Tyler took an aggressive step toward him. Then another. "I said, make me get out of your way."

Esme had released Tyler's shirt.

Patrick's mouth opened and closed. And then those twitchy fingers of his did exactly what Tyler had expected. They went for the gun.

FBI agent, my ass.

Tyler leapt for him. Even as Patrick hauled out the weapon, Tyler grabbed his hand. He shoved Patrick back, and he rammed Patrick's hand against the side of the open door. Once. Twice. The gun clattered to the floor on the third hit. It also fired off a shot *before* it dropped.

Esme screamed.

Tyler's blood iced. He knew the bullet had missed her. It had blasted out and slammed into the wall. But what if it *had* hit her? What if Tyler hadn't come back into interrogation to go over his rules? What if she'd been in there alone when this jerk arrived?

Dammit, a real Fed *should* have been guarding the door

to interrogation. Patrick—or whoever the hell he was—should not have gotten inside to Esme.

Tyler drew back his fist, and he plowed it hard into the face of the bastard who'd thought he would just waltz in and *take* Esme. "Over my dead body," Tyler rasped.

Pounding footsteps rushed toward him. Tyler hit the pretend agent a second time. The prick slumped bonelessly and slid down to the floor. Blood trickled from his nose and busted lip. His glasses sat askew on his face.

"*What in the hell is happening here?*" Gray bellowed.

Tyler looked over at him. Gray's gun was out and currently aimed at the man sprawled on the floor. "He said you gave him orders to transport Esme." Tyler's head whipped around so that he could find Esme.

She'd pressed her back to the mirror. Her skin had gone too pale, and her eyes were way too wide. He didn't like the look of fear on her face. Not at all.

"You're the only one with orders to transport her." Gray crouched next to the beaten man even as the jerk's eyes blearily blinked open. "Who are you?" Gray demanded.

"F-FBI—" the man began.

"Fuck that shit," Tyler snarled. "He pulled his gun on me. He came to take her. He knew *your* name, Gray. This whole place is compromised." He marched for Esme. Held out his hand.

She stared at his fingers. Then Esme put her hand over his palm.

"I'm getting you the hell out of here."

"He's *not* FBI." Gray sounded adamant.

"No shit," Tyler returned. His stare bored into Esme's. "You're coming with me."

A nod. "I am so glad I married you," she whispered.

His fingers closed around hers. Carefully, though, so he

didn't hurt her. He spun back for the door. Saw that a swarm of agents were behind Gray. And the man on the floor? He'd already been cuffed. Gray had the guy's badge in his hand and a look of disgust on his face.

"Real ballsy to just waltz into a Fed's office," Gray announced. Not an admiring tone. A pissed one. "You seriously thought you'd get away with that shit?"

"I-I'm so sorry, Agent Stone," a fresh-faced agent with blood-red cheeks stammered. "He said you wanted me to come into the conference room for a meeting, so I left my post. H-he said he was supposed to take over guard duty here. I saw his badge and he looked legit, and I—"

Tyler's growl cut through the apologizing agent's words. *He was the one who should have been watching the interrogation room.* Tyler recognized the green agent. He'd walked past him a few times earlier.

So much for top-of-the-line security. The place felt more like a joke than anything else. There was a reason why he hadn't become a Fed. Two reasons, actually. *Too much red tape. Too much bullshit.* "Clear a path," Tyler barked. "*Now.*"

The man in cuffs laughed. "Five million." He smiled, revealing the blood on his teeth from his busted lip. "Like I'll be the only one who comes for her with that much cash on the table."

A path had been cleared. But Tyler stopped in front of the grinning jackass. He kept his grip on Esme's hand. "Hey, dumbass," Tyler said to him. "You just confessed to being a hitman. A confession you made in front of at least five agents. You attempted to assault a U.S. Marshal. Just when do you think you'll be able to see the light of day again?"

That wiped the smile off the creep's face.

"Someone did not think this through," Tyler noted. "Your mistake."

But five million dollars could just be too tempting to pass up. The hitman must have been close by, and he'd seized his opportunity when he'd received word about the five-million-dollar pay day. And the damn thing was...

What if I hadn't been in the room with her? Shit. In a freaking FBI office, this prick could have killed Esme.

Enough of this crap. His path was clear. And he was taking his charge the hell out of there. He strode forward. Esme's heels hurriedly tapped as she followed him.

"Uh, Tyler?" Gray cleared his throat. "We need to talk more. I need—"

"*I* need to get her the hell away. That's a hitman cuffed near you. And that's a bullet hole in the wall." He threw a glare at his friend. "She's mine to protect, so let *me* do my damn job."

A grudging nod from Gray. "Fine, but first..." His stare darted to Esme. "I'm gonna need some intel from her."

* * *

"I WANT TO SEE HER."

Grayson glanced up from the paperwork on his desk. A freaking mound of paperwork. Because a sonofabitch hitman had stormed into the FBI field office and nearly taken their prime witness in an international criminal investigation. That attack had led to hours of a paperwork nightmare.

And now...

Grayson sighed.

Now he had Jorlan Rodgers in his space. The man had lawyers on either side of him. Expensive ones that

Grayson recognized from their billboards and commercials.

"Hello, Jorlan." Grayson kept his tone civil. "Just who is it that you want to see?" As if he didn't know.

"Esme Laurent." Bitten off with fury. "Right now."

Grayson glanced around his office. "I don't think she's here."

"Don't give me that bullshit!" Jorlan lunged forward. One of the lawyers grabbed his arm. Jorlan heaved out a breath. "I know you arrested her. She attempted to steal from me, and I want to confront her. I want to know how the hell she thought she could get away with taking what's *mine*."

Grayson closed the file he'd been studying. Then he slowly rose to his feet. "There's been a mistake."

"Hell, yes, there has been." Jorlan's nostrils flared. "No one steals from me and walks away."

"I'm not sure where you are getting your intel." Again, Grayson kept his voice civil. "But Esme Laurent has not been charged with any crimes. The scene at your home was very chaotic and confusing so I'm afraid some details may have been erroneously spread."

"Bullshit."

"Esme *did* assist in recovering your diamonds." *Because they were strapped to her thigh and their recovery was made by Tyler Barrett right in front of me.*

"What?" Jorlan's jaw nearly hit the floor. "Recovering them?"

The lawyer on his right—an older male with carefully styled, silver hair—leaned forward and whispered in Jorlan's ear.

"Fuck that," Jorlan blasted back at what had obviously

been an attempt by the other man to calm his client. "I want to see Esme, right the hell now!"

"I wish I could help you." Grayson lifted his hands and then let them fall back to his sides in one of those *so-sorry* gestures. "But Esme left hours ago. Her father is the French Ambassador, you know. He wanted his daughter away from the spotlight. Perhaps you could try calling her?"

Rage flashed on Jorlan's face. A savage, chilling rage.

His lawyer whispered to him again.

Jorlan's chin notched up. "I will absolutely call her." A cold promise. "Thank you for letting me know about the confusion." He turned on his heel and marched for the door.

Grayson waited until the guy was *almost* out of his office and then, acting on a hunch, he asked, "Was there anything else of value in your safe?"

Jorlan stilled.

"Anything else taken that you would like to report to the Feds?"

Jorlan turned. Stared at him. "Esme Laurent is not here."

"Yes, that's what I said." *She's flying away as we speak.*

"I believe that I will be handling my own affairs from here on out. It's so hard to find good help in order to get a job done."

There was something about those low words...

Good help. Fuck. Grayson was around his desk in an instant. "Did you send that sonofabitch?"

Both suit-clad lawyers jumped between Grayson and Jorlan.

Over their shoulders, Jorlan gave a little wave. "See you soon, Agent Stone."

And he walked right the hell out, whistling as he left.

* * *

Jorlan climbed into the back of his limo. The fool lawyers tried to climb in with him, but he waved them away. "Shut the damn door!" he ordered his driver.

The door shut.

A few moments later, the limo was shooting down the road and leaving the lawyers in his dust. Jorlan's right hand fisted.

The bitch thinks she's getting away from me? Rage churned in his gut. Oh, hell, no. No one played him for a fool. No one screwed with his business. No one *touched* what belonged to him.

Esme Laurent wasn't just going to disappear into the sunset.

He'd hunt her down. He'd rip apart her world.

And then she would be very, very sorry that she'd ever tried to play games with him.

Too bad the hitman he'd tipped off with Esme's location at the FBI office hadn't gotten the job done properly. Jorlan yanked his phone from his pocket. He made a fast call because loose ends truly were a pain in his ass. The call was answered on the first ring.

He appreciated promptness in a business associate.

"What can I do for you?" No other greeting. Just that.

"Snip the loose end."

"Done."

He hung up. The failed hitman would be eliminated soon enough. No ties back to him. And now Jorlan could focus once more on the beautiful Esme.

His thumb scrolled across the pictures on his phone. Stopped when he came to her. Her dimpled smile stared back at him. So deceptively beautiful. And with just the right hint of evil inside. He'd thought they might be a perfect match.

Too bad she'd screwed him over.

Too bad he'd have to make her pay.

Too bad he'd have to kill her.

But...

No one steals from me. You were warned, Esme. You should have listened to my warning.

He'd find her. No matter where she went, there would be no escape. Not with his money and his reach. The authorities could be bought. More hunters and hitmen brought in to track her. She'd be hunted down like the prey she was.

In the end, she'd beg his forgiveness.

Too bad for Esme that he never forgave anyone.

Chapter Six

Esme was incredibly comfortable. Granted, her pillow was as hard as a rock, but she felt warm and protected. And being *protected*? Safe? That was a very new feeling for her. She'd fallen into a deep sleep shortly after the plane took off. Plane rides always made her sleepy. And she *had* been up for more hours than she could clearly recall.

So, she'd drifted off.

And had some very steamy dreams about a certain U.S. Marshal.

Her eyes opened. Her head turned. And she realized that her pillow? Her ever-so-hard pillow? That would be his thigh. She was actually stretched out across the seats, and her head was on his rock-hard thigh. When she turned her head, she found herself staring straight up at him.

Grimly, he stared down at her.

"So..." Esme cleared her throat. "I don't actually recall how I got in this position."

He kept staring back.

She should get up. She would. Her head moved and...

Oh.

"Ahem." Esme winced. "I'll get up...carefully, shall I?"

His jaw could not possibly clench any harder.

She got up, carefully, because there had been a very aroused cock not far from her head. Once she was securely in *her* seat again, Esme discovered that the skirt of her dress had hiked way, way up. She pushed it down, extremely aware of the silence from the stone-faced man beside her. "Plane rides make me sleepy."

"Um."

"Though, for the record, I can't remember ever just making the passenger next to me into my own personal pillow. You're the first on that count."

His eyes were on her. So very watchful. "Good to know."

"Guess you're special?" She tried a smile.

He didn't smile back. "You were slumped on my arm. Your neck was all twisted."

Now that he mentioned it, her neck did ache a bit.

"I put you down so you'd be more comfortable."

He had? She couldn't control her beaming grin. "That was incredibly thoughtful of you." Her fingers skimmed up his arm. *So warm.* "Thank you, Ty."

"Tyler."

"That's what I said."

"No, you called me Ty."

She waited. With brows expectantly raised and everything.

He didn't speak.

This man. Shaking her head, she politely inquired, "Do you have a problem with being called Ty?"

"It's not my name."

Playing with him was too fun. "It's a shortened version

of your name." The man was precious. "Do you not have any friends who call you Ty?"

"*No one calls me Ty*."

"Well, all right then. Jeez. Don't have to get all growly, *Tyler*." She was still stroking his arm, but since he was being bitey, she pulled her hand back. No strokes should be given when someone was being rude. "I was just trying to get into my new role. As your loving wife, I would think it would be okay for me to call you by a nickname. But if you don't like Ty—"

"I don't."

So huffy. "Then I'll just call you something else. Darling. Sweetheart. Love of my life. Best sex ever." She shrugged one shoulder. "I'll think of something that works. No worries."

"Is everything a joke to you?"

"Are you saying that you will not be the best sex ever for me?" They were the only ones on the plane. Well, other than the two pilots up front. She and Tyler were the only ones *in the back* of the plane. So it wasn't as if she had to worry that they were being overheard. "This news greatly disappoints me. I had very high expectations where you were concerned. Especially when I woke up, and there was a giant cock so close to my face."

He sucked in a breath. "My job is to protect you. Not to fuck you."

She made a distinct point of *not* looking down at his giant dick. "But you want to fuck me."

"It is a *physical* response," he gritted.

"Well, yes, lust is very physical." As if she'd argue that point. "You don't have to get snippy about it."

"Snippy?" Tyler seemed to be choking.

She hadn't stuttered, so Esme knew he'd understood. It

was time for him to understand something else. "I want you, too. Or do you think I just go around kissing every man I meet?"

Silence.

"Oh, bad form," she whispered. Her chest ached. "You do think I kiss every man I meet." Very insulting. And hurtful. "You are wrong. I happen to be very choosy about my partners. I like you. I was simply being honest and telling you how I felt." She rose.

He immediately threw out a hand to block her path.

She looked at the hand. Then at him. "Is there a problem?"

"Where are you going?"

"Well, considering that I am trapped in mid-air with you, I'm obviously not going far. Not like I plan to jump out of the plane. I seem to be without a parachute." She sniffed. "But your kind FBI friend *did* bring me a bag." One that was currently in the overhead compartment. "I assume it has clothing inside it. I was going to change out of this fabulous dress and into another outfit. That way, I'd be less likely to attract attention when we get to our mystery destination." Because he hadn't told her where they were going.

Probably for the best.

His gaze could not get harder. Or hotter. That blue seemed to blaze.

His hand lowered.

She maneuvered past him. Tried to, anyway. Their bodies brushed a great deal because he was unnecessarily large. At one point, she basically straddled him. A fun position for another time.

"Stop."

Her hands came down on his shoulders. "It's not my fault you're so big."

"I'll get up." His hands closed around her waist. He lifted her up as he rose. Turned and a moment or so later, she was in the narrow aisle. Tyler even reached up and snagged her bag for her.

"Aren't you the gentlemen? *Merci, monsieur.*"

The faint lines near his mouth tightened. "You...don't have to speak French."

"It's my native tongue. Sometimes, it just slips out." But she was intrigued. She pressed closer to him. "Or do you like it too much when I speak French?" A teasing murmur.

Faster than any striking snake could be, his hand flew out. Curled around her shoulder. "You have to stop playing with me."

But she wasn't playing. When would he get a clue on that score?

"You don't want to fuck me. Despite what you said *in French* at the station. And what you just said here and now."

"How do you know what I want?"

"I'm part of the game you're working. You think I don't know a con artist when I see one?"

She leaned closer to him. Parted her lips.

His gaze was on her mouth. Totally focused.

"That is an *asshole* thing to say," Esme informed him. "Absolute asshole. Here's a helpful tip about me. I don't always lie." In fact, she tried to tell the truth the majority of the time. "Wasn't I helpful to your friend at the FBI? Before we left, didn't I give him reliable intel that he could use to solve several big crimes?" She had. She'd considered the info as a down payment on her protection plan. "Those offshore accounts *will* check out. And the locations I gave him that had stolen artifacts? All legitimate. I was helping."

"The very fact that you knew that information means you're involved in illegal activities up to your gorgeous eyes."

She batted her lashes. "You like my eyes? Good to know. At this point, we've established you like both my eyes and my ass. Thank you. To be fair, I also like your eyes. I find it particularly charming when they blaze with heat and go all molten blue."

"I don't think molten blue is a thing," he muttered.

"Then clearly you have never seen your eyes when you are battling a hard case of lust." Esme cleared her throat. "I suppose you have an okay ass, too."

"You were just...honest with me."

"No, I wasn't. I was lying." A wince. "Your ass is actually far better than okay."

"*Esme.*"

"I'm not a villainess. Don't make me out to be one." Another bit of honesty. "You're the hero, though. That is plain for anyone to see. Surely, I'm not the first woman who has been attracted to you. Not all women go for the bad guys. Some of us have other preferences."

"You want to fuck me...because I'm *good?* Baby, you could not be more wrong about me."

"Are you getting into the role of my loving husband? Or did that endearment just slip out accidentally?"

He blinked.

"I'll assume that we keep our first names during the course of this undercover operation. Easier for us to fall into character, yes? If we keep using our real first names?" Esme tapped her chin with her right index finger. "But what will our last names be?"

"Hollow."

She nodded. "Esme and Tyler Hollow. Fair enough. After I get back from changing, you'll have to tell me all about our cover story." She took the bag from him. Their fingers brushed. A bolt of heat shot through her, but she refused to acknowledge it. She'd told him how she felt. He'd have to make the next move. She couldn't very well do all the romantic heavy lifting herself. A woman did like some pursuit. "I am hoping you have some marvelously splendid how-we-met story that you are planning to share with me. And your proposal to me?" She swung away from him. "Has to be epic. People aren't going to believe we have some super passionate marriage if we are not epic." She made her way down the plane's aisle and toward the small bathroom.

"Esme."

His voice stopped her just as she reached for the bathroom door.

"I should have told you that another one of my rules was no lying. You can't manipulate me. You can't pretend with me. I'm the man saving that sweet ass of yours. I have to know everything about you."

No one knew everything about her. "You stood between me and a gun today." She peered back at him.

"You had already done the same for me."

Yes, but the gun *he'd* stood in front of had actually been loaded. The one she'd stood in front of hadn't been. Something she wondered if he knew. Surely his FBI buddies had told him that fact already? "You're the hero. Not me." A warning for him.

"You told me you weren't a villainess."

Yes, but not being a villain didn't necessarily make you into the good girl, either. "Shades of gray." She bobbed her head. "I've got to ditch these heels. They are killing my feet.

See you soon." She opened the door. Crept into the small bathroom. And her first order of business? She did ditch the heels. Then she bent and twisted the bottom of the right shoe. The heel opened because it had been hollow. A perfect hiding space. The small USB drive fell into her palm. "Hello, gorgeous," she whispered.

As if she'd waste her time stealing something as boring as diamonds. Please. She could get diamonds any day of the week. But the USB drive? Oh, it was special. Worth killing for, in fact.

Her fingers closed around the drive. Now the big question...had Jorlan realized what she'd done? And just how long did she have before he started to hunt her? Probably not long at all.

And that's why it is such a good thing that I have my own personal U.S. Marshal for protection.

Such a very, very good thing...because recently, Esme may have done a few very, very wicked things.

* * *

"So WHERE EXACTLY ARE WE HEADED?" The plane had touched down an hour ago on a deserted air-strip. She'd been whisked out of the plane and into a dark SUV in record time. Esme had barely had a chance to wave goodbye to the pilots before Tyler had been hitting the road. Hard.

The darkness of night surrounded her, and he hadn't taken anything close to a main road, so there had been no road signs for her to see. In fact, when she squinted hard enough, all she could see in the dark were the twisting outlines of trees. Lots and lots of trees.

He took me to the middle of nowhere, check.

"Where are we headed?" she repeated her question.

"And do tell me our delicious cover story." Because he had not shared it on the plane. When she'd gone back to the seat, Tyler had been dead silent. "Did we meet in Paris? Beneath the Eiffel Tower? Did you take one look at me and fall hopelessly in love?"

"I fell into something, all right."

Her gaze whipped away from the trees and onto him. They narrowed suspiciously. "Are you making a joke? Because I had no clue you were the joking kind."

"There's going to be no talk of France, Esme. Not when we share our, uh, backstory with people. And since you are so good at not having any accent at all, go with that," he ordered her. "Don't slip up and speak any French."

"I'm sure I can manage to avoid slipups." Not like the man was talking to some kind of amateur. She yawned. The plane flight had actually been pretty short, and though she'd slept, she could use a good five or six hours more of rest time. Before they'd boarded the plane, Tyler had whisked her through Miami and in and out of several different locations in what she suspected had been an attempt to throw any other tracking hitmen off their trail. Hours had drifted by. He'd fed her some takeout, they'd waited for the plane to be ready, and now—nightfall. Nightfall plus her new home. "I've got our last names. How about we flesh out more of our story since you're not telling me where we're headed?" How many times did a woman have to ask for details?

"No need to flesh it out. I've got a full file for you in my bag. After we get to the house, you can read over it all tonight, or you can check it out first thing in the morning."

"A whole file, huh? Someone works fast." Her fingers tapped against her leg. "Why don't you give me a few highlights?"

"You just don't want to ride in silence, do you?"

Actually, she didn't. Besides, she'd already had plenty of silence on the plane, thank you very much. "I may look all bold on the outside, but I'm quite shaken, if you want the truth. It's not every day that a man bursts into an interrogation room and tries to kill you." She swallowed and could have sworn she tasted the bitterness of fear on her tongue. Fear was bitter. Lust was spicy. Love? She had to guess on that one, but Esme thought it would taste sweet. Maybe one day she'd find out. But, back to business. "There is the matter of the five million dollars on my head. That amount of money tells me that more bad guys will be coming after me. The life I knew before is over." Dead and buried. A good thing.

"They aren't going to get you." Grim. "They'd have to go through me first."

Oh, wow, but he was sweet.

"I'm not easy to get through," Tyler added. "I'll rip them apart before they ever so much as touch you."

So, sweet was probably not the right word for him. *Bloodthirsty*. That fit much better. "Where have you been all my life?"

A shake of his head. "You're not going to manipulate me, Esme."

He kept saying that, but, alas, Tyler was wrong. She already was manipulating him. "I really like the way you say my name, FYI. It's all hot and dark and rumbling. Pretty much how I'd imagine you'd say it if we were in bed together."

He sucked in a breath, then rasped, "*Not going to manipulate me.*"

"Who's manipulating? I'm stating a fact." She went back to peering through the windshield. "I swear, I haven't seen a single sign of *anyone*. Are you taking me deep into the woods? Are we going to be all isolated and have to share one bed because that's the only thing available and you just can't keep those wicked hands of yours off my body when we are thrust together into such close, intimate confines?"

More silence. Hadn't she told him that she didn't enjoy silence?

Silence made her think too much. She didn't want to think right then. If she thought too much, she'd realize just how screwed she was. *Tyler is the only thing standing between me and some extreme danger*. Good thing he was so bloodthirsty.

"There's gonna be more than one bed," he finally said.

"Oh." A sigh. "That's disappointing."

"What?"

"You heard me. Don't pretend you didn't."

He cleared his throat. "The house was set up on short notice. I didn't want to go through the usual channels."

Once more, her attention shifted back to him.

"So I pulled strings. I'm not exactly sure what all I'll be facing on this case, and I needed to have some people I trusted close by."

Okay, that all sounded good to her.

"We're almost there." He turned the SUV to the right.

How had he known when to turn? She could see nothing, but, sure enough, they were on another road.

"And since you are so eager for details...you and I are newlyweds."

She couldn't help her smile. "Delightful." A nod. "We are passionately-in-love newlyweds. We can't keep our hands off each other. Check." Her fingers were itching to touch him, but she was holding herself back.

"We wanted to get out of the big city because we want to raise our future kids in a small town."

"Oh my!" A thrilled exclamation from her. "This is sounding like one of my favorite Hallmark movies. Pinch me because I have to be dreaming."

He growled.

A little glow spilled inside her. She liked his growls far too much. Other men would not be able to pull off those deep, rumbling sounds. Tyler did. He made them ridiculously sexy.

"We rented property in town because I have an old Marine buddy in the area who gave us a great deal on the house. We're going to fix it up a bit. Make it our own. Turn it into a home and raise a family."

Okay, the glow had changed, and damn if she didn't feel wistful. "Is it going to be a picket-fence place? With flowers in the yard? Cute shutters on the windows?"

"Ah, not exactly."

She waved that away. "I'm sure it will be amazing."

He coughed.

"What is it that I do in this amazing life of ours?"

"You're an interior designer."

Esme nodded. "That's why I'm so keen to fix up the place." She could get into this role. "And what about you?"

"Private security. We'll say I manage a cyber company. I work from home, and that's how I'll be able to stay close to you day and night."

They were going through some sort of town. Finally. She could barely make out the buildings. Excitement pumped through her because this was actually happening. She'd kissed her old life goodbye. She was starting fresh with her marshal. Good things were going to happen. She could do good, or at least, fake doing good.

When the SUV pulled to a stop about ten minutes later, she jumped from the vehicle. The headlights were still on so she could see...

Her shoulders slumped.

No picket fence. No flowers. No shutters.

Instead, the house sat, seemingly forgotten and alone, in the dark. Big, looming, with a sloping roof and twisting trees that surrounded it, as if fighting to consume the home.

It was stark. Intense. Slightly scary.

Her new home sweet home.

"I'll get the bags," Tyler said from right behind her. She hadn't heard him leave the SUV, so Esme gave a little jump. And not like she wanted him taking *her* bag, so she rushed to snag it herself.

He followed her as she cautiously made her way up the steps in front of the house. They creaked beneath her feet. Spooky. She could have sworn that the wind was even howling as she crept toward the front door.

Tyler dropped his bag on the porch. She was pretty sure that dust shot into the air around them when it dropped. He pulled out a key and opened the door a moment later. His hand waved. "Ladies first."

She didn't go first. She did look around. There was another house—she could see the dim light from it—about fifty yards away. A neighbor. "People can always be watching." Even when you thought you were safe and alone.

"What? Uh, no, no one is watching."

Esme still did not advance. Her right foot tapped. "I think you're supposed to carry me over the threshold."

She caught his curse. Esme bit back a smile.

"You like messing with me, don't you?" Tyler suddenly accused.

To be honest, it was one of the few things bringing her joy at the moment.

"If you're not strong enough to carry me, it's okay," she assured him in a placating tone. "I'll just tell any neighbors who ask that you threw out your back a few days ago. Because of that, we now have to be careful with strenuous activities when it comes to you—" The last bit ended on a gasp because he'd swung her into his arms.

Yes, please. This was what she'd wanted.

He held her easily. And, oh, indeed, it was hot. Sexy. Because Tyler strode across the threshold as if carrying her was no problem whatsoever. As if her weight didn't matter at all. She could feel his strength all around her. She dropped her bag as soon as they swept inside, and her arm looped around his neck. He was walking forward into the dark with her held tenderly in his arms, and her head tipped back.

This man was so very different from the people who usually inhabited her world. He was the hero. The good guy. Who would have thought that the good guy would make her want to do so many very bad things?

Tyler's head had turned toward her. And, granted, it was dark, but she was pretty sure his eyes were on her mouth. Her eyes were definitely on his mouth. And her fingers might just be applying the smallest amount of pressure on the back of his neck in order to get him to bend his head so that those slightly cruel— but ever so sexy—lips of his would press to hers.

Come on. Come on. Just a little closer.

Their lips were so close that she could almost taste him. *Spicy.* Because lust was, indeed, spicy and rich and somehow decadent all at the same time. At least, with Tyler, it was.

Her mouth parted—

And he dropped her.

She bounced when she hit the couch. A couch that had been covered by a giant, white cloth.

"Welcome home, wife." He swung away and turned on the lights.

The bright illumination had her flinching. "Thanks so much, husband."

"The bedrooms are upstairs. One for you, and one for me. You can take your pick first. I want to check the perimeter." He didn't even look back at her as he marched out of the room.

So much for having a romantic moment. How many times did a woman have to make a move before she got tired of rejection? Fine. She could take a hint.

Or a giant, flashing sign that said the man wasn't interested.

Esme climbed off the cloth-covered couch. She swept a glance around the den, then went to collect her bag. At the foot of the stairs, she paused just a moment.

Then she began to climb. One step at a time.

* * *

I WANT HER MOUTH.

Tyler stalked around the perimeter of the house. All of the security cameras were in place. Fully functional. He'd engaged the system moments before—right after he'd basically run out of the home in order to get away from Esme.

Or rather, in order to get away so he didn't do all the things he wanted to do with Esme.

Her mouth had been less than an inch from his. He'd

wanted to kiss her. To taste her. To make her moan. He'd wanted *her*.

To fuck her and claim her and have her scratching her nails down his back as she begged for more.

He'd never crossed a line on any case. But with her, that was all he wanted to do. Cross lines. Break rules. Take. Her.

And she knows it. Esme knew how sexy she was. It was a game to her. Her seduction was a power play. He had to remember that. No matter how damn cute and engaging she looked when she flashed her dimples at him. He could not trust her.

Con artist. Thief. Criminal.

He knew what she was.

The problem?

His body didn't seem to *care.*

Satisfied that the location was, in fact, safe, he headed back into the home. Locked the door. Set the system for the remainder of the night. The interior lights were still on, blazing, but there was no sign of Esme in the den. Good. She'd gone to bed. One less problem for him to face.

"Oh, Tyler!"

Shit.

He looked up.

Esme stood at the top of the stairs. She'd changed clothes. Put on some silky pajama top. *Where was the pajama bottom to match the top?* "Aren't you missing pants?" he rumbled.

She laughed and darted down a few of the steps. Her bare feet skated over the stairs. "The top is long enough to cover me."

No, it wasn't. It stopped mid-thigh.

"We have bigger problems," she told him.

His body instantly went on alert. Well, a different kind

of alert because his dick had already decided to salute the moment he'd seen her standing at the top of the stairs in that silky top.

He rushed up the stairs and met her half-way. "What's wrong?" Dammit, he'd been so busy checking outside. He should have looked *inside* first. But he hadn't thought the place could be compromised so quickly. Only a select few trusted individuals knew he'd been planning to arrive at the house with Esme.

"You've been misled." Her hands were tucked behind her back. The placement stretched the fabric of the black, silk pajama top across her breasts.

Misled? Tell me something I didn't already figure out, sweetheart. Like he and Gray didn't realize the woman was working her own agenda? Not their first ballgame. But he'd decided to play along. He had two jobs on this case.

Job one...Keep Esme alive. Protect her. He would absolutely get that job done. No one would hurt her on his watch.

Job two? That was a little more complicated. Because job two involved him getting close to her and discovering every single secret that Esme possessed. The Feds and the CIA wanted her intel. He was the guy who was supposed to deliver those juicy secrets to them on a silver platter. In order to do that, though, Tyler had to make Esme trust him completely.

He suspected Esme didn't trust easily.

He'd stopped a few stairs below her, but she still had to tip her head back just a little to stare up at him. Her eyes were big and deep and so dark. If a man looked into them too long, he might just lose his soul.

So why am I looking so long? "How was I misled?" Was she already about to confess?

She looked both innocent and tempting as she stood on the stairs. Innocent because her hands were behind her back. Her eyes so wide.

Tempting because...it was Esme. And she appeared to only wear a top, dammit. Did she even have on a bra beneath that top? Panties?

Sweet hell. Esme...with no panties. His back teeth clenched.

Her hands came up. Curled around his shoulders. "We have a problem," she whispered.

Battle-ready tension flooded through him. As if he hadn't already been tense enough.

"There are two bedrooms upstairs," she informed him. "But one is completely empty. No furniture at all. Just a big, empty space."

What? His brows shot up.

"So, I regret to inform you, Mr. U.S. Marshal..." Her fingers bit lightly into his shoulders through the t-shirt that he wore. "We are, in fact, in a one-bed situation."

Fuck.

"I really hope you don't snore," she added sweetly.

Chapter Seven

"Good morning, sunshine."

Her bright voice had his eyes flaring open. She beamed down at him, her hair falling forward because she was bent very close to stare at him.

"Was the floor as uncomfortable as it looks?" Esme continued in a slightly sing-song voice. Damn if she didn't look perky and well-rested and just the faintest bit evil as she motioned toward his body and the hardwood floor. "I get that the couch was too small for your very large form. But there was a perfectly good bed upstairs that I was willing to share with you."

He sat up. Growled.

"There it is," she enthused. "The sound I live for. Guess that means the floor is, indeed, as uncomfortable as it looks."

He opened his mouth to reply. *Fuck yes, it was uncomfortable.* But not just because the floor had been unyielding and stupid hard, but because he'd spent way too much time thinking about her during the night. Realizing that she was just up the stairs. That she'd left the bedroom door unlocked. That she'd *invited* him into her bed.

And he'd so wanted to take her up on that invitation. But not because he wanted to sleep. He wanted in the bed with her because he wanted to fuck Esme until neither one of them could move.

But he didn't get the chance to actually say anything because Esme thrust a cup of coffee into his hand. "Made this for you. It's probably horrible, full disclosure, because the stuff in the kitchen looked ancient, but I like to start my day with a good deed."

He took the mug of steaming coffee from her. Their fingers brushed. Yep. There it was. The spark of awareness that ignited each time they touched. How long would that last?

"Good to know you feel it, too," she nodded, as if satisfied. "Even if you apparently aren't going to do jack about the situation."

His brows rose.

"Hope you like your coffee black. There was no milk or sugar in the kitchen. We should probably go shopping soon." She put a hand to her heart. "Our first grocery trip as man and wife."

"Why do you start each day with a good deed?" Time for him to cut through her BS and get to know the real woman.

Her lashes flickered. "Because if I try to do good, it balances out the bad that is sure to follow later on. After all, I'm incredibly bad, right?" She stood, and he realized that she was wearing faded jeans. A light blue top. The jeans hugged her hips and thighs, and the top flowed over her chest like some kind of soft, silky waterfall. "You think I'm bad. You think I'm a thief."

"You *are* a thief." He sipped the coffee. It was—surprisingly—damn good. "I caught you red-handed, remember?" Which brought up a point he wanted to discuss. "How the hell did you make that walk on the ledge? Weren't you terrified? And, dammit, Esme, it was raining and slippery. You could have fallen to your death. For what? Diamonds? Your family is already rich as sin."

"So are you. You pretend to be the poor, former Marine, but I know different." Her gaze wasn't on his face. It was on his chest. His bare chest. He'd ditched his shirt, socks, and shoes, and slept in his jeans. Her hand flew out and touched a scar near his shoulder. "From a bullet?"

Her touch electrified him. "Yes," he hissed.

Her fingers trailed lower. Close to his right side. "This look likes the slash from a knife." She caressed him.

He put the mug down, fast. Not like he wanted to singe himself because she was making him twitchy with her touches. "It *was* from a knife."

Her hand dipped down—

His hand flew out and curled around her fingers. "I think that's enough exploration, don't you?"

Her long lashes lifted. "You have a lot of scars."

"Yeah, I'm sure they are a real turnoff to someone like you."

"What's that supposed to mean?"

"Fucking perfection, that's what I mean." Enough games. Enough playing. They were away from the rest of the world. He rose. So did she. She kinda had to rise fully since he still had his grip on her wrist. "You're all gloss and glamour."

Those long lashes flickered once more. "I see."

"You can drop your act, you know." He should let her go. He didn't. His thumb slid along her inner wrist. "There's no one here to see you but me. You don't have to pretend to be someone you're not. Drop the good deed BS. Drop the pretense that you want me. I'm here to protect you. Fucking me will not be necessary in order to get me on the job. I'm already committed to your case."

She sucked in a breath. And she also yanked her hand away from him. "I have just learned several important things about you." Her chin tipped up. "You like your coffee black."

Yeah, he did.

"You have far too many scars on your body."

Like he could help that shit. "Came from doing the job. When you risk your life, you have to be ready for pain."

Her delicate jaw hardened. "And you are an absolute *asshole* first thing in the morning. I'll be sure to remember that."

"Esme..."

"Here are some things for you to remember about me. What did I learn? Three things about you?" Before he could respond, she bobbed her head in a jerky nod. "Right. Three. So I'll tell you three things about me." One index finger shot into the air. "One. I actually *do* try to start my day with a good deed. It's something that my mom taught me. Do something nice first thing. No matter how small. Because, after all, who wants to be an *asshole* first thing in the morning? Oh, right. You do."

"Esme—"

"Two." A second finger joined the first. "I don't have any problem with your scars. Wait. Scratch that. I do. I'm sorry that you were hurt. But they are not a turnoff. Quite the opposite. They show me that you're strong and that you're a fighter and that even when you get hurt, you keep going. I find your scars unbelievably sexy."

He swallowed. "Esme..." Softer now.

"Three." Not soft at all. A third finger joined the others.

"I only *fuck* someone because I want to do it. I don't fuck in order to manipulate or get protection or for any other ridiculous reason that you can suggest. I thought you felt the same heat that flares between us. I *thought* you might be someone I could respect. Instead, I see that you're indeed... *an early morning asshole.*" Two of her fingers immediately lowered so that only one remained. A very prominent one. "Fuck you," she said sweetly. Then she snatched up his cup of coffee and marched into the kitchen.

She marched fast, and he shook his head to get out of his stupor as he charged after her. "Esme!"

She dumped the coffee down the drain. Such a profound waste. Then whirled to face him. "I'm sure you can make your own coffee." Her hands curled around the counter behind her. "Oh, whoops. There is no more coffee in the house. Too bad."

He stalked forward.

There was no place for her to go.

Her breath heaved in and out. Her eyes gleamed. Fury had brought faint red color to her cheeks.

His hands flew out and clamped on the counter near her body. He caged her there. And all he wanted was to kiss her.

Do. Not.

What got him—what *really got him*—was that he was certain he'd seen actual hurt flare in her eyes. And Tyler didn't like it when Esme hurt. "I'm sorry," he rasped.

"Didn't quite hear that. Want to try again?"

"I'm *sorry.*" Louder. Well, rougher, anyway.

"What, exactly, are you sorry for?"

She was too freaking gorgeous. "For being an early morning asshole." Having her pissed at him was no way to build trust.

She searched his eyes. Then shook her head. "It won't work."

"Excuse me?" Her scent had filled his nostrils. That delicious scent.

"You, pretending to be sorry in order to get back in my good graces so that you can manipulate me. It's not going to work. I mean, sure, maybe it would work on the women you are used to scamming."

"*Scamming?*"

"But I'm not like them. I'm very good at reading people. It's a particular talent I have. And I know your apology isn't legit. You're just trying to get under my skin. You think if you get close enough to me, I'll reveal all of my deep, dark secrets to you."

He was so close that their bodies were brushing. So close that it would barely take an inch more, and he could have his mouth on hers. "You're supposed to reveal all of your deep, dark secrets to the Feds," he reminded her. "It's part of your protection deal. You stay alive, and in return, you share those secrets."

Her right hand flew up. Pressed against his jaw. "But there are secrets..." Soft. "And then there are *secrets*."

"What the hell does that mean?"

"Figure it out."

"I can't figure out anything about you yet." He was trying, though.

"Give yourself some time. You will. I have faith in you."

He sucked in a breath and lurched back as if she'd just burned him.

Esme glowered. "What is it now?"

"I—"

His phone rang. Vibrating and pealing from back in the den. But he hesitated.

"Oh, please." Esme rolled her eyes. "Don't let me hold you up. Go grab the call. I'm sure only a very select few have your number and the call no doubt has something to do with *my* case." She shooed him with her hands.

"We're not done," he warned grimly.

"I don't think we're ever starting but, whatever."

The phone pealed again.

He stalked back to the den and scooped up the phone. She'd been right. Only a select few individuals did have this particular number, and Gray was one of those few. Tyler put the phone to his ear. "Checking in already?"

"I've got a dead man in a cell," Gray returned bluntly.

"What?" Tyler's grip tightened on the phone.

"Your lady's would-be hitman? The prick who pretended to be a Fed? Found him dead in a cell this morning. Looks like he was shanked, only are you ready for the fun part?"

"There *is* a fun part?"

"He was alone in the fucking cell. All night. I'd given strict orders for him to be kept away from any other prisoners. And the security camera for his area went off-line just after midnight. A security failure that wasn't discovered until this morning."

"Shit."

"Exactly. This mess is screaming inside job, and you know how I hate it when things get fucked to hell that way." A long exhale from Gray. "Thought you might also like to know that the five-million-dollar bounty on your lady's head?"

"She's not mine."

A sniff.

His head whipped to the side. Esme was right there. As

in less than three feet away. Clearly close enough to hear his words.

Her arms were crossed over her chest. "I'm not exactly claiming you, either," she informed him with a glower.

"How the hell do you keep getting so close without making a sound?" Tyler demanded.

She shrugged.

"Uh, Tyler? You listening to me?" Gray asked. "Because this is kind of important, but sure, I can hold if you need to deal with some domestic crap right now."

Tyler kept his eyes on Esme. Just how much of the conversation was she overhearing?

Probably everything. Gray's voice could damn well carry. Hell. No choice. "Keep talking," he told Gray.

"It's not five million any longer."

"Okay, okay, that's good news, at least." A bright spot. "So the Feds worked their magic and started scrubbing her info from the dark web—"

"It's seven million. The bounty on her has increased, and clearly, with this prisoner's death, we have to believe that law enforcement members may be involved. That means you and I need to be extremely careful about who we trust. And you had better be staying *extra* close to Esme."

Her arms moved to wrap around her body.

"Someone powerful wants her dead." Gray wasn't sugarcoating anything. "Get her to tell you *why*. I need more information from her."

"On it."

"Do whatever you have to do," Gray continued in his carrying voice. "Seduce the woman. Make her fall in love with you. Worm your way into her cold, cold heart."

Her eyes could not narrow more. Yep, she was definitely picking up on Gray's words and not liking what she heard.

"Get the job done." A flat order from Gray. "She's sitting on a pile of secrets, and I need to know every single one."

"Go investigate the dead guy," Tyler advised him. "You leave her to me." He hung up even as he wondered how in the hell he could possibly smooth this situation over with Esme. Should he just begin by announcing that Gray could be an idiot? His buddy could be. A loud-mouthed idiot.

"The hitman is dead?" A quiet, careful question from Esme. Her arms were still wrapped around her body in what looked like a gesture designed to either comfort or shield herself.

"Yes."

"He was killed while in federal custody?"

"Yes."

A quick exhale. "So should I assume that this location is already compromised?" Very, very careful words as her eyes darted around the house.

"No, you should—"

The doorbell rang.

Her lips parted. Esme's head swung toward the door. Her hair flew over her shoulder. "Company?" A gasp.

Screw that. He had *not* invited any company over. Tyler bent down and picked up the gun that he'd tucked beneath the couch before he'd gone to sleep last night.

"When did you get that?" Esme squeaked.

He shot her a you've-got-to-be-kidding look. "I'm a U.S. Marshal, sweetheart. I always have a gun." He headed for the door.

She lunged out and grabbed his arm. "You can't just meet our neighbor *armed*. That is not friendly."

"No prick should be at our door right now. We were just told that a hitman was killed while in federal custody.

You think I'm just gonna stroll out, unarmed, and see who is knocking at our safe house?"

She nibbled on her lower lip.

"You need to go hide," he informed her. "*Now.*"

"But—"

"You follow my orders, Esme. That was part of my conditions, remember? Non-negotiable."

The doorbell rang again.

She jumped. "Fine. But be careful. And don't be afraid to shoot if that is, in fact, a bad guy at the door."

Oh, sweetness, I never am afraid.

Then she surprised the hell out of him by leaning forward and pressing a quick kiss to his lips. Esme bounded away in the next moment—moving in absolute silence as she headed for the kitchen. He strode for the front door. But he pulled out his phone before opening that door. He tapped a few times and had the front porch video feed popping up on his screen.

And Tyler instantly recognized the SOB on his doorstep.

Eyes narrowing, Tyler tucked the gun into the back waistband of his jeans. He disengaged the alarm and hauled open the door. "What in the hell are you doing here?"

The man on his porch raised a large welcome basket. "Hi, friend. Long time, no see." He thrust the basket into Tyler's arms. "Welcome to the neighborhood." He smiled at Tyler, and the badge on his chest gleamed in the sunlight. A gun was holstered at his hip. "Thought I'd come by and introduce myself to your new wife."

Sheriff Clay Banks. Tyler knew him well.

"Get your ass inside," Tyler groused.

The sheriff got his ass inside. Clay kicked the door shut and surveyed the scene even as Tyler dumped the basket on the nearby, still cloth-covered entrance table. White cloths covered basically every piece of furniture on the lower level of the house.

A low whistle came from Clay. "You're in town one night and you're already in the dog house?" He motioned toward the pillow and blanket on the floor. "What kind of wife has her husband sleeping on the floor on their first night in town? Huh." He sawed a hand over his jaw. "If I didn't know better, I would think you weren't involved in a real marriage. That this might just be some crazy setup."

"Don't be a dick." Did it look like he was in the mood for the sheriff's crap?

"Where is the mystery wife? I would love to meet—" Clay's words stopped. Mostly because Esme had just strolled out of the kitchen.

Hadn't Tyler told the woman to *hide?* A direct order, one she'd ignored. They really needed to discuss the meaning of the term *non-negotiable.*

Because there she was. Looking sexy and charming with her smile and...

Shit. She had a massive butcher knife gripped in her hand, and Esme was heading straight for the sheriff.

Chapter Eight

"Sweetheart!" Tyler jumped into her path. "I thought you were busy in the kitchen." He reached out and his fingers curled around hers as she gripped the butcher knife.

"Sweetheart," she cooed right back at him. "I thought you might need me out here."

"Got it all under control." He tugged the knife from her.

She let him take it. Not like she'd actually been planning to lunge at the man with the sheriff's star gleaming on his nicely pressed uniform. Esme would hardly make such a mistake. She'd merely wanted to check on her husband. And she believed in being prepared, so she'd checked on him with a knife at the ready.

Maybe they should talk about her also getting a gun? She made a mental note to revisit the gun situation when she and Tyler were alone.

Tyler put the knife onto a nearby end table. But he kept his grip on her hand. "Our neighbor came by with a welcome basket."

She peeked around Tyler and sent a smile at the sheriff who watched her so intently. "Incredibly thoughtful of you." She twisted around Tyler and strode toward the sheriff. Since Tyler didn't let her go, she dragged him with her. But, after three steps, he did release her hand.

She extended said hand to the sheriff. "Esme Hollow. Pleasure to meet you."

The sheriff was a devilishly handsome man with brown hair, green eyes, and tan skin. He was about Tyler's height, but smaller in the shoulders. A much sleeker build. His hand reached out to take hers. Not in a handshake, as she'd expected. Instead, he caught her hand and lifted it up toward his face, as if he'd kiss her knuckles.

She was used to the gesture in Europe. But in the US? Not so much.

Then she realized he wasn't going to kiss her knuckles. He was busy staring at her fingers. Or rather…

"No ring," he murmured. "Yeah, hate to be the one to tell you, but that shit is a dead giveaway that you aren't actually married."

He dropped her hand. *His* hand went toward his holster.

Oh, no. Esme gulped. "I took off my ring while I was washing dishes." A light laugh slipped from her. "I'll just go get it." She spun to dash back to the kitchen, but she basically slammed into Tyler.

Tyler's hands closed around her shoulders. "He's being a dick, darling."

First "sweetheart" and now "darling" as an endearment? Oh, they were on a roll. "I don't think you're supposed to call the sheriff a 'dick,' darling," she returned without missing a beat. "At least not to his face."

"Yes, well, in my experience," the sheriff drawled—and there was definitely a faint southern drawl that dipped and pitched in his voice, "Tyler never does what he's supposed to do."

Her head whipped back toward the sheriff. "You two know each other?"

"Served together once upon a time. Semper Fi." Both of the sheriff's hands were at his sides now. "When Tyler called and said he needed a safe place to crash for a few days, I was happy to offer this place. Not like I was doing a damn thing with it."

She quickly realigned her ideas about the sheriff. He was not a bad guy there to sniff them out. He was...Tyler's friend? This man had not come up in her recon/intel work. But there were only so many classified files that a woman could access. Only so many secrets that she could unearth. Especially in a world where people's actions were buried by the government. Pasts were erased. And new lives were created.

Case in point, I'm now a married woman.

The sheriff grimaced. "No ring. A pillow and blanket on the floor. Not like I want to tell you how to do your job, Tyler, but I'm pretty sure this isn't the way to run an operation."

Tyler let her go.

"If I had been a real neighbor—you have some of those, by the way, and you should expect to meet them eventually. People in Asylum tend to be a curious lot. If I had been a *real* neighbor and was supposed to buy that you were madly-in-love newlyweds, I would have some questions."

"Excuse me." Esme cleared her throat. "Asylum? As in...insane asylum?" Where on earth had Tyler taken her?

The sheriff—she still had not caught his name—laughed. It was a warm, rich sound. "We prefer to think of it as a place where people are given shelter. Right now, in case your hubby hasn't informed you and it seems he has *not*, you are in Asylum, Alabama. We're a small little town nestled along Mobile Bay. Tight-knit. Quiet." A pause. "Safe."

She could use some safety.

"I'm Clay Banks." His head dipped toward her. "And I hear you've got yourself into a bit of trouble."

Not exactly a bit.

"This won't cut it." Clay motioned toward the blanket and pillow. "And you are not acting like a husband at all, Tyler. Even in small towns, folks notice when shit is off. I get that you're usually delivering prisoners and dropping off witnesses to their new lives, so you don't have a lot of experience at playing parts." He ambled around the room. Tugged sheets off furniture and tossed the balled-up material to the side. "But here are a few pro tips for you. One, don't sleep on the den floor when you have a gorgeous bride upstairs."

"Oh, darling..." She reached out and patted Tyler's arm. "Your sheriff friend is absolutely charming and so insightful."

"Put a ring on her finger," Clay continued. "That's pro tip number two."

She stopped patting Tyler's arm and instead lifted her hand so she could wiggle her ringless fingers at her husband.

Tyler's jaw tightened.

"Number three? Maybe act like you can't stand to keep your hands off her. You're tense and glaring. Body language speaks volumes. Yours is screaming at me right now. Change it up. She's the love of your life, remember?"

"That's me." Esme touched her heart. "Love of your life." She batted her lashes at Tyler.

A muscle jerked along his clenched jaw.

"He's not a morning person," she explained to Clay.

"Yeah, tell me some shit I don't know." He thrust back his shoulders as he kept his eyes on Tyler. "Hit town soon so we can go ahead and get this cover established for you. Come to the station, and I'll introduce you as an old Marine buddy. I'll let word spread that I've rented the house to you and your new bride." He sauntered back toward the door. He tipped his head to Esme. "Nice meeting you."

"The pleasure was all mine."

His gaze swept over her. "Out of curiosity, what were you thinking to do with the knife?"

She didn't blink. "I forgot I was even carrying it. I just came out to say hello."

"Right. Sure. And if I'd been a bad guy when you came out to say hello, would that knife have wound up in my chest?"

It was her turn to give a soft ring of laughter. Though her laughter was forced, and she didn't think the sheriff's had been. "You aren't a bad guy, are you? So I guess we'll never know."

His brows rose. But the sheriff just saluted Tyler and ambled out the door.

Only after Tyler had locked the door did Esme's breath ease out. Tyler didn't face her, not at first. His back was to her as his right palm pressed to the doorframe. "Thought I told you to hide."

Uh, oh. She caught the thread of steel beneath those words. An angry thread. "I did hide. I went into the kitchen. Didn't you see me go?" Speaking of going...Esme spun on her heel and began to hurry toward the kitchen again.

She didn't get far.

Tyler snagged her wrist and spun her around to face him. "Repeat after me, Esme. *I will follow Tyler's rules.*"

"Fine," she huffed out. What in the hell was she? A child? "I will follow Tyler's rules."

"Because if I don't," he continued, voice even darker, "then I'll be dead. And Tyler has many skills, but he can't bring me back from the dead."

Her heart slammed into her chest. "Do I have to worry about your *friend* the sheriff killing me?"

"A seven-million-dollar bounty is on your head. Plenty of people would sell out their own mothers for that kind of money."

Yes, she was aware. She'd caught that snippet from his phone conversation. Something else she'd caught? "The man who tried to kill me at the FBI office is dead."

"He was murdered while in custody." Tyler's hold tightened on her. "That means whoever killed him either works at the Bureau or has significant pull. Enough pull to get someone murdered when the target was surrounded by law enforcement." A rough exhale. "We have to be very careful who we trust."

She licked her lips and had to say the part that worried her. "Grayson works at the Bureau."

His head tilted the smallest fraction. "Gray isn't selling us out."

"Not even for seven million dollars? Because that's the kind of money that can buy someone a new life." And this absolutely terrified her, but she had to ask, "Is it the kind of money that could buy *you* a new life?"

And the tension between them got very, very thick.

She tugged her wrist free of his grip. Esme backed away

from him. His expression had absolutely locked down, and that lack of emotion scared her. She'd tried to research him, but, as much as she hated to admit it, Esme had been wrong before. If she was wrong this time, she was a dead woman.

She retreated, but she'd misjudged where she was going, and her back hit the wall.

Tyler glanced at the very large knife on the table near him. He picked it up. Turned it so that the light hit the blade.

She really, really needed a gun. Though this did not seem to be the moment to bring up that conversational topic.

"You think I'll sell you out, Esme?"

With her whole heart, she hoped he wouldn't.

"Is that why you're suddenly looking so worried as you stare at me with those big, dark eyes of yours? Because you realize I've taken you away from everything you've known. Every friend you had."

She didn't have a ton of those. Getting close enough for friendship was dangerous in her world.

He turned the knife in his hand. The blade was wickedly sharp and terrifying. "You realize that you are alone with me. It's you and me, and it would be very easy for me to say...sneak up on you when you're sleeping and get myself seven million dollars."

"Stop."

"Or, why bother with sleeping?" He'd been staring at the knife, but now he looked up at her. "I could get myself seven million dollars right now. You conveniently provided the weapon. It's right here in my hand. Think you could stop me if I came at you?"

Her breath shuddered in and out.

"Fuck." He dropped the knife back onto the table. In a flash, he'd eliminated the distance between them. Tyler didn't touch her. He just stood right in front of her. Towered over her. "You get to play every game you want, but the minute I do...*dammit, don't look at me that way.*"

What way was she looking at him?

"You picked me," Tyler said with certainty. "You knew you were going to use me even before you said those first words to me at Jorlan's, didn't you?"

Her lips pressed together.

"Dammit, *answer me.*" Not loud. Low and lethal and somehow even scarier for it. His hands flew out, but, again, not to touch her. To press to the wall on either side of her as he caged her in place. "I am here to protect you. I'd take a bullet for you."

Her head moved in a hard, instinctive, negative jerk.

"Kinda the job description, sweetheart. But instead of getting shot, I prefer to do the shooting. So how about I clarify things for you a bit?"

Her heart needed to stop its frantic racing.

"I will stop anyone who comes to attack you. I will *kill* to keep you safe. Better?"

Much better. So why wouldn't her heart slow its wild beat?

"I deserve honesty from you. If I'm guarding that gorgeous body of yours, day and night, then you stop the games you're playing with me."

"What if I don't know how to stop?" The minute the words were out, Esme wished she could take them back. But they were true. She'd been pretending for so long that she wasn't even sure who she truly was any longer.

Socialite.

Spoiled rich daughter.

Thief.

Criminal.

"I'll help you," he told her.

"You don't even like me," she whispered back.

Tyler blinked. "Maybe I like you too damn much."

Had he really said those words? Or had she just imagined them because she would love to hear words like those from him?

"Time for truth," Tyler bit out. "You picked me, didn't you? Before we even met?"

"It wasn't exactly a spur of the moment decision." Could she slip under his arm and dash upstairs? They needed some distance. She needed to get her control back. She was revealing things that she should not. And why was it so hot in there? Did the house's AC system not work?

"You knew who I was before you approached me at Jorlan's. You didn't just look at me and realize I didn't fit in with the too rich crowd. You knew I was undercover before you even said a word to me."

She could lie. Absolutely, she could lie. And lie well. Without batting an eyelash. She could stare straight into his steely blue eyes and lie her brittle heart out. But... "Yes." A sigh. A confession. "Yes, I knew who you were."

"How?"

Had he leaned a little closer? Esme was pretty certain he had. "I couldn't leave my safety to just anyone. I mean, it's my life we're talking about here. Sort of important to me, wouldn't you say?"

"*Esme...*"

"Do you intend to sound so sexy when you rumble my name that way? If so, stop. It's distracting, and I'm trying to bare my soul to you. I don't do that often, so it's rather a struggle for me."

He sucked in a breath.

"I have lots of contacts in this world. Some good and some bad." For once, she spoke flatly. All bravado and coyness gone. Just quiet. Almost tired. She'd been tired for a long time, but Esme always had to pretend she wasn't. With him, in this instance, she was done with the pretense. "One of those contacts owed me a great deal. I understood that trouble was coming my way, and I knew I would need protection. But, as you just pointed out, some people would sell out their own mothers for the kind of money that is currently on my head." She licked her lower lip. "I needed someone who could not be bought. Someone who actually takes being *good* seriously. Someone who would never be swayed or tempted." She'd thought for sure that someone was him but, again...*I have been wrong before.* So she'd gotten scared when he held the knife and seemed so cold and distant. "But you're not tempted," she said mostly to just hear the words. *I am not wrong about you.*

"Oh, I'm fucking tempted," he returned in a deep, dark growl.

Her lips parted.

"Not by money, sweetness." Another growl that rolled right through her. "By you, and that's a very dangerous situation." A muscle flexed near his jaw. "Let me make sure I've got all of this straight. You got some criminal buddy of yours to dig into my life and find out that I could be trusted?"

Oh, she'd done a bit more than that. And she'd never said it was a criminal buddy. Hadn't she told him that she had good and bad contacts? "I arranged for you to be placed on the team at Jorlan's house. I needed to see you in action for myself, after all."

His eyes widened. "Thousands of people in the world

and you picked me to be your protector? *Why?*" He appeared stunned.

She had that effect on some people. Unfortunately. But as to the why, well, she'd already started going down the truth road, so she'd just continue on this path. "Ten years ago, a hurricane slammed into a small southern town. Nearly wiped the place out. Marines rushed in to help the survivors. A picture circulated online of a man who was pulling a terrified family through waist-high water in a small boat. The boat the family huddled in was an old rowboat. Only no oars were in sight. The man was just walking. Pulling them. Not stopping."

"That fucking picture."

The picture had been of a younger Tyler. He'd been the one pulling the rowboat by hand through the water and helping the family. That picture was burned in her mind. She inclined her head. "Let's talk about that same Marine, a few years later."

Tension coiled around his body.

And hers. "A bomb went off in a Paris café." The memory could still make her shudder. "Some Marines were in town, on leave, and they ran toward the explosion. They pulled out three survivors before the entire building collapsed. You were one of those Marines."

"You have been doing your research. Consider me impressed."

"I was in Paris that day." Again, the words just slipped out. "I saw you."

His eyes narrowed. Then widened. His stare swept over her. So intense. So sharp. So...

Her breath rushed out. It was almost a relief to get this out in the open. "I know sign language because right after the blast, I couldn't hear. Not for several weeks, actually. I think that is probably why silence makes me uncomfortable. It takes me back to one of the worst times in my life."

"No." He backed away. "No fucking way."

"Yes, yes, fucking way. I look different, of course." She stepped away from the wall. Motioned toward herself. "At the time, I was in my blond hair period, though I doubt you noticed since I was covered in blood and ash and blackened debris." Another heave of her breath. "It's hard to look your best when you are at death's door. So don't hold that against me."

Shock covered his face. "I-I tried to find you after—"

"After you put me in the ambulance? Yes, I know. But my father didn't want me to be found. I wasn't supposed to be at that café, you see. So I wasn't. He erased me. And it's not like the brave Marine who saved my life was being chatty with the press. Instead, he was finishing up his service, and, lo and behold, he soon got the position he wanted with the U.S. Marshal's office. He deserved that position. He deserved a lot of things."

Tyler swiped a hand over his hard jaw. "Wait. You're saying that *you* got me that position?"

"It was the least I could do." She'd had to be careful and pull lots of strings without letting anyone know that *she* was the one working behind the scenes. "Without you, I would have died that day. I would have been buried beneath all of the debris and forgotten."

His gaze slid over her. And then...

Tyler grabbed the hem of her shirt. Lifted it up.

"You should at least ask first," she murmured. "Manners, you know. Personal space and all that. Not very gentlemanly to just lift up a woman's shirt without asking permission first. Unless we are in the middle of a very sexy and intense scene, and we are currently not."

"You have the scar." His fingers skimmed over the puckered line on her stomach. A line that snaked and twisted near her belly button. "*You were bleeding so much.* You were covered in blood and ash."

"Told you before." Esme ignored the way her stomach seemed to be flipping and churning as he touched her. "I don't mind scars. Not at all."

"Fuck."

He was staring at her as if he'd just seen a ghost.

"Fuck," he bit off again.

"You said that already," she pointed out. "Such dirty talk."

His hand flew back.

"Once a hero, always a hero," she told him. "At least, that was what I was hoping would be the case with you. I just needed to have that acquaintance of mine dig a little to see what you'd been doing since our paths last crossed."

The shock had faded from his face, but Tyler still appeared dazed. Trapped between his memory of the past and her in the present. "You never opened your eyes. I never saw your eyes."

"My eyes are open now." Open and on him. "I needed a hero, so I found myself one." Trips down memory road sucked, so she preferred to skip them whenever possible. "Despite the brief hesitation earlier—I'll blame that on the large butcher knife and me not having enough sleep—I truly don't think you're the kind of man who would sell out his charge for seven million dollars. I don't think you're the kind of man that would *ever* sell out anyone. You're a very rare breed. And you're exactly what I need."

"*They told me you died.*"

"Yes, that would be what I meant when I said my father erased me. A false name. A dead woman who wasn't. And no one learned the truth. A very important man's daughter was never in the café. She couldn't be tied to what happened. Her father could be safe from the mob of the press. So could she."

"You're telling me the truth."

She was. Esme nodded.

"What is going on?" Tyler demanded. "You pulled me in your web and now you tell me everything."

She would tell the most important thing. But he already knew it, didn't he? "Powerful people want me dead."

"*Were you the target in the Paris bombing?*"

She'd revealed enough for now. Big revelations were exhausting. "According to the press, that was a terror attack." And she still fought the terror that rolled through her whenever she heard loud noises. "The perpetrators were caught. Sentenced. They should never get out again."

"Then why did your father hide the fact that you were there for all this time? Why the lies?"

"Because fate is funny." Hilarious some days. Horrible on others. "I was meeting with someone...let's just say this individual could have caused a great deal of trouble in the international world. He had proof that certain powerful individuals were involved in a massive weapons and drug trade. If that proof had gotten into the right hands..." There was no point in the "if" talk. Her gaze darted away from Tyler and skimmed around the den. Paused a moment on the blanket and the pillow. "The proof was destroyed in the explosion." Suddenly very weary, Esme headed for the stairs. "Lots of things were destroyed in that explosion." Including the person she'd been before the world had erupted around her.

"Esme."

Her hand reached for the banister.

"Were your hands the right ones? Is that why you were in the café? Were you the one who should have gotten the intel?"

She looked at her hand as it pressed to the wood.

"Were your hands the right ones?" Tyler asked again.

"Not then." Because her job hadn't been to make sure that proof got out...

Watch him, Esme. Stop him. Report back.

Her eyes closed. "You're the hero, remember? Not me. Don't ever forget that." Enough sharing for the day. It was morning, and yet she was already soul weary. Esme climbed up the stairs and left her hero behind.

Oh, who was she kidding? She'd never been able to really leave him behind. For years, he'd stayed in her head.

When a man saved your life, you tended to never forget him.

* * *

"They're here," Clay Banks said into his phone. He sat behind the wheel of his patrol car, and his eyes were on the house that waited about twenty yards away. "Got eyes on their place right now."

"And Tyler is staying close to her?"

He thought about the way Tyler had watched the woman. "Pretty sure you can count on him staying close."

"The cameras are in place?"

He'd been the one to install them, so... "Yes."

"You'll report to me on everything that happens?"

Now this was the part that made him feel like shit. "Tyler is a friend of mine."

"And you want your friend to stay alive, don't you?"

Yeah, he damn well did.

"Seven million dollars is a lot of money."

Under-freaking-statement.

"Report to me. The sharks will be closing in."

Right. His fingers tapped on the steering wheel. For that much money, he expected a great white to be swimming through his town any minute.

Chapter Nine

"Do you mind if I turn on the radio?" Esme's voice was muted. After their talk in the den, some of her vibrancy had vanished, and frankly, Tyler hated that shit.

He wanted flippant Esme back.

Smiling and charming and seducing and over-the-top Esme.

"Go ahead." He sounded like a freaking bear. His hold tightened on the steering wheel. Tyler cleared his throat and tried again. "Turn on anything you want." They were almost to the main part of town but if she wanted music, she could blast it as loudly as she wanted.

Hours had passed before Esme had come down the stairs again. She'd looked just as beautiful as ever, but the unease in his gut warned Tyler that maybe she'd been crying. Hell, there was no maybe about it.

She'd cried alone, upstairs. As if she hadn't wanted him to see her tears.

Esme is the woman I carried out of that hellhole in Paris? He'd thought of her too many times over the years. The woman who'd seemed so fragile in his arms. She'd been trapped beneath the rubble, and he'd had to heave half of a damn wall off her body. Her eyes hadn't opened. She'd been limp as he carried her out. He'd worried so much about a spinal injury but leaving her hadn't been a possibility. The whole place had shuddered around them. He'd had to pick her up and rush through the wreckage.

He'd barely gotten out and then...

I'll never forget the sound of that building collapsing completely. The dust and ash had choked him. He'd stumbled forward with her cradled in his arms. EMTs had pulled her from him. Tucked her into the back of the bright ambulance. The siren had wailed but he'd barely heard it. And he hadn't seen her again.

Rock music filled the car. Not soft rock. *Hard rock.* Of course, that somehow seemed perfectly Esme.

"Cute town." Her head had turned as she gazed out at the main hub that was Asylum, Alabama. "Ohmygosh. Look at the gazebo in the middle of that park. I bet they put Christmas lights all around it for the holidays." She sucked in a breath. "I bet they have a whole tree lighting ceremony here! That's what they do in small towns, right?" She bounced. Some of her light was coming back, and the tightness in his chest seemed to ease even as Esme excitedly continued, "They probably have a whole event that everyone comes to attend with carols and hot chocolate and—"

"Esme." A smile tugged at his mouth. "We're at the bottom of Alabama. Do you really think it gets cold enough down here for hot chocolate, ever?"

She rolled one shoulder. "I can drink it and still sweat." Her head craned as she took in the sights. "Those buildings are adorable. Is that a tea shop?"

It was.

"An art gallery?"

"Try not to get sticky fingers."

She sniffed. "You take one Rembrandt..."

He slammed on the brakes. "*What?*"

"And suddenly someone thinks you just steal everything you see. Relax, handsome. I'll be on my best behavior."

Had she really stolen a Rembrandt? But Tyler bit back the question as he drove forward. Tyler was curious about what Esme's best behavior entailed. "We're going to the hardware store. Our cover is that we're updating the house, so we need to pick up some paint and a few supplies. Then we'll hit the grocery store. We're only paying in cash. Keep to our story line. Don't go getting overly chatty with anyone."

"Yes, sir."

They'd check in at the sheriff's station soon enough so that Clay could help spread word that Tyler was an old Marine buddy. But first, Tyler thought he and Esme should be spotted doing "normal" things in the area. He parked in front of the hardware store. She started to hop out immediately. "Nope." He leaned over her and opened the glove box. "A few things to handle first." He slapped a cap on her head.

"I'm a football fan now?"

"Hardcore." He studied her critically.

"I can cut my hair. Change the color. Probably should have done that before we came to town, though." Esme nibbled on her delectable lower lip.

"You're perfect as you are." She'd braided her hair. Loose tendrils tickled her cheeks. Golden hoop earrings curled from her lobes. Had Gray packed the earrings for her? If so, his buddy had been thorough. Esme was dressed casually in jeans and a white t-shirt. Her voice held zero accent, and when she grinned at him the way she was currently doing...

My dick could not salute her more. Dammit.

"You just need one more thing." Tyler slammed the glove box closed and dug into his pocket. A few seconds later, he had the ring in his hand. A simple gold band. Actually, two of them. One for him. One for her. He reached for her fingers.

"It's so sudden," she demurred.

"Cute, Esme." He slid the ring into place.

Before he could put his on, she took it from him. She pushed it onto his left ring finger.

For some reason, his chest got a little tight.

"Guess we're official now?" Her smile flashed at him.

Killer smile. His gaze swept carefully over her face. "Your nose is different from the way it looked back in Paris."

Her smile dimmed. "Different bad or different good?"

"Don't know that there could ever be anything bad about how you look. You're beautiful, Esme."

Her hand slid from his. Her index finger ran down the bridge of her nose. "Don't know how much you recall, but my nose was broken. That probably was why so much blood was on my face. I'm sure when you saw me, my nose had to be horribly swollen. Maybe twisted. No worries, it was one of the first things the doctors fixed for me." She grabbed for the passenger door handle.

"Sometimes, it's easier to fix the stuff on the outside."

Her knuckles whitened around the handle. "Are you saying that you think I'm broken inside? Because that's not a very kind thing to tell a woman. Hardly charming."

"I don't think there is anything broken about you."

Quite the contrary. She might just be one of the strongest people he'd ever met.

She cleared her throat. "Elizabeth."

She'd lost him. "Excuse me?"

"I think that, instead of being called Esme, when we're in public, you should call me Elizabeth. I know the general routine is to keep first names, if possible, when you're in witness protection, but I think Esme might stand out a bit too much. We'll have to be sure and tell your sheriff buddy about the change. I'll be Elizabeth from here on out."

Okay, first, she was wrong about the general routine. "You don't *have* to keep your first name. You can. Or you can change it. Your choice. I'll call you whatever the hell you want. But you have to be able to answer to the name. I can't be shouting Elizabeth, and you just walk past me, humming."

"I won't walk past you."

He didn't think she would.

"But I will still be Esme to you," she added quickly. "This is just a public thing. In private, I'm your Esme. Because I absolutely love the way you say my name. Makes me want to jump you."

"Esme—"

A shiver slid over her. "Not now. We have paint and groceries to buy, lover. Save it for later." She shoved open the door.

He climbed from the vehicle, too. Took his time walking to her side. And when they were close, he leaned in and rasped near her ear, "How many times do I have to tell you, don't play with me?"

"And how many times do I have to assure you...I'm not playing?"

* * *

"TELL me again why you insisted we get so much black paint."

Esme tossed angel hair pasta into the buggy. "Because it's like the song goes, 'I see a red door and my black heart wants it painted black.'" She snagged pasta sauce. Nodded in approval before putting it in her buggy. Then she continued strolling down the aisle.

"I don't think that's how the song goes," he assured her.

"No? Probably close enough though, yes?" She paused in front of the coffee. "Okay, what is the best for your black-coffee-loving self?"

He snagged his favorite coffee. Tossed it in the buggy and was oddly warmed that she'd remembered he needed it.

Music played on the store's speakers, and every few moments Esme would hum along to the beat. Damn if he didn't find her hums oddly charming.

She grabbed bread.

Then some super, super sugar-heavy cereal that was covered in chocolate.

He stocked up on protein for them. Steaks.

"You grilling?" she asked with a bat of her lashes.

"You've never tasted heaven until you've sampled my steaks."

She laughed and he smiled back and holy shit...*this feels too real.* Esme wasn't pretentious or cold or...hell, he didn't know what he'd really expected her to be. The woman had acted like an excited kid in a candy store when they'd gone to pick up the paint supplies. And, honestly, she was pretty close to acting the same way as they shopped for food.

A random and startling thought struck him.

"Sweetheart, you *have* gone to a grocery store before, haven't you?"

Laughter sputtered out of her. "What kind of question is that?" She turned for the next aisle.

It was the kind of question she had not answered. She did that a lot. Evaded. Sneakily.

He caught her arm. Pulled her closer. "Let me rephrase." A pause. "Sweetheart, *have* you gone to a grocery store before?"

"There are a lot of open markets where I used to live. But, FYI, yes, I have been to a grocery store before. Excuse me for enjoying myself."

He considered her words. "I kind of think you might enjoy yourself everywhere you go."

"Well, it's better than hating every moment of your life."

Uh, yes. He supposed it was.

They continued. She hummed. Stopped in front of a freezer. "What is your favorite ice cream?"

"Vanilla."

More laughter rang from her even as she took out the vanilla ice cream.

"Care to share the joke?"

Two people had turned at the sound of her laughter. One looked like a college kid. The other appeared to be in his early fifties. Both let their stares linger a bit too long on Esme.

Tyler moved to block their view.

"Sure. I'll share." Her eyes danced. "If I had to describe you and your taste...well, I never, ever would have taken you for a vanilla kind of guy."

She was talking about sex. It was Esme. Of *course*, she

was talking about sex. In the frozen section of the grocery store.

"No handcuffs? No kink at all?" She clicked her tongue. "I am shocked. Especially considering the way you eagerly slapped those cuffs on me not too long ago."

"*Sweetheart.*"

"What? I spoke in a whisper. No one heard."

He'd heard.

And, blessedly, she was done with her shopping extravaganza. They wheeled toward the checkout. One lady was in front of them. A woman in blue scrubs who had her daughter seated in the buggy. The girl's braids swung around her head as she twisted to take in everything around her. The girl was around three years old. Maybe four. She clutched a small teddy bear in her hands.

"Doctor Bear," she announced.

Esme frowned at the child.

"He's Doctor Bear, and he can make you feel better." A wide grin to reveal a mouthful of baby teeth.

"Doctor Bear looks amazing," Esme assured her. She gave the little girl—and the bear—a wave.

The mom finished paying and stacking her bags into the buggy. She glanced over at Esme and Tyler. "We have to take Doctor Bear with us *everywhere,*" she explained to them. "Everywhere."

"Oh, look, honey, he has his own stethoscope," Esme breathed. "That is adorable."

The mom laughed. "I'm a doctor, and my baby girl insisted on getting him as soon as she saw him in the store. Said he was just like me."

"He can fix anyone," the girl boasted with no small amount of pride.

"I am absolutely certain he can." Esme nodded. And as

the mom and daughter wheeled away, Tyler could have sworn he saw a hint of wistfulness on Esme's face. He touched her shoulder.

She just flashed a megawatt smile his way.

The clerk began swiping their items. "You two must be the couple who moved into the sheriff's old family place."

The words had him glancing at the woman behind the counter. Her shrewd gaze swept them.

"Guilty," Esme responded happily.

His fingers squeezed her shoulder.

"How'd you know?" Esme asked.

"It's a small town. New people always stand out." The scanner beeped as she rolled items right past it. "Hear that you're friends with the sheriff?"

"My husband is," Esme helpfully clarified before Tyler could respond. "Such good friends. And I am thrilled to be down here. Can't wait to get all settled in. Tell me, what is your absolute favorite thing to do in town?"

The woman blinked. Stopped scanning. Then nodded as if she'd reached a decision. "Catch the sunset on the bay. That's my favorite. You see the sunset from the pier, and it'll bring peace to your soul."

Esme's throat moved the tiniest bit. "I could use a little peace. Thank you."

The cashier finished ringing up their items, Tyler paid in cash, and—

"Chocolate chips!" Esme rounded on him in dismay. "I forgot them."

"We don't need them." He pushed the buggy toward the automatic doors at the front of the store.

"Um, yes, we do. Tyler, please, go snag some for me? I'll stay with the buggy. I swear, I'll be good. Just get my chocolate chips, would you? They're needed for my recipe."

Great. She looked so hopeful. She'd been so damn happy in the store, and...*I keep seeing her after the blast.* It was almost impossible to match up the two images in his head. Beautiful, bold Esme as she was now. And the battered, lifeless body he'd held in the wreckage of that café.

Tyler swallowed. He liked the happy Esme. The bold and sparkling one. "I'll be right back."

"I will be on my best behavior. Promise." She rose onto her toes and skimmed a kiss over his cheek. "Thank you. Best husband ever, that's you."

Jaw locking, he hurried back through the store.

* * *

SHE HADN'T WANTED to block the doors, so Esme pushed her buggy outside and eased next to a display of charcoal and tiki torches that waited in front of the grocery store. Her gaze scanned the parking lot.

She caught sight of the doctor loading her groceries into the back of a mini-van. The little girl was spinning in circles near her mother's feet. And...

The little girl took off running—heading back for the store.

Esme's eyes widened.

The mother hadn't noticed that her little girl was gone.

The child seemed locked and intense on her goal. Esme's mouth dropped open when she realized that the teddy bear the child had been clutching was on the pavement near the store's entrance. The girl was going straight for it.

And an engine was growling.

Esme's head whipped to the right. A big, souped up truck raced forward—rolling right toward the bear and going far too fast in the parking lot. What looked like a teenager was behind the wheel, but his head was turned and he was laughing with a friend who sat in the passenger seat.

Everything seemed to happen both incredibly slowly and incredibly quickly.

The little girl ran forward with a burst of speed. A mad dive for the bear.

The truck's engine growled as the big vehicle barreled straight ahead.

Esme screamed and the sound just seemed to echo and echo in her own head even as she lunged forward. Her arms were outstretched as she tried to grab the child.

Then she heard the screech of brakes. The wail of metal. And she felt the bone-jarring thud as her body slammed down onto the pavement.

Chapter Ten

"There's blood everywhere!" A yell.

Tyler's head whipped up.

A frantic teenager rushed toward the line of registers. "Call the cops!" he blasted. "A lady needs help outside!"

Tyler dropped the chocolate chips. He raced toward the front doors and shoved through the crowd of customers who were suddenly all scrambling to get out. As soon as he cleared the doors and erupted outside...

Esme, Esme, where are you?

A big truck had slammed into one of the pillars near the entrance to the grocery store. A buggy had gotten pinned near the truck's massive grille. The buggy was smashed and bent and...

Red.

Everywhere. Red was *everywhere.*

For a minute, Tyler could have sworn his heart stopped. The contents of the buggy...His mind clicked through them. The ice cream. The coffee. The freaking angel hair pasta. *Esme's buggy.*

Only there was no Esme to be seen.

"I'm so sorry!" It was the teenager. Bobbing and weaving and shaking near Tyler. "I-I didn't see her. She ran right in front of me!"

Tyler shoved the kid away from him. Heart now racing in a double-time rhythm, Tyler leapt to the opposite side of the truck. A small throng of nervous onlookers had gathered over there. He recognized the doctor in her scrubs and—

Esme.

On the ground. Curled in a ball. Tyler didn't realize he'd roared her name until she turned slowly and looked back at him.

I'm okay. He couldn't hear those words from her. Not over the thunder of his heartbeat, but he saw the movement of her lips and the world stopped imploding. At least a little.

Tyler rushed to her just as Esme opened her arms and a crying girl lurched out of them. The girl flew at her mother.

And Esme fell back against the black pavement.

"I'm really okay," she told Tyler as he came to a shuddering halt beside her. "The driver looked up and saw me at the last second. He rammed into the pillar instead of hitting me and the kid."

"You saved my girl." The doctor clutched her daughter tightly. "You saved her!"

Tyler swept his gaze over Esme. He could see blood on one of her hands. And her jeans were torn at the knee. More blood. "Sweetheart?"

She lifted a hand toward him. Except that hand clutched a decidedly beat-up-looking teddy bear. "Give this to her, would you?"

He took the bear. Handed it to the mom.

The girl stopped crying.

More people gathered.

"We should call an ambulance," someone said.

"What if her back is broken?" From someone else.

"What's up with all the blood?" A third voice. Younger. Cracking.

"Pretty sure that's my pasta sauce." Esme curled her fingers around Tyler's hand. "Help me up, would you? So unglamorous to be sprawled this way in front of everyone."

Screw glamour. He didn't just help her up. He lifted her and cradled her against his chest. Tyler was aware that his whole body seemed to shake. And, fuck it, he'd called her Esme in front of the crowd. She'd asked to be called Elizabeth, and *he'd* been the one to screw up. So not like him.

But these weren't normal circumstances. *Esme could have been killed.*

Her lashes lifted as she peered at him. "You all right?"

No. For a moment there, he'd been afraid she was dead. He pressed a kiss to her temple. A worried husband would do that, wouldn't he? Kiss his wife. Hold her like he'd never let go. Feel fear sink into his very bones.

It's just a role. I'm doing this for the audience.

So why did it all feel real? In her ear, he whispered, "This really how you keep a low profile?"

Esme trembled. "I fucked up."

Yeah.

All eyes were on her.

"But if I had to," she told him, voice husky, "I'd do it all over again in a heartbeat."

A siren cut through the curious voices. Then, a few moments later, a door slammed. Rushing footsteps joined the party, and Tyler wasn't overly surprised when he heard Clay demand, *"What in the hell is happening here?"*

* * *

"People hiding out in safe houses are supposed to keep low profiles." Clay paced in front of the old fireplace in the den of their safe house. "They don't attract attention. They blend." He stopped and pointed at Esme as she sat on the couch. "You do not blend."

She bit her lower lip. "Sorry, but, ah, not sorry, too." Like she could regret saving that adorable girl.

A long exhale came from Clay even as his hands fell to perch on his hips. "Bobby Miller wasn't paying enough damn attention. Little Kady Jo was too freaking small—he wouldn't have seen her in time. You saved her life."

Her knee still ached. So did her palms. And Esme shifted uncomfortably on the couch. "It wasn't a big deal."

Clay stared at her. "You get that if Bobby hadn't finally turned his head in the right direction, he would have hit you? That you'd be seriously hurt, if not dead right now?"

She swallowed. "Yeah, I get it. But thanks for the reminder."

Clay's attention shifted to Tyler. "I thought she was supposed to be some master criminal."

Her shoulders stiffened.

"What's the deal?" Clay demanded. "Because right now, my whole freaking town thinks she's a hero."

"Never been that before." Esme rose. "Should be a fun change of pace, don't you think? Especially for a master criminal like me. I'm second only to the wicked witch, you know. Absolutely heartless." Her gaze darted to Tyler. *Is that what you told him I was?* "Excuse me. It's been a big day." It had been. Tyler had insisted she get checked out by an EMT even though she'd been fine. Just a little bruised and banged up. No biggie. Then they'd gone to the sheriff's station. There had been questions. So many of them.

And, of course, they'd had to pick up groceries again. Though the store had given them to her for free, so...win.

In the end, the whole day had slipped away. Now she wanted to escape from the men and their grilling and their accusations and go upstairs. "I think I'll take a shower and turn in. Night, gentlemen." She headed for the stairs.

Surprise, surprise, Tyler stepped into her path. "You're not the wicked witch."

"Oh, stop. Your compliments will overwhelm me." She was so done, and he didn't even get it. How could he? He'd forgotten her after Paris, while she'd built him up in her head as being this incredible white knight. She'd thought of him nearly every single day. *Obsession much, Esme?*

She'd been so sure that he would be the answer to her troubles. Someone she could trust. Someone who would help her and never be tempted to betray her.

Yes, she had a problem with high expectations. Sue her.

But there was only so much one woman could take. And the big truck with its gleaming grill? That would be another image that she added to her nightmares. She'd held her shit together all day. Even as she'd felt like she was shaking apart on the inside. The master criminal crack from the sheriff had been the final straw for her.

You're smart if you believe absolutely nothing that you hear and only about half of what your eyes can see...

But what if the part you saw was the truth?

"Scoot, Tyler." Esme waved her hand in a shooing motion.

He didn't scoot or shoo. He stood right there, the big, unmovable object that he was.

"You're too pale."

"Stop. Really. More compliments?" Esme shook her

head. "How does any woman resist you and that killer charm you possess?"

"Your fingers are shaking."

Indeed, they were. She curled her hands into fists. "My blood sugar must be low."

He didn't appear to buy that excuse. "Are you coming off an adrenaline crash?"

Well, she had almost been run down, so, yes, probably. But her chin lifted. "No, I'm just absolutely bored and ready for bed. Only there is a six-foot-three marshal in my way."

He stared at her.

She glared at him.

His body seemed to stiffen more with every moment that passed. She truly did not think the man was going to move when—

"I'll be joining you in a few minutes, Esme." He stepped to the side.

"Really, how odd. I don't remember giving you an invitation to join me." She skirted around him and hopped up the steps. A twinge shot through her knee, but she ignored the brief flash of pain.

"One bed, sweetheart. One bed."

Esme glanced back.

"See you soon." His eyes *blazed.*

* * *

TYLER WAITED until Esme reached the top of the stairs. He kept his eyes on her every single second.

"Look, you need to—"

Tyler held up a hand, indicating that Clay needed to stop talking. His friend stopped.

A few moments later, Tyler heard the bedroom door shut upstairs. He dropped his hand and fired an angry glare at Clay. "Don't ever call her a criminal again."

Clay's green eyes seemed to double in size. "Uh, that's what she *is*. You're the one who told me that trivia fact! Remember? When you contacted me and asked if I could get this old house ready?"

"I was wrong. Things are more complicated than they first appeared to be." His hands had clenched. He hadn't liked the look in Esme's eyes. *Pain*. He wanted to take every bit of her pain away.

"Complicated, my ass. You told me that you caught the woman with diamonds strapped to her thigh. She's tied to dozens of thefts and currently wanted on the dark web for a stupid amount of money. You don't get a bounty like that on your head when you live a life of virtue and grace."

That crap wasn't funny. "Don't call her a criminal again. You do, and we'll have a problem."

Clay edged toward him. His eyebrows beetled down in concern. "Did you hit your head at some point today?"

"Fuck off."

"Huh. Okay. Maybe not your head. Are you just thinking with your dick all of a sudden?"

Tyler sucked in a breath. "We're about to have that problem I mentioned." He'd warned Clay, but if the other man chose to ignore the warning—that was just on him.

"Look, we both need to take a minute." Wisely, Clay took both a minute and a step back from Tyler. "I'm confused as hell about Esme, too. She saved Kady Jo! You know I freaking love that kid. I'm trying to convince her mom to marry me, but so far Vanessa has resisted my charms." He blew out a breath. "So I'm now grateful to a crimin—okay! Jeez, breathe!" He'd retreated fast when

Tyler surged toward him. "Didn't mean to say the c-word. It slipped out!"

It had better not slip out again. "Esme could have been hit by that truck. She could have died."

"Bobby was driving too damn fast. It was a parking lot, for goodness' sake. He was rolling through there like a dumbass, and he could have seriously hurt someone. If your Esme hadn't been there, hell, I don't want to imagine what I might be doing right now." Clay raked a hand through his already disheveled brown hair. "So, whatever else she's done, for the moment, definitely consider me on Esme's team."

"Like you weren't on her team before?"

Clay waited a beat. "Like *you* were? Like you are not seriously working an angle and trying to manipulate that woman so you can get intel for your federal buddies?"

Shit.

And a door opened and then immediately clicked closed upstairs. Sonofabitch. He'd been afraid of that. *Esme was listening to us talk.* The first time she'd shut the door, it had just been a ruse. To make him think she'd gone into the bedroom. When, really, she'd lingered to eavesdrop. Of course, Clay had just blurted out the worst possible accusation. "I am on her team. She's *it*. My goal. I keep her safe."

"Because she's the assignment."

"Because she's Esme." There'd been a dramatic shift in their relationship. And he didn't even know how to process everything that was changing inside of him. All he knew was that...

Esme isn't going to die. Esme isn't going to be hurt. I will never rush toward her prone body again and feel fear and anger and grief pour through me because I think she's gone.

"Aw, hell. Like that? Seriously?"

Tyler rolled back his shoulders. "Are we back to our problem?"

Clay swallowed. His Adam's apple bobbed. "You know I've followed you to hell and back before. I'll do it again. But, let's try to avoid getting burned as much as possible, okay?"

It was hard not to get burned when the fire was so tempting.

After Clay left, Tyler secured the front door. Then he glanced upstairs. Did he hear the faint sound of running water? Had Esme climbed into the shower? He pulled out his phone and made a quick, necessary call.

Gray answered on the first ring. "Tell me that we don't have a problem already."

"Nothing I can't handle."

"Good." A relieved sigh. "Because I need that woman to continue being alive and to continue cooperating. The stuff she shared before leaving with you? Freaking gold mine already. The CIA is about to piss themselves. And I know that is just the tip of the iceberg when it comes to what she knows. We need her talking and cooperating fully. You have to break through her walls and get her to tell you every single secret that she has."

His jaw ached because he'd clenched his back teeth so hard. Did everyone think he was just going to seduce Esme to get intel? With an effort, he forced himself to relax. "What's happening with the hit on her? You find out who put up the bounty?"

"Look, I'm still trying to find out who the hell killed the bastard in our custody. Kinda got a lot of work going on here, my friend. I've been grilling suspects all day, and let me just tell you, the other Feds don't like it when you question them. That kind of thing makes you very unpopular at the office."

"Too bad. I don't like it when other Feds are dirty."

"You and me both." An exhale. "Jorlan came to visit me, did I tell you that already?"

No, he damn well had not.

"Guy was pretty pissed. Kept demanding to see Esme. Got to say, for someone who had his diamonds located, he sure seemed real twitchy."

Tyler waited. He knew there would be more. With Gray, there always was.

"Twitchy in a way that told me more was at play. I called in some favors from the local PD. Got a tail on him. You're not gonna like this but...the guy took off in his private jet first thing this morning."

"And where the hell did he go?" Shit.

"The plane landed in Vegas. Except I can't actually find anyone there who has *seen* Jorlan."

Great. "Are we compromised?"

"Be on guard. No need to relocate yet. You have friends in that area, we both know it. They can watch your six."

"Just how many enemies are going to be closing in on my Esme?"

"Uh, *your* Esme?"

A slipup. "She's my charge, isn't she?" *And she's wearing my ring.* Okay, yeah, he needed to cool his ass down. The ring was just a prop. The relationship was pretend. The job? Real. Keeping her safe? A very, very real priority. No, a necessity.

"She's your charge, all right," Gray agreed readily enough. "And don't you wonder why she was so dead set on *you* being her companion?" Curiosity darkened the words.

Tyler knew why she'd wanted him. For some reason, he

didn't share their past with Gray. Instead, Tyler asked, "How many enemies are closing in?"

"I don't know! Find out from her. This would be the whole *get close* business I was referring to moments ago. For seven million dollars, every eager hitman in the world will be gunning for her. You know this. So, if I were you, I'd probably lock the woman inside the safe house. Keep her fully secure and under watch at all times."

Lock up Esme? He almost snorted. "A little late for that." She'd already been out and about and catching plenty of attention from the locals. Her low profile was a thing of the past.

"Tyler, do *not* tell me something that will make my blood pressure go up even more than it already is."

Fine. He wouldn't tell Gray about the supermarket incident.

"It's not the number of enemies that concern me," Gray continued doggedly. "It's *who* has enough cash to actually put seven million on her head. And when I think about that, I keep going back to one man."

Like Tyler hadn't already made the connection. "Jorlan."

"Right. The psycho bastard has money to burn. You know I think he's been tied to murder, drug deals, and the weapons trade. Getting the charges to stick, though? Whole different matter."

The task force hadn't just been about stopping the jewel theft ring. That had been the story Tyler and Gray had sold to Jorlan. The real truth was that they'd been looking for evidence to use against the SOB. They'd wanted to catch the thieves, and they'd wanted to take down Jorlan.

The first part of the mission had been achieved. As for

stopping Jorlan? That hadn't happened. And now, "He's vanished." A very bad sign.

"He won't come for her himself."

Nah. Jorlan didn't seem like the kind to get his hands dirty. "Thus, the seven million hit."

A grunt from Gray. "Unless *your* Esme has made some other insane billionaire furious with her. It's your job to find out the truth. So go and act like you think the woman is amazing. Pretend that you've fallen under her witchy spell or some shit. Play the player and get the mission accomplished."

"You did not just say that to me. 'Play the player.' Are you drunk?"

"I saw the way she looked at you." No humor in Gray's words. "Use it, okay?"

How had Esme looked at him?

"Just make sure that she doesn't use *you* along the way, got it? Stay emotionally detached or you'll never get the job done."

Esme was the job. "Don't worry about me. I can handle her."

"Good."

Tyler hung up. After a few moments, he made sure all the alarms were set, and he turned off the lights downstairs. He didn't intend to bunk down on the floor again.

With slow, deliberate steps, he made his way upstairs. He went straight to the bedroom on the right. The bedroom that he knew Esme had selected the night before. The door was shut. His hand lifted, and his knuckles rapped against the door.

No answer. But when he reached down, the knob turned easily. Not locked. He opened the door. "Esme?"

Again, no answer. He pushed open the door more.

Eased inside. The lamp beside the bed had been left on, and it spilled a soft glow onto the big bed. An old brass bed. Certainly large enough for two. But the bed was empty.

The bathroom door creaked open. Automatically, his head turned toward that door. Steam drifted around Esme as she stood there, with a white towel wrapped around her body. Her gaze swept over him.

He should speak. And pick up his jaw from the floor. "You, ah, you saved that girl today."

Soft laughter slipped from her as she strolled toward him. "Stop giving me credit I don't deserve." Esme stopped right in front of him and tipped back her head. Her wet hair slid over her shoulders. "I knew there was plenty of time to get out of that truck's way. He really wasn't going that fast. I wanted the people in town to like me, so, goal achieved." Her hand rose, and she gave his cheek a little pat. "You are so gullible. It's almost charming." A soft sigh. She turned away. Headed for the bed. With her back to him, she dropped the towel and provided him with a truly impressive view of her fine ass. "Feel free to join me in bed. There's certainly enough room for two." She slid beneath the covers.

He wasn't breathing.

"Oh, by the way..." Her voice floated to him. "I hope you had a great chat on the phone with your federal buddy."

Could the woman hear everything?

"Tell me, was it anything like the glorious chat you and your sheriff friend had about me? Always great to know that you're in the game of manipulation so that you can learn all of my dark and naughty secrets."

Fuck.

Esme was pissed. And he was screwed.

* * *

The day had been entirely too freaking long. Grayson grabbed his coat off the back of his chair, flipped off his desk light, and headed for his door.

But the door opened before he could reach it.

His boss stared back at him. "Ah, Agent Stone!" Thaddeus Caldwell cleared his throat. "There's someone here to see you."

Now? But if his boss was making an appearance, the someone there to see him had to be a BFD. So he stepped back and put a smile on his face as he got ready to meet the Big Fucking Deal in question.

His boss entered the office first.

Thaddeus was followed immediately by a hulking guy in black. *Bodyguard? Hired muscle? That's what the man screams.*

Then...

An older man, silver at his temples, hair perfectly trimmed, and wearing a suit that appeared to cost more than a month of Grayson's salary. The man's dark eyes swept assessingly over Grayson. "Special Agent Stone."

"That's me." He inclined his head. "And you are...?" But he already knew. Because he had this man's picture—and his file—in his top desk drawer.

"I'm Etienne Laurent, and I want my daughter."

Oh, damn. "Your daughter?" he echoed. He did not look at his boss.

"Don't insult either of us, *s'il vous plaît.* I know that you were the agent who arrested my daughter in that bit of confusion that occurred at Jorlan's residence. I've spoken with him, and he has assured me that he has no intention of pressing charges against my Esme for something that was simply a miscommunication."

Grayson rubbed the back of his neck. "When, exactly, did you speak with Jorlan?"

"This evening, when I was flying to the country because some foolish FBI agent had erroneously arrested my daughter. The daughter of a diplomat." His dark stare was unblinking. And icy cold. "I'd certainly better not learn that you've been keeping my daughter locked up this entire time."

His boss really needed to give him some kind of signal on how to proceed here. But Thaddeus remained silent and stoic. *Great, just gonna let this shit hit the fan, huh?*

"Esme," Etienne said. "Now."

So, since Thaddeus wasn't offering a lifeline, Grayson would just go with the story they'd established previously and hope like hell that his boss had not changed his mind. "Esme was released long ago. She's certainly not in any cell."

Still no blinks from the French Ambassador. "So where is she?"

"Uh, have you tried calling her?"

"*Oui,* I've tried calling her, and I've tried tracking her cell. It isn't on."

"You didn't get any texts from her?" An agent should have texted the man—acting as Esme and saying that she was going out of town for a bit to decompress.

"I have not received texts from my daughter. Just some bullshit from a federal agent pretending to be my Esme."

Uh, oh.

Finally, his boss stepped forward. "I told the ambassador I had no idea what he was talking about."

Way to cover your own ass. Grayson straightened his

shoulders. "I certainly don't have any idea, either. If you got a text from your daughter—well, sorry you didn't like what she had to say, but that's not the FBI's problem." Playing nicely with this man wasn't going to be an option. There was something cold and hard about him. And his eyes were like pure black ice. "Esme Laurent is not being held in a cell anywhere." Complete truth. Esme was in a safe house, not a cell. "She told me she wanted to find some peace and quiet. That's what I hope she found."

"Esme isn't one for peace. And she hates the quiet. Came from briefly losing her hearing a few years ago."

Surprise rolled through him.

"But you didn't know that." Etienne seemed satisfied. "Because you are not one of her confidants. I see that I've misjudged the situation. *Je regrette.*" He turned on his heel. His bodyguard instantly fell in line behind him.

"Wait!" What in the hell was going on? Grayson had the uneasy feeling he'd just been thoroughly interrogated, and he hadn't even realized the interrogation was occurring until it ended.

Etienne gripped the wooden doorframe. "There something you need, Agent Stone?"

He needed lots of answers. "Just how close are you and Jorlan Rodgers?" He'd start with that inquiry. Jorlan was as dirty as they came. And the way this man was talking had alarm bells ringing in Grayson's head.

Etienne turned and smiled at him. "As close as I suppose a man can be to his future son-in-law."

Grayson let the surprise show on his face. "Esme and Jorlan are engaged?" Since when? "Neither one mentioned that to me."

"They are not officially engaged yet. Simply a matter of time, though. They've been involved before. They break apart. Then come back together. They can't stay away from one another. Some things and people are just meant to be." A brief hesitation. "*Au revoir*."

"Yeah, *au revoir*."

His boss hurried to follow the ambassador out. The door clicked closed behind them.

Grayson stayed put, with his mind absolutely whirling. *Is Esme conning us all? Is she fucking Jorlan and playing the Feds?* If so, dammit, Tyler could be in danger.

Fuck, fuck.

A few minutes later...

His door swung open. Then slammed shut again. "Did you know that?" Thaddeus demanded. "Did you *know* that Esme and Jorlan were romantically involved? What in the hell? How screwed are we?"

His breath expelled. *Very* screwed. But only if what the ambassador said was true.

So...was it true?

One man would be able to find out for him. Except Grayson wasn't about to call Tyler with Thaddeus standing in front of him. *Because I don't trust my boss. Not completely.*

"Get Jorlan's file," Thaddeus barked. "And Esme's. We're going over them right the hell now. No one uses me and my team. *No one*."

Chapter Eleven

THE GIANT, BLACK TRUCK WAS COMING AT HER TOO fast. Music blared from the interior even as the engine growled, and Esme knew that she was *not* going to make it to the little girl in time. Or, even if she did make it, the truck was going to hit her. She and the girl would both die. The mother was close, screaming because she'd realized what was happening, but it was too late. Far too late.

The heat from the truck lanced over her, and it was almost like a fire.

Like a bomb.

Like—

Esme jerked awake. Her eyes flew open even as her breath heaved in and out. In and out. Because her heart raced so hard, she automatically put a hand to her chest. The sheet tangled between her fingers, and it took her a moment to process just where she was and what was happening.

The bedroom of the safe house.

Just a nightmare. That's all. A nightmare. Because the

little girl was okay. The truck hadn't hit either of them. *Everything is fine. Fine.*

And...Esme was a world-class liar.

She stared up at the dark ceiling even as her heart continued to race. She'd totally lied to Tyler's face. When she'd run for the little girl, Esme had only been focused on getting to her. Saving her. Not seeing a kid die right in front of her mom.

She's not dead. She's okay. You did one good thing, Esme.

And her mother's voice drifted through her mind...

Start each day with one good deed.

Good deeds had just always been so hard for her. It was the wicked deeds that came easier.

Thus, the naked stroll in front of Tyler. The lie to his face because she'd heard what he said to Clay. As if she hadn't already known that the man was playing her. No way that a guy like Tyler would ever really want *her*. Not for more than some hot and dirty sex, anyway. The forever kind of want? Not happening. He wouldn't end up with a master criminal.

And she wouldn't end up with some morally upright and uptight marshal. Vanilla, indeed.

But she did lean over the side of the bed. Peek down at the floor. Because Tyler wasn't sleeping downstairs that night. He'd taken a pillow and an extra blanket and he'd bunked down right beside her. She squinted at his shadowy form, trying to make him out in the darkness.

"Did you have a bad dream, sweetheart?"

"*Mon Dieu!*" Her whole body jolted.

"You're not supposed to slip into French, remember?"

Her heartbeat had gone right back to galloping. "You're not supposed to try scaring me to death, either."

"I wasn't trying to scare you. I was trying to check on

you. You gasped a few moments ago. Then you were almost falling on top of me. I thought it seemed appropriate to ask if you were okay."

How was his voice so calm and controlled? How was he always in perfect control? Something that drove her crazy. "I wasn't *falling* on top of you." A sniff. "I was checking to make sure you were all right. I thought I heard *you* cry out. As if you'd had a nightmare."

"Can't have a nightmare if you haven't been to sleep yet."

She peered down at him again. Her hair slid forward. "Why haven't you been to sleep?"

"Because this drop-dead sexy woman I know flashed her curvy ass at me and made my dick so hard that sleep is a bit difficult." Rough. Not as calm. A little ragged around the edges.

"Oh." Her mouth had gone dry. She swallowed. Twice. Didn't really help the dryness.

"Uh, huh. So, why don't you lean back in bed? Go back to sleep."

She didn't lean back. She might have leaned forward a little more. Definitely hanging half off the bed now. Possibly in danger of falling down on him.

"If you don't want to go back to sleep," Tyler added gruffly, "you could always tell me about your bad dream."

"What bad dream?" she asked.

Deep, rumbling laughter came from him. "You really think I can't see through your lies?"

She certainly hoped he could not. She worked extremely hard to make sure that no one could see through her.

"Hate to break it to you, sweetness, but I can see you for exactly who you are."

Sweetheart. Darling. Sweetness. He certainly used a variety of endearments. None of which he actually meant. Instead, when he thought of her, she knew he thought... "A criminal mastermind."

"Like that's all you are."

So he hadn't denied the charge.

"But there's more to you than that," he surprised her by adding. "In my experience, people are very rarely just one thing in this world. Hell, even serial killers have families. A man who has killed four people could still be the most devoted father you ever saw. A guy who goes to every soccer game that his son has. Never misses a family dinner."

It took her a moment to actually be able to speak. "Are you comparing me to a serial killer?" Just so they were clear.

"Nah. Because you aren't evil."

Her breath rushed out. "Well, that's something, I suppose. But, please, try not to overwhelm me with your fancy compliments." *He doesn't think you're a serial killer, so, that's something. Something crappy.*

"It's like armor, isn't it, Esme? The way you just toss out your flippant comments to disarm and distract people."

She heard the faint rustle of the blanket below her. When she strained her eyes, she was pretty sure that she could see that he'd shifted around a bit. Were his hands behind his head now as he just relaxed and stared up at her and absolutely picked her world apart?

"Are you scared for people to see the real you, Esme?"

"Didn't realize I'd wake up and stumble into a late-night psychological evaluation. If I'd known that, I would have stuck to my nightmare." She flopped back on the bed. Pulled the covers up to her chin and glared at the ceiling.

His soft laughter followed her. "Hardly a psych

evaluation, but I think I am getting a pretty good handle on the real you."

No, you're not. "Do tell." *Don't. Don't say anything else, would you?*

"How about we start with this? You had no clue if you could get to the girl in time."

Esme swallowed. She also didn't deny his words. How could she? They were dead accurate. *Dead.* Terrible key word.

"You didn't know if the truck would stop or if it would roll right over you. See, you didn't have time to think about all of that stuff. No way in hell did you have time to think about it."

That had sounded like real anger breaking through in his voice. Esme rolled onto her side, but she did not poke her head over the edge of the bed again.

"I heard the mother talking to Clay. She said she looked up, saw her daughter going back for the teddy bear, and she could barely even get out a scream. Her daughter was too close to the truck."

Esme blinked quickly. In the dark, he wouldn't be able to see that her eyes had just filled with tears. Not that he could see her, anyway, not from her position. Because she'd hidden herself from him. *I hide from everyone.*

"You just ran out to grab her, didn't you?" Tyler continued, relentless. "With no other thought except that a kid was going to die. You saw the girl. You saw the truck. And you knew you were the only one close enough to save her. But you *didn't* know if you could both get away from the truck in time."

"What can I say?" Soft. Mocking because that was all she could afford to be. "You should probably start calling me a hero. Maybe the town will throw me a parade."

Silence.

I hate the silence. Hate it. At first, when she'd woken in that private hospital, it had been all she knew. She'd seen people talking. Seen their mouths moving. But there had been nothing for her to hear.

Then, after days—weeks—she'd heard what sounded like the ocean. A dull roar in her ears. It had shaken her nerves even as it both gave her hope and terrified her.

She would always hate silence. Esme scrambled for something to say. "Any word on the dead hitman?"

"No."

Well, okay, that had hardly been a conversation starter.

The silence came again. Dammit. "Tyler..."

"Tell me about your nightmare."

She didn't want to do that. "Why don't you tell me about one of yours?" Now she did poke her head over the bed once more. Almost as if she couldn't help herself. Because she couldn't. "Mr. Big, Bad U.S. Marshal. Surely you have the occasional nightmare, too? You tell me yours, and I'll tell you mine."

"You trying to find out what I fear so that you can manipulate me?"

"Well, no." She hadn't been. "I actually didn't realize you feared anything."

"We're all afraid of something. Even tough talking, sexy-as-hell con artists and criminal masterminds."

"You say the sweetest things." Her teeth snapped together.

"I fear walking out of a damn grocery store, holding fucking chocolate chips, and finding you dead on the pavement." Flat.

She shivered.

"I fear running to you and turning you over only to see

that you have blood all over you. That your bones are broken and smashed. And that your eyes—the most gorgeous eyes I've ever seen in my life—are closed. That they will always be closed. Because you left me. Because I didn't do my one job. I didn't protect you. I fear fucking up and *losing you*."

Wow. That had been surprisingly deep. She pushed a little more off the bed because she wanted to see him so badly.

He grabbed her. His hands flew up, curled around her, and in the next instant, she was tumbling right off that bed and into his arms. Her breath left her in a rush even as her body collided with his.

"I fear something happening to you," he rasped.

Her upper body pressed against his powerful chest. Her legs straddled his hips, and there was no missing the hard, thrusting proof of his arousal. His hands remained curled around her shoulders.

"I fear you dying on my watch when there isn't a damn thing I can do to protect you." His hands slid down. Moved to curl around her hips.

Her hands pressed into the floor on either side of him, and she lifted up just enough that she could peer down at his face. "You're really good at protection," she murmured. She wanted his mouth.

No, I want him.

"And you're good at breaking my control," he returned in a tone that made a shiver slide over her body.

And with that, his mouth took hers. He closed the last bit of distance between them. His mouth pressed to hers. His tongue thrust inside. He tasted her. He took. He commanded a response.

A flood of need burst through her. Her emotions—

already so tightly wound—seemed to explode. Leftover adrenaline? Fear? Who cared what it was? Suddenly, her nails were biting into him even as a moan stirred in her throat. She'd crawled into bed naked. A taunt to him. And when he'd pulled her off that bed, she'd still been naked. Her hips rocked against his thick dick, and the only thing separating them was the blanket he'd been using.

And—as she discovered when her hand slid down between them—his jeans.

Why did the man still have on his jeans? She could help him ditch those. Her mouth pulled from his as she pushed herself up. The move just had her hips rubbing harder against his cock. Her breath seemed way too loud as it heaved in and out.

Darkness.

She couldn't see him clearly.

But she could feel her own arousal. Just from a kiss, and she'd gotten wet for him. Her breasts ached. She wanted Tyler to touch them. To tease her nipples. To touch her, everywhere. But she also had no intention of being the man's regret come morning.

Her hands splayed across his chest. Her traitorous hips might have been arching against him. "Is this the part," her voice was too husky, "where you're going to tell me that if we have sex, it will change nothing?"

"Esme."

"Because I can beat you to that point." Her chin lifted even as she still tasted him. "It will mean nothing. It will change nothing. Just hot, dirty sex in the dark."

His hands were curled around her waist. Holding tightly. "Wrong."

Wait, what?

He lifted her up. Moved with that casual, powerful strength of his, and in the next second, she found herself on the bed again. She bounced and stared up at his shadowy form as he towered over the side of the bed. No, as he towered over her. Her fingers flew out and grabbed for a sheet. Too dark for him to see her, but the man had just rejected her in record time, so no way did she want to be naked in front of him. Darkness or not. "Change your mind already? The good guy just can't stand the thought of fucking the bad girl?" Mocking. Maybe. Maybe there was also a hint of pain beneath her words.

"Oh, I can stand the thought. In fact, it's basically all I could think about for the last three hours while you slept. Especially after that little strip show before you climbed into bed. You want me?"

Yes.

"Then I am absolutely going to fuck you." A savage promise. "But it will change everything."

A tremble of fear might have gone through her heart.

"You think I'll fuck you once and walk away?"

She actually hadn't thought beyond the immediate fuck. *Or...yes, I have thought beyond it. I know he'll have to walk away eventually.*

"Not happening. You're going to be mine, Esme. I protect what's mine."

Her tongue swiped over her lips. "I thought you already were protecting me."

"Because you're already mine. You just didn't fucking know it. You will now. Before I'm done, there will be no doubt." And he caught her legs. He pulled them to the side of the bed. Pulled her there. "I've been dying to taste what's mine."

Her lips parted in surprise.

Then he put his mouth on her. Right where she ached the most for him. He devoured her.

Chapter Twelve

HER TASTE DROVE HIM INSANE. HIS HOLD ON HER waist was probably too tight, but Tyler couldn't let go. Just like he couldn't stop licking her. Taking more and more of her. Her hands flew over his shoulders even as she arched her hips against him. Not to get away. To get closer.

Then she screamed his name. He could swear he tasted her pleasure as she came for him. Against his lips and tongue. He didn't stop. Just lapped her up greedily because he wanted every fucking drop of her bliss.

Esme is mine.

It was time for her to realize that.

"Tyler?" Soft. Broken.

He'd never have her broken. One more lick—one that made her shiver—and his head rose.

"I'm not...still dreaming, am I?" Her breath panted in and out. "Because I don't usually have sex dreams that are this good."

It felt like a dream to him. The most erotic of his life. But it wasn't. "I'm going to fuck you until you scream my name again."

"Promises, promises..."

Yeah, it was a promise.

He stood. Backed away. Then he hit the light on the lamp beside the bed. Immediately, a soft glow of illumination spilled onto Esme.

She blinked, and her hand flew out to grab one of the tangled sheets. She yanked it over her body.

Why the hell would she do something like that? His hands had gone to the waist of his jeans. At her move, though, he stilled. "Shy, Esme? Now?"

She clutched the sheet tighter. Then, slowly, she let it go. As she did, he saw the scar on her stomach. A line that stretched and twisted.

She'd walked toward the bed and tempted him earlier, showing him her perfect ass. But he realized that she'd hidden her scar from him. Odd. Damn unnecessary, too. "Thought you didn't mind scars."

"I don't mind *your* scars." A hitch in her breathing. "But I—"

He kissed her scar. Pressed his mouth to the line that marked her and tried not to remember the day she'd gotten that scar. The way she'd been so still in his arms. Her body so limp. *Never again.*

"Tyler."

His head lifted.

"What's changed?" A soft question from Esme.

Everything. He straightened once more. Then he opened the nightstand drawer. He'd put his weapon in that drawer earlier. His weapon. His phone. His wallet. Now he pulled out the condom that had been tucked into his wallet. He dropped it onto the top of the nightstand. His gaze slid back to Esme, and he found her eyes on the condom.

"Tell me no if you don't want this. Us." He didn't move.

"It can end now, Esme." But once they crossed this line, it would be too late.

"I don't want it to end now." She moved to her knees before him. Her hand pressed to his chest. "You kissed my scar. Do I get to kiss yours?"

"Esme..."

Too late. She was kissing them. Brushing her lips over wounds that had stopped hurting long ago. Using such care. Tenderness. When was the last time he'd had tenderness? There wasn't a hell of a lot of that in his world.

There was violence. There was punishment. There was evil.

Tenderness? That just came with Esme.

Her fingers went to the top of his jeans. Unhooked the snap. Pulled down the zipper.

His hand closed around her wrist. "I don't have scars down there."

"I should check, just in case." She leaned down. Her mouth feathered over his dick. Her breath blew lightly against the sensitive head.

He was fully erect. So hard he hurt. All he wanted to do was shove deep and hard into her core and make her scream for him again.

Then she took his dick into her mouth.

He locked his legs. Stared down at the sexiest sight in the world and tried to not come right then and there. But seeing his dick slide past her plump lips, seeing her take him inside shredded his control.

So. Fucking. Hot.

"Esme."

Her tongue rolled over him.

He was *done.* He pushed her back onto the bed. A light, sexy laugh spilled from her. No laughter came from him.

Tyler was too far gone, and he knew it. He ditched his jeans and kicked them away. He grabbed the condom. Rolled it on. No words came from him. Not like he could manage speech. Though he probably did growl as he came down on top of her.

Esme reached for him eagerly. A mistake, that. Because her eagerness just made him want her all the more. Her legs were parted, and he went right between them. He put the tip of his dick against her straining core. Her hands grabbed his shoulders, and her nails bit lightly into his skin.

He should ask if she was ready. If she could take him.

"Don't make me wait any longer," Esme breathed.

Yeah, right. Like he could. He thrust deep into her. Hard and deep and...*fucking fuck*. She was tight. Squeezing all along the length of his dick and it was all he could do not to come right the hell then. She felt like a hot, tight paradise. Heaven. Clamping along every single inch of his dick and making him lose his mind.

She'd gone still beneath him. Tense.

Too tense.

"Esme," he snarled her name. Snarls and growls and grunts were all he could manage.

Her eyes opened. Her breath came out in quick heaves.

Had he hurt her? *Can't hurt Esme. Never her*.

"Give me just a sec." A quick, nervous smile came and went. Her smile made his heart feel funny. "Been a while. And you are...way big."

He growled.

Her eyes widened. "Did you just get *bigger?*"

Yeah. For her. Every instinct he had demanded that he withdraw, then plunge again. Thrust frantically toward a savage, brutal release that would rock them both.

But she wasn't ready.

She's not ready. If Esme wasn't with him, he would take no pleasure. One hand maneuvered between their bodies. He pushed down to her clit. Rubbed. Stroked. Kept his hips absolutely still. *Do not thrust. Do not withdraw. Fuck me, she feels too good.*

The tenseness slowly fled from her body. Esme sighed out his name. Her legs wrapped around his hips. "Give me everything," she tempted.

He did.

A chain seemed to break inside of him. Tyler withdrew, then thrust. Over and over. His thrusts lifted her off the bed, and she just moaned with pleasure. He grabbed her legs. Threw them over his shoulders so he could get in her even more. So that he could take and take and she was completely open to him.

She jerked and heaved beneath him. Screamed his name. Her hands clawed down his arms.

He kept thrusting. His orgasm bore down on him with feverish intensity, but he didn't want to stop thrusting. She felt too good. Fit him too perfectly. Tight. Hot. Esme.

"*Esme!*" The orgasm barreled into him, and Tyler exploded in her.

* * *

"Who is the first target?" The man stared at the two photos that had been placed before him. "The lady or the bastard?"

Jorlan hunched his shoulders. It had been damn fucking hard to arrange this meeting. The guy in front of him was a shadow. A whisper. One of the freaking scary stories that you hoped wasn't real.

He's real. I paid too much for this meeting. He'd better be real.

"You're to take out the man first. Then bring the woman to me. I need her alive."

Rusty laughter answered his order, and that laughter was somehow scary. Odd because Jorlan was very rarely scared.

"That's gonna be a problem." Cold, mocking words. "Because I've been told I can get a cool seven million if I take *her* out. The bounty is on her being dead, not alive."

"The plan has changed." He could feel his heart slamming into his chest. "But don't worry, I'm giving you a tip that other hunters won't have. You'll be at an advantage."

The hunter stared back at him.

Jorlan waved toward Tyler Barrett's picture. "No one else knows that she's currently with him. You find the man, and you'll find her, too."

A gloved hand touched the picture of Esme. "How do *you* know that she is with him?"

"Because he vanished. Right after she did. No fucking coincidence. He's hiding her, and if you know him, you can find her." A pause. "You *know* him, don't you?"

Icy blue eyes met his stare.

Yes, you know him. I have my own intel that says you do. That was the reason he'd fought so hard to get this meeting arranged in such a short time. "You can hunt Tyler Barrett. You can take him out. He's the only thing standing between her and me." Tyler was the real threat. Jorlan should have put the pieces together sooner. As soon as the prick showed up asking for an invitation to his party and acting like he was there to *help*. Such bullshit. "Get rid of him and give her to me. *Alive.* I just need Esme."

Jorlan had two men at his back. Two men armed with guns. He should have felt safe with them right there. But as he peered into that arctic blue stare, a shiver skated down his spine. He knew death when he saw it.

Jorlan licked his lips. "I've offered you a great deal of money. I'm giving you a tip that none of the other hunters have. Are you going to take the deal or not?"

"I'm confused." But he didn't sound confused. He seemed vaguely intrigued. Maybe a little bored. "Why put the bounty on her head originally if you just want her alive now? Something change? And you don't know how to call back the hounds so you're trying to use me to do the dirty work for you?"

"I never said I was the one who put the original hit on her." Sweat soaked his back. "The seven-million-dollar hit, if you recall, is for the death of the Fox."

"Esme Laurent is the Fox."

"Is she?"

Unblinking blue eyes stared back at Jorlan. "You want to add more on that or just be all suspenseful-like?"

No, he didn't want to add more. He just wanted to get his hands on Esme. "You in or out?"

If the bastard was out, the prick was dead. Jorlan had already given orders for his men to shoot him. Immediately. He couldn't afford any other loose ends. Jorlan held his breath.

"I'm in."

Yes.

The bastard in front of him was supposed to be the best tracker there was. Tracker, killer.

"I'll get rid of him." A cold smile curved the hunter's lips. "Then bring her to you alive. When you're done with her, I'll kill her right in front of you." A pause. "And I'll be taking that big seven-million-dollar payday while her blood is still warm."

"Nice visual," Jorlan muttered. *You won't be taking any money. Because I'll kill you as soon as I have Esme.* He extended his hand. "Do we have a deal?"

The gloved hand closed around his. "Absolutely."

* * *

He walked into hell. Fire raged. Smoke billowed around him. Screams seemed to echo, but were those real screams or the sounds of the old building as it groaned and shifted around him?

"*We have to get out!*" A cry from his friend. "*Place is gonna collapse!*"

It was. They had to go.

But...

He saw her arm. Saw her. Trapped beneath what appeared to be half a freaking wall. His heart raced as he ran to her. He heaved and shoved and got her free. Her head fell back, like a flower on a broken stem.

So much smoke. Ash? Hard to see. He scooped her into his arms even as his friend roared for him to flee. The screams weren't from the survivors–it was the building screaming. Falling down around them. He held the woman tighter in his arms. They burst out just as the remainder of the café seemed to collapse behind them. Tyler stumbled forward, and he held tightly to the woman in his arms.

Her long hair fanned around her as he hurtled toward the pavement. So much blood. It covered her face. Trickled from her ears. And...

Her white shirt was covered in red.

She wasn't moving. Was far too still. Her eyes were

closed, and no breath came from her pale lips. "Help!" Tyler roared.

Ambulance sirens wailed.

"Help!" Tyler staggered back to his feet. He lumbered toward the ambulance. "Victim!"

"Alive or dead?" A fast retort from the man in uniform.

"*Alive.*" She had to be alive.

The EMT took her. Shook his head. "No, she's dead."

"No! No, put her in the fucking ambulance—*she's alive!*"

But the EMT lowered her to the pavement. He shook his head again. "Can't you see her?"

He could. She was all he could see. The blood on her face. In her hair. He should have seen it sooner. It was Esme. His Esme.

"She's already dead. You just don't know it."

What?

"Already dead—"

"*Esme!*"

Chapter Thirteen

"I'M RIGHT HERE."

Tyler jerked. His eyes flew open. His head turned.

The lamp was still on. It fell onto Esme as she stared worriedly back at him. "You called out my name."

Fuck.

"It wasn't exactly a happy call." Her hand touched his shoulder. "Did you have a nightmare?"

Tyler swallowed.

"Because I thought you didn't have those."

"Everyone has those." Even bastards like him.

"Did I do something bad in your dream?"

"Yes," he gritted out. His hands reached for her. "Very, very fucking bad." He caught her and pulled her on top of him. Her eyes widened as she straddled him. "Promise to never do it again," he ordered.

"Wh-what did I do?" Her hands pressed lightly to his chest.

You died, Esme. I didn't save you in time. You died, and I couldn't bring you back. But as he stared up at her, he couldn't say the words. Because saying them would make the dream too real.

It hadn't been real. Esme wasn't dead. She was alive. Warm and sexy and right in front of him. Right on top of him.

Her hair slid over her shoulders as she shook her head. "I can't make a promise if you don't tell me what I did."

"Open the nightstand drawer," he ordered.

Her eyes widened, then she reached over. Her breasts did a delicious jiggle, and he had to lean up and lick one. Suck it.

"Tyler!"

He nipped lightly and felt her sex get wet on his dick. Nothing separated them. If he just thrust up, he could sink straight into her tight core again. *Want in. Need in.* "Condoms inside. Get one."

"You have more condoms in your wallet?"

"Not the wallet." He'd already used the only one in there. "Inside the bottom drawer."

"Uh, how are there condoms in the drawer?" And, sure enough, she shimmied and twisted, and pulled out a box. She shook the box at him. "Planned this already, did you?" Her voice seemed oddly flat. "Did you tell your friend to have them in the bottom drawer before we arrived?"

"I put them in there. Got them at the grocery store." He hadn't pulled them out earlier because he'd thought seeing an entire box might freak her out the first time they had sex.

Her eyes widened.

"Got them on our second trip." She'd been talking to Clay. Tyler had thrown as much into the buggy as he could and hauled ass out of the place.

"You...you knew you were going to fuck me then?" She

was back to straddling him. Her silken folds slid over his dick, but she didn't take him inside.

Need to put on the condom. But, wait, she'd asked him about fucking her. A rough laugh broke from him. "I knew I wanted to fuck you the minute you first told me that you were trouble—that was back at Jorlan's BS party."

She opened one packet and slid back so she was resting on his thighs. "I didn't tell you I was trouble." Slowly, inch by torturous inch, she rolled the condom onto his dick.

His back teeth clenched.

"Do you think I'm trouble?" Esme asked him.

He stared into her eyes. Eyes gone even darker. And he thought about his nightmare. "Yes." Rasped. "You are the worst kind of trouble." The kind that could wreck a man.

What could have been pain flashed in her stare. He couldn't have that. He tumbled her back onto the bed. His mouth pressed to hers. Claimed. Possessed. She gave the little moan that was quickly coming to addict him, and then he was kissing a path down her neck.

Something within him felt *marked* by her. Changed.

And he wanted to mark her.

His mouth pressed harder to her neck.

"That feels so good." She whimpered. "Tyler, fuck me."

Like he wanted to do anything else. The condom was on. Her legs were spread, her hips were rocking eagerly against him, and he sank in deep.

Her head tipped back against the mattress. Her breasts thrust toward him, and he had to taste. To lick. Even as his hips pistoned against her. Over and over, he drove into her hot, tight body. Sanity slipped away as he hurtled toward the release that waited for him.

The bed heaved beneath them. Her gasps filled his ears. His mouth was on her breast. One hand strummed her clit.

And when she came, she squeezed his dick so hard that he lost his breath.

Fucking perfection.

There was no more holding back. There was only the fierce, driving need that consumed him. For the first time in his life, he let go completely. His self-control snapped as he fucked her. As he sent them both straight into brutal oblivion. The pleasure consumed and seemed to burn everything else away until the only thing that existed?

Esme.

* * *

SHE COULDN'T CATCH her breath. Aftershocks of pleasure still pulsed in her sex, and Esme's heartbeat still hadn't returned to normal.

He'd pulled out of her. Ditched his condom in the bathroom.

Then came back to the bed.

His arms were around her. He held her close, like she mattered to him, and she didn't say a word. A woman who hated silence, but she found she couldn't talk. Why? Because sex with Tyler had just wrecked her. In the best possible way.

Sex had never been that good for her. So good that she'd lost herself completely. The orgasm hadn't been for a beat of time. It had gone on and on and on, wringing her out. Leaving her sated and limp. And, possibly, utterly destroyed for other men. Dammit.

Her eyes closed. Sleep pulled at her. For the first time in a very, very long while, she actually felt safe. How could she not? She was in her marshal's arms. He'd sworn to protect her. And after what they'd just done, she couldn't merely be a case to him. Not anymore.

Hope flickered. The dream she'd had for so long.

Her heartbeat finally began to settle.

"When are you going to tell me the truth?"

Her eyes had just been sagging closed. At his low question, they flew right back open again. The lamp was off. Darkness surrounded her.

"You weren't after diamonds at Jorlan's party, were you?"

She could not move. He had to feel the tension in her body. Anger built inside of her. The twisting, stabbing pain of betrayal grew stronger with each tick of time that passed. *Don't do this, Tyler. Not now.*

"Jorlan is pissed, Esme."

Had he just kissed the back of her head?

"He came looking for you at Gray's office. Demanded to talk to you. And now he's gone missing."

Oh, no. Her breath shuddered out. *Jorlan can't find me.*

"Why does he want you so badly? Can't be just about the diamonds. We took those from you. They're safe. The diamonds were flash, weren't they? They were to distract everyone from noticing what you really wanted. What you took."

The anger inside was getting worse. As was the stab of betrayal. So much for the best sex ever. "Your post-sex chitchat needs a whole lot of work." She tried to pull away.

He didn't let her go. "You trusted me enough to fuck me."

Yes, she had.

"Trust me enough to handle your secrets."

She didn't trust anyone with those. She turned in his arms. Their faces were close. "I have no secrets." A whisper.

"Liar." But the word sounded like a caress, not a condemnation.

Weird. "You know exactly what I am. I've never pretended to be anything else with you." She'd told him the truth from the first moment. *Sometimes, you meet someone... and you know right away that the person is trouble.* She hadn't been saying that Tyler was trouble. She'd been trying to warn him that she was trouble.

"You went outside on that ledge at Jorlan's place. You walked in the rain."

"Light rain at the time. Hardly a sprinkle," she dismissed. She wouldn't remember the fear she'd felt. Or the way her left foot had slipped off the ledge on her way back to the library.

"You risked your life. You didn't do that for diamonds."

"No?"

"Something more valuable was waiting for you in that safe. *Tell me, Esme.*"

Her chest ached. "Did you think if you fucked me that I'd suddenly reveal every deep, dark secret that I have? The sex was good, but not that good." And, furious, she rolled once more–this time, away from him. She sat up and shot off the bed.

But he grabbed her wrist. "It wasn't good."

Her jaw dropped. The hell it hadn't been. He'd better not pretend that the sex between them had not been *phenomenal.*

"It wasn't good. It was the best I've ever had. The only reason I'm not fucking you again–right now–is because I know I hurt you."

Her lips pressed together.

"You were damn tight. You said it had been a while for you. How long, Esme?"

Her chin lifted even though he couldn't see the move. "Am I grilling you? Asking about your ex lovers? Tacky, Tyler, very tacky. Again, your post-sex talk is abysmal. Work on it."

"How long." Not a question. A very rough demand.

Jeez. "Two years." A beat. "How long for you?"

"Six months."

Do not think of Tyler having sex with anyone else. Her fingers might have curled into claws. "Are we done sharing about our exes now? Or do you want me to type up a list with names? Maybe want me to write a full report for you?"

"I don't want to know the assholes. That will just make we want to beat the hell out of them." His thumb slid along her inner wrist.

She forced her fingers to relax. To, ah, declaw. "Why would you want to do that?"*For the same reason I want to attack your exes? Stupid jealousy?*

"Because no one else should have you. Just me."

"Sounds awful possessive for a pretend husband." *Remember that, Esme. It's pretend. Just because you had an insane O, don't go getting all confused and overly emotional. He doesn't really care about you. It's just an act.*

"I am possessive." No denial from Tyler. "Get back in bed."

"So you can grill me again?"

"So I can hold you."

A pang slid through her. It would be nice to be held.

"You're tired. You nearly got run over today. Adrenaline wrecked you. And then I fucked you." A pause. "Twice."

She'd come more than twice. Not something she cared to share at the moment.

"I can be a gentleman for the rest of the night. Hell, you

can take the bed, and I'll go back to bunking on the floor if that's what you want."

"Not necessary." She eased back into the bed. He kept right on holding her wrist. Stroking over her pulse point. "I'm sure you can maintain control. Not like you'll go all lust-crazed on me."

"You have no idea." A mutter.

"What?"

"I'll keep you safe while you sleep, Esme."

Yes, she thought he would.

Her eyes closed. Was she hiding from him? Or from herself?

"And when you wake up..." Low, but this time, she understood him perfectly. "I'll still be keeping you safe."

* * *

SHE WASN'T IN BED.

Tyler shot upright. "Esme!" Sunlight trickled through the curtains on the other side of the room. His gaze frantically flew around every nook and cranny in the space.

No Esme.

How the hell had she slipped away from him? He usually woke at the slightest sound. But she'd left the bed. Left him, and he leapt across the room and yanked open the bedroom door. His steps thundered down the stairs as a surge of fear spiked through him. "Esme!" A bellow. He hit the landing and turned to—

Esme strolled out of the kitchen. She carried a covered plate in her hands. She was fully dressed—jeans, a black top, matching black tennis shoes, every hair in place, light make-up on her face and soft pink tint on her lips. Gold hoops hung from her delicate earlobes. A little frown pulled at her eyebrows. "Do you have to yell? This grumpy morning asshole routine of yours has to stop."

His breath shuddered out. "You weren't in bed."

"Absolutely correct." Her gaze darted down his body. His naked body. Her eyes widened, then her stare whipped right back up. *"You're naked."*

"Because I came looking for you!" He sawed a hand over his jaw. It grated against the stubble. "You weren't in bed."

"You said that already." Her gaze darted down once more. Then right back up. "You need clothes. And you, ah, well, at least we can now say for certain that one part of you wakes up in a good mood, eh?"

"Esme."

"You looked so peaceful sleeping in the bed. I didn't want to disturb you." A shrug. "So I crept out of the room on my tippy toes. No big deal."

It was a big deal. She shouldn't have been able to get away from him. He should have heard something. Tyler closed in on her. "How the hell do you slip past my guard? I'm an extremely light sleeper. As soon as you climbed from the bed, my eyes should have been open."

"Technically, I had to first pry your arm off me, then I climbed from bed. Someone is a bit possessive in his sleep."

He stopped right in front of her.

"Someone is also not very shy." She nodded. "Another fun point to know about you. You like being naked, huh? Not that I am complaining. Not at all. I support this life choice that you have." Again, her stare dropped. Only this time, it didn't rise. It lingered with definite appreciation.

One part of him had certainly risen to the occasion. How could his dick not salute? Esme was right there. And the memories of what they'd done the previous night burned in his mind.

She's distracting you. Hell, the woman distracted him by breathing. "How'd you get away without waking me?" A point he needed to understand.

"I moved your hand. I rolled to the right. I tiptoed out. Done. Well, I did pause to dress first so..."

And he'd missed all of that?

One of Esme's hands continued to hold the covered plate. The other rose to lightly tap his cheek. "Don't worry. I won't tell the other U.S. Marshals that you slept on the job. No one will kick you out of the cool club." Soft laughter. "It's really all right that you didn't wake up. Even tough guys like you need their beauty sleep." Her hand fell. "Now, if you will excuse me, I have that good deed to go do."

What the fuck?

When she moved to the side, so did he. No way was he getting out of her way. "You're a perfect thief."

A sigh slipped from her. "This early in the day, and we've already started with the name calling?"

"You move soundlessly. *When* you want to," he amended as he turned over memories in his mind. "A very impressive trick. I want to know who taught it to you."

She stared back at him.

"Master thieves aren't born, Esme. They're made. Who made you?"

Her delicate jaw hardened. "I was a gymnast until I has fifteen. You learn all sorts of things about movement when you're training five hours a day, five days a week." A quick rush of air burst from her in an angry exhale. "Happy now?"

"No." Far from it. "Because you're lying to me.

Someone taught you how to be a thief. I want to know who the hell it was." Though he had a suspicion.

She leaned toward him. "I have got to say, your morning-after routine sucks as much as your post-sex talk. This is not the way to make a marriage work, my love."

My love. His chest ached. "Esme—"

"I have a delivery to make." She lifted the plate. "Fresh chocolate chip croissants. I think our neighbor will love them, don't you?"

What was happening? His gaze jerked to the plate. And he became aware of the absolutely delicious scent wafting toward him. *Chocolate chip croissants.* "I'll take one."

"Don't remember offering you one." She took a step back and dropped the plate lower. Probably trying to get it out of his reach. "Though there *is* coffee in the kitchen for you." A grudging admission.

He fought a smile. "You made me coffee again?"

"Yes, but that was before I knew you'd wake up and be a total ass accusing me of being some criminal-in-training my whole life."

They stared at each other. He had obviously stepped over a line and pissed her off. Time to regroup. Maybe restart?

"Chocolate chip croissants will be wasted on Clay," he finally told her in a careful voice. "Guy can't stand chocolate." Total lie. Clay loved chocolate.

"I'm not taking these to Clay. He's not technically a neighbor, by the way. He lives too far away for that classification. Though he did assure me that he could be here within ten minutes if we ever need him."

When in the hell had Clay told her that?

She skirted around Tyler. "We do have *real* neighbors, you know. Not just a sheriff who is pretending to drop by for a neighborly visit." She made her way to the door as he gaped after her.

It was only when Esme *opened* the door that he realized she truly intended to waltz out. He bounded forward before she could actually leave and slammed his hand against the wood, shoving the door closed again. "Have you forgotten the little matter of a seven-million-dollar bounty on your head? You can't just go skipping to random houses alone!"

Her head turned. Her mouth was kissably close. "Clay told me that we have a neighbor to the left of us. A single guy who is also fairly new to town. He told me that the man was probably lonely, and that it would be neighborly to say hi."

Clay, you sonofabitch. "Oh, he told you all that, did he? *When?*"

"During the insanely unnecessary question-and-answer session after that wee mishap at the grocery store. He got all chatty with me. Clay specifically said it would be *fine* for me to go over. That he'd already checked out the neighbor and that he was safe. No red flags flying." She inched a little closer to Tyler. "Speaking of things flying, I'm pretty sure I feel your dick poking at me."

Yeah, because it was flying. "Do *not* leave this house without me."

"Well, then you had better put on some clothes because if you rush out naked, I am sure word will spread all around town about the fact that I have an exhibitionist husband." Her eye lashes fluttered. "Not to tell you how to handle your business, but I don't believe that's the way to keep a low profile."

Deliberately, he took the plate from her. Put it on the nearby table. Then he turned her around so that she had to fully face him. His body before her. The door at her back. "You think I'm going to ignore what happened?"

Her chin tipped up even as her dark eyes flashed at him. "Dirty sex in the middle of the night doesn't change anything. We already covered this point, remember?"

He shook his head. "Wrong, sweetheart. I told you that it would change everything."

Did a flicker of fear come and go in the darkness of her eyes? He thought it had. Dammit, she should not be afraid of him. Hadn't they covered that point, too? Wanting a reaction from her, needing it, he said, "I've got scratch marks on my arms and back from you."

Her lips parted. "Want me to apologize?"

"No, I want to fuck you up against the door. Right now. And let you mark me more."

He could see the pulse drumming madly at the base of her throat. Grimly, he smiled. *Hello, reaction.* "And you want that, too, don't you, my Esme?"

"I...want to deliver a gift to the neighbor."

That sonofabitch. "Liar, liar." Almost a caress. "I can see the lies easier now. Your mask is wearing thin when it comes to me. That's a warning for you." One hand rose and curled lightly around her throat. His touch was extra careful as his thumb stroked along the slender column. "You're not the only one who left a mark." He remembered exactly when he'd put *his* mark on her. "Told you last night, you're mine."

Her lower lip trembled.

A movement that surprised him. "Esme?"

"Until the case is over? Is that how long I'll be yours? Until you get the master thief out of your life?" Her hands rose and pushed against his chest. "Until you learn all of my secrets? Is seducing them out of me the technique that you think will work best?"

He didn't back away. "You're mine, Esme. I will protect what's mine."

"Even if you find out something terrible about me?" That tremble of her lip again. He didn't think the tremble was part of any act. He thought it was real fear. "If you find out something horrible about me, will you throw me to the wolves?"

Is that what she thought would happen? "No." Flat. "I could find out that you stabbed a man in the heart, and I still wouldn't leave you to the wolves. That's not who I am."

"Stabbed a man in the heart, huh?" Her right hand pressed just over his heart. "You think I'm cold enough to do that?"

A phone was ringing somewhere in the house. Shit. It was his phone. Ringing upstairs.

"Better answer that," she murmured. "We both know only a select few have this number."

It rang again.

"Could be an emergency," Esme added as her head cocked to the right. "A matter of life and death. My death, most likely."

"Do *not* leave this house without me, Esme." He wasn't moving until he got her promise.

"Clay said it was safe to visit the neighbor."

The phone rang again.

"Not without me." He stared into her eyes. "You do not leave without me."

"Fine." Grudging. Very bit out.

"Thanks so much, sweetheart. It's part of the twenty-four, seven protection rule. I want to be right next to that sweet ass of yours wherever you go." He backed away. He also swiped a croissant as he ran up the stairs. He bit into it even as he shoved open the bedroom door.

Holy shit, this is heaven. The croissant was light and flaky and the chocolate chips melted in his mouth. Esme had some serious skills.

Like I didn't know that already.

He swiped up the phone. Gray was calling. *Don't be life or death. Don't be.* His finger slid over the screen even as he put the phone to his ear. "Yo." He wanted to devour the rest of the croissant. Then he wanted to go and devour Esme.

"We have a problem."

Dammit.

"Did you *know* that Esme was planning to marry Jorlan Rodgers?"

The croissant lodged in his throat.

"And that she'd been fucking him?" Gray snapped out.

The phone nearly shattered in Tyler's hand.

Chapter Fourteen

Something was wrong with Tyler.

As they stood on their neighbor's porch, Esme cast a quick glance Tyler's way. He'd bounded down the stairs fast enough after his phone call. He'd dressed in jeans and a gray shirt. Black boots covered his feet. A baseball cap—one that he'd turned around backwards—rested on his head. He'd barely spoken to her as they made their way to their mystery neighbor's house.

But she could feel tension boiling off him.

He pounded on the neighbor's door. Not some friendly little rap. More like he was trying to beat the door down.

"Uh, Tyler?" She sent him a nervous smile. "We're trying to make a good impression, remember? Friendly couple and all that? Maybe don't try so hard to break down the man's door."

His gaze glittered at her. His face was completely impassive, and goosebumps rose on her arms, even though the day was plenty warm.

Something had happened during the course of that phone call. Something that had changed the way Tyler looked at her. Because the fury in his eyes? It unnerved her. "Tyler..."

The door flew open. A gruff, male voice demanded, "What in the hell is happening out here?"

Her head swung back around. A tall, black-haired bear of a guy stood in the doorway. He pretty much *filled* the doorway. His shoulders nearly touched the wood on either side of him. His shirt was covered in paint splotches and his jeans were, too. His hazel eyes swept both Esme and Tyler suspiciously.

She shoved up her plate of croissants. "Hi, neighbor." She tried a bright smile. He did not smile in return. "I'm..." *Uh, oh.* Was she Esme or Elizabeth? Hadn't they bounced both names around the previous day? But when the big crowd had been gathered at the grocery store, she was pretty sure Tyler had called her—

"This is *my* wife, Esme," Tyler said, a hint of possession in his voice. "And I'm Tyler. She baked."

The bear squinted at her. "Baked what?"

"Chocolate chip croissants," Esme told him with the tiniest bit of pride. She really loved her croissants. The recipe had been passed down from her *grand-mère*. The plate was right in front of their neighbor, yet he made no move to take her offering. "We're, ah, new to the town." Now she started to ramble. "Clay told me that you were new, too. So I thought it would be great for my husband and I to come and say hello." He still hadn't taken the plate. "Hello," she said.

One dark eyebrow quirked.

"Oh, for shit's sake," Tyler fumed. "Step back and act like you're inviting us in. Let's get this crap over with. I have other things to do."

What?

But the other man stepped back. He waved them inside. And Esme realized that... *dammit, Clay set me up.* Something she could almost admire.

Once they were inside the house, Tyler kicked the door shut behind them. "Any sign of watchers?"

She just stood there, clutching her plate, as her eyes swung between the two men. Two men who were obviously not strangers.

"Nothing out of the ordinary." Their *neighbor* crossed his arms over his impressive chest. "It's a quiet street. No cars came by last night that shouldn't be here. As far as I know, the cover is holding, and all is well. Though why in the hell you two are on my doorstep, I have no clue."

"I was being neighborly," Esme mumbled. She kept right on holding her croissants. She'd spent so much time carefully preparing them.

"Clay wanted her to meet you. Prick told her to come by and say hello. She goes nowhere without me." Tyler peeked out a curtain. "You getting the security feed okay over here?"

"Perfectly." The stranger turned and headed toward the room on the right.

Curious, Esme followed him. She drew up short in the doorway, though, when she saw the massive computer setup inside. Lots of monitors. And on those monitors, she could see lots of images focusing on her safe house. All exterior shots. "You don't, um...happen to have cameras *in* the house, do you?" She looked away from the monitors and found the neighbor's intent gaze on her. "Because that could be awkward." In so many ways.

"Outside only," he assured her.

Great. Provided, of course, she could believe him.

"So whatever you and Tyler are doing—*or did, all night*

long—that's your business." His hazel eyes were on Esme's throat and on the faint mark that she could suddenly feel burning. "But there is undercover work, there is carrying on a pretense...and there is taking the cover way, way too far."

She slapped down the plate on the desk that waited in the middle of what was...a study? An observation room? Whatever. Esme could feel flames in her cheeks. *He didn't see anything. Stay focused. You are okay. He's just making judgy comments.*

"You're not usually one to cross a line, Tyler." The neighbor's attention had shifted to a glowering Tyler. "This case getting personal for you?"

Say yes. The thought just flew through her mind. She wanted him to say—

"There is absolutely nothing personal happening between me and Esme." Tyler looked straight at her as he made that ice-cold announcement. Then his stare flickered toward the neighbor. "Don't worry about me, buddy. I haven't been compromised. I will not be. I know how to work a case."

Esme automatically glanced down at her chest. Just to make sure there wasn't a knife sticking out of it. But, nope, there wasn't. It just felt as if Tyler had picked up a knife and stabbed her right in her brittle heart.

Hearing those savage words come out of his mouth *hurt.* The pain was much deeper than she'd expected. She considered pasting a big, fake smile on her face. Tossing out something about how nothing was ever personal for her, either.

But she was just too tired. Too done. She was so tired of pretending that nothing mattered. Especially when too much did matter to her.

I need to get away and get myself together.

"I know we haven't exchanged names," Esme said with very careful politeness as she focused on the neighbor. "Though it is obvious you know exactly who I am."

"Esme Laurent."

Her head inclined toward him. "In the flesh." Her hands twisted in front of her. "Do you mind if I use your restroom for a moment?"

"Down the hall to the right."

"Thanks so much." She backed away. Turned on her heel. Absolutely refused to hurry. Her steps were slow and certain. And as soon as she entered the bathroom, she shut the door with the softest of clicks.

Esme looked into the mirror.

Just as a teardrop slid down her cheek. A real one this time. Not the dramatic tears that she could so effortlessly fake. Real tears.

That was why she'd wanted to slip away from the men. It was fine for the world to see her fake tears. Fake tears didn't matter.

But real ones?

No one got to see those. No one but her.

That bastard Tyler had just broken her heart.

I said it wouldn't matter. I told him it wouldn't. She'd said they could have sex and nothing would change.

Just another lie. The bitter truth was that Tyler had mattered to her for a very long time. Only now it was apparent that she would never matter to him. As for the things he'd said the previous night—*can't trust them. They weren't real.* In the heat of the moment, men often said things they didn't mean. She didn't belong to Tyler.

He didn't belong to her.

Nothing personal.

* * *

"I MEAN, YOU COULD HAVE CALLED."

Tyler thrust back his shoulders as he faced off with Kane Harte. "Is that shit supposed to be funny?"

"No, it's just the polite dictates of a well-meaning society. Haven't you heard? Dropping by unannounced is a real pain in the ass for most people. So you call, first."

Tyler grunted. He also edged close to the hallway so he could look for Esme.

"Got to say, that was a dick move."

"Dropping by unannounced?" The dude was harping. "You'll get over it. You had to make contact with Esme sooner or later."

"I'm not talking about your unexpected visit. I'm talking about the way you just broke that woman's heart."

Tyler swung around in a flash. "Bullshit." He hadn't broken anything. He would never break Esme. *Never*.

Kane let out a low whistle. "Ten to one odds say she is crying in the bathroom. You were staring straight at her when you carved out her heart. I mean, are you seriously this clueless with women? You can't be. Or *can* you be?"

Tyler didn't waste more words with Kane. Instead, he stalked to the bathroom. Pounded on the door.

"Occupied!" Esme called out.

He damn well knew it was occupied. "Open up."

"No. I am busy."

Was she crying? Didn't sound like it but unease slithered down his spine. "Open. Up."

"Busy!" Esme shouted back. And there was a definite sniff.

Oh, fuck. Oh, no. "*Are you crying?*"

He heard the sound of the sink running. He gripped the

doorframe fiercely and waited for the door to open. To open...

You can't kick down the door. She's not crying. You didn't break her heart.

The door opened. There was water on Esme's cheeks.

"I splashed a little cold water on my face. I was feeling a bit sleepy. Thought it would wake me up." Her smile dipped toward him as she waved one hand. "Are you having some sort of emergency? Please, go right ahead and take the bathroom, I'm done."

He didn't move. "You weren't crying."

"You're in my way."

"You...wouldn't run away to cry."

Her eyes rolled. "Tell me more about what I would and would not do. So sexy."

"You're fucking Jorlan."

Her mouth dropped open.

Wait. Shit. He had *not* meant to say those words right then. Absolutely not. But...*I am not in control.* Ever since Gray had made his big reveal, rage and jealousy had been twisting in Tyler's gut. He'd intended to wait until he and Esme were alone again, until he'd cooled the hell down, and then he'd planned to carefully question her about her involvement with a man who was as freaking deranged and diabolical as they come.

But...here they were.

Her mouth snapped closed. Her nostrils flared. A jerky nod, and then, "The phone call." A long exhale. "Had to be Grayson calling. Let me guess, he had some new intel to share? Intel about *moi?*"

"Esme."

"I believe I warned you before about that old saying. Don't you recall? I specifically told you that if you were smart, you'd believe absolutely nothing that you hear and only about half of..." She stopped. "Screw it. You know the rest. But at the first whisper of a rumor, you go all in and believe exactly whatever BS Grayson is spouting. So annoying. Get out of my way. I'm not in the mood to be trapped by a jerk and held prisoner in a bathroom of all places."

Slowly, he backed away.

Her spine was straight, her chin was up, and she did not deign to glance his way as Esme made her way back to the front of the house and to a waiting and clearly curious Kane. Even though Tyler followed her every step of the way.

Esme extended her hand to their neighbor. "I don't believe I caught your name."

"Kane." His hand swallowed hers in a brief shake.

Her hand fell back to her side. "And, Kane, I'm to assume that you're on my protection detail, too?" Her head angled to the side. "Another U.S. Marshal? Or are you part of Tyler's former Marine crew?"

"Why don't you tell me?" Kane's eyes assessed her. "Because I think you have already figured it out, haven't you?"

"Semper Fi," she murmured.

"All day long."

Finally, *finally*, Esme glanced back at Tyler. "He was already in place? Before we came here, he was already in Asylum? How is that possible?"

"Kane moved to town about a month ago. He's in between jobs, and Clay had always tried to get us all to come visit this area. Said the fishing was fantastic." The guy used to brag about his catches in the bay for hours on end.

"In between jobs..." Esme seemed to taste those words.

Her focus shifted back to Kane. "Will you tell me what sort of jobs you normally do?"

Kane shoved his hands into his pockets. "Afraid that intel is classified, ma'am."

"Of course. It would be, wouldn't it?"

"But you can rest assured that I know how to watch Tyler's six and yours. No one is gonna slip up on you while you're in that safe house down the road."

Tyler knew he needed to speak. "I was aware that Kane was here. Hell, he's the main reason I decided to bring you to Asylum. Knew he would be here. Knew Clay was here. I had a ready-made operation in place. Besides, Kane is practically a one-man security team. Even better at ass-kicking than I am."

"Stop." Kane rolled back his massive shoulders. "You'll make me blush."

Nothing made that prick blush. "I trust him with my life," Tyler added. A grim truth.

"And with mine?" Esme inquired in an emotionless voice. Then she brushed away the question. "Don't worry, you don't actually need to answer that. Besides, I am quite aware of Kane Harte's impressive talents."

Tyler tensed. Kane hadn't given Esme his last name.

"He was with you in Paris." She turned away from Kane and headed back toward the front of the house. "Pulled out a young mother and her son. Carried them both to safety. Incredibly brave."

"How the fuck does she know that?" Kane fired softly. "You tell her? You don't usually share our secrets."

Tyler shook his head. He hadn't told her. Esme had just been doing her research.

"Figured you would turn up, sooner or later. Just didn't expect to see you this morning. Since you are notoriously camera-averse, it took me a moment to connect the dots with you. But when you gave me your name, everything clicked. A reporter caught your name at the sight of the explosion in Paris. First name only, of course. I read your name in the paper and never forgot you."

If she'd had his name, then in Esme-speak, that meant she'd probably tried to dig up as many secrets on Kane as she could.

Esme paused in front of a bookshelf in the den. Tyler had thought she'd exit the house. Instead, she'd strolled into the den as cool-as-you-please and was poking around. "The two of you have certainly stayed in close contact over the years, and when it comes to his six, Kane is right. Tyler can trust you with his life. You've never let him down before." Her fingers skimmed over the spines of the books. "Mind if I ask a favor of you, Kane? I know we just met, so feel free to deny me."

"Who the hell is this woman?" Kane trailed beside Tyler as they closed in on Esme.

She straightened and turned to smile at him. Her double-dimple smile. The one that meant absolute trouble. Tyler knew this was the part where she would wrap Kane around her little finger. "It's a really simple favor, I promise."

Tyler slanted a glance at his friend. Sure enough, Kane now seemed blinded by her smile.

Her hands dropped to her sides. "If it ever comes down to a choice of saving me or saving Tyler, choose your friend, would you?"

What. The. Fuck? Tyler surged toward her.

"Easy enough to do." She seemed so casual. "Tyler's job is to protect me. To keep me alive. So how about *you* focus less on me, hmm, Kane? Can you do that? You focus on your friend. You make sure he lives and that the trouble chasing me doesn't take him out."

Kane studied her. Then glanced over at Tyler. He shook his head. "Did what she just say make you feel like absolute shit? Because it should. She's worried about your fool ass, and you're busy cutting out her heart."

"He's...not cutting out my heart." Halting from Esme. "I think you're confused."

"No, I think I'm right as rain. Tyler is a dumbass, but I suspect you know plenty about him, don't you? Like the fact that trust is damn near impossible for him because of what happened to his family. Hell, I'm pretty sure there are only a handful of people in this world that Tyler actually does trust, and I'm one of those fortunate few. When your whole world implodes on you, it changes who you are. Changes the way you look at people. You expect the worst. So that's what you see."

She edged right next to Tyler. Her arm brushed against his. That sweet scent of hers teased him. "Do you see the worst when you look at me?"

When he looked at her, Tyler saw everything that he wanted. *Fuck.* His teeth ground together.

"I will take that as a yes." Her lips pulled down. "Of course. Well, *c'est la vie.*"

"Esme..."

"My bad. The old saying just slipped out. Luckily, only one of your team members heard me." She nodded toward Kane. "Do me that favor, will you? In return, I'll be forever in your debt. And try a croissant. Tastes divine." She looked at her wrist. No watch was there. "Got to go. Schemes to hatch, you know. But it was great meeting you. Always nice to meet a true friend of Tyler's."

"Very interesting to meet you, too, Esme."

Esme ambled toward the door.

Nope. Tyler closed the distance between them in about three fast steps. His hand flew out and curled around her wrist. "Not so fast, sweetheart." He felt the jump of her pulse beneath his touch.

Her head turned toward him. "As if I would dream of leaving without my twenty-four, seven protection."

"We aren't leaving. Not yet." He shot a glance at Kane. "Gonna need to use your tech room for a bit. Make yourself scarce, would you?"

"Ah, you're telling me to make myself scarce, in my own home?"

"Glad we understand each other." Tyler used his grip on Esme's wrist to tug her after him as he marched for the tech room. Tech room. Study. Whatever the hell Kane wanted to call the hub with all his screens and computers. Once inside, Tyler shut the door. And locked it.

Esme's gaze lingered on the lock before she slowly shifted her attention to him. "Is there something I'm missing?"

"We're not done here yet."

"No? We're not? Why? Did you want a private space so you could snarl at me about sleeping with Jorlan again?"

Fuck. A black wave of jealousy rose within him. "Did you?" Had Esme slept with that bastard? *Want to break him into a thousand pieces.*

"Did *you* just pull me in this room to grill me about past lovers? We *could* have this discussion in the privacy of our safe house."

They needed to have this discussion right where they were. He'd just gotten derailed, dammit.

With her free hand, Esme brushed back a lock of hair.

"Besides, I thought you said—quite clearly last night—that you didn't want to know about my exes."

"Jorlan isn't just an ex. He's a suspected murderer, arms runner, drug dealer, and all-around freaking *menace to the whole world.*" And he couldn't stand the idea of Jorlan's pampered hands being on her body. "He was a prick in boarding school, and he's a monster now. Why the hell would you ever get involved with someone like him?"

"Some women like a bad boy." She tugged against his hold. "You can let me go now. The door is locked. I'm not planning to run away."

He let her go, but he didn't back away. "Do you like playing with bad men, Esme?" He just wanted the truth from her. Why was that so much to ask?

"Not particularly. It's too easy to get hurt with them."

"Are you sleeping with Jorlan?" Tyler bit off.

"Told you last night—I haven't been with anyone in over two years. So, no, I am not sleeping with Jorlan. I am sleeping with you. Now, can we leave?"

No. "Gray says you're going to marry the sonofabitch."

She sucked in a breath. "Where would he get an idea like that?"

"From your father."

Her shoulders rammed into the closed door as she whipped back. "Gray has been talking to my father?"

A note of fear had definitely entered her voice. *Why is Esme scared of her father?* Though he'd already had suspicions forming. Time to push more. "Your dad is the one who told Gray that you were involved with Jorlan. On and off is the way he described it. Why would your father say that if it wasn't true?"

"Why, indeed? Maybe some people just like to lie."

Esme's father is important. "How did you get the invitation to Jorlan's party?"

Her shoulders still pressed into the wood of the door. "He personally extended the invitation to me. I'm popular. People invite me to parties. In fact, some would even go so far as to say I am the actual *life* of a party."

He was sure plenty of people said that. She was bright and shining and she could disarm with a smile. In the real world, she'd never be with someone like him.

Fuck. This is real. I am protecting her. No, he was doing one hell of a lot more than that. But he needed answers. "How did you know about the secret passageway? Did Jorlan tell you about it?"

She didn't look away from him. "No, I discovered the passageway when I got the schematics for the house. I was doing some recon work. Had to figure out how best to take those diamonds."

Enough. "Sweet liar." His hand drove into the pocket of his jeans. His fist came back up and went right between them. "You didn't give a shit about the diamonds." And then he opened his hand. "You were after this."

A USB drive rested in the palm of his hand.

"Want to tell me the truth now?" Tyler pressed. "Or shall I just go ahead and pop this into a computer so we can see—together—exactly what is on the drive? So *I* can see what you were willing to risk your life to steal?"

All of the color fled from her face.

* * *

The drive was fucking not there. He'd searched fast and hard. He'd ripped apart the luggage bags. Searched the drawers in the bedroom. Gone through every item that

Esme and Tyler had brought to the safe house, but he'd turned up absolutely *nothing*.

Sweat beaded his brow. *Where the hell is it?*

He didn't have much time to waste. He couldn't be found in the house. And he'd left wreckage in his wake. Not like he'd had time for a *clean* search.

His breath sawed in and out.

He picked up Esme's shoes. Expensive as hell heels—and one of the heels turned in his tight grip. Frowning, he peered down and saw the hollow opening hidden in the heel.

But nothing was inside that opening.

Though his gut told him something *had* been inside those heels. Once upon a time.

So where in the fuck is the drive now?

Chapter Fifteen

There were several ways that she could play this scene. Unfortunately, none of those ways seemed promising. Esme swore she could feel her head spinning, and the last thing she wanted to do was pass out while Tyler glared at her. "You should smile more," she blurted as her mind kept right on whirling. "Makes you look so much less scary."

His glare intensified. So much for following her stellar advice.

Her gaze zipped down to the USB drive in his hand. "Where did you get that?"

"It was tucked inside one of your bras."

Dammit. That had been her hiding spot. A man was not supposed to go plundering in a woman's personal space. "Why on earth would you be searching inside one of my bras?"

"Because I knew you'd taken something other than those diamonds from Jorlan. My job is to figure out your secrets, remember?"

As if she could forget. "Yes, I remember. You must

uncover all of my deep, dark secrets, even if you have to fuck them out of me." Horror filled her. "*Mon Dieu.* That's what you did, isn't it? After we...last night...when I fell asleep with you—*you searched then, didn't you?*" The betrayal she felt was staggering. Betrayal, followed swiftly by rage.

He didn't speak.

She shoved against his chest, and he took a step back. "Asshole!" A very loud yell.

He didn't flinch.

"You *used* me. I thought that what we did meant something, but you were just trying to fuck me into oblivion so you could search my stuff!"

"What's on the drive, Esme?"

Rage and pain and fear swirled within her. All of her careful plans were in ashes. "Heroes aren't supposed to do things like that." She swiped at her cheek. "Such an utter disappointment."

"*Are you crying?*"

"Yes, dammit!" Another disappointment. "And I can't march to the bathroom and cry in peace because some jackass locked the door and I'm trapped in here with him!" Another swipe at her cheek. "Can't believe you did this to me. I *trusted* you! Heroes don't do this. Heroes don't—"

"Sweetheart, heroes will do anything to get the job done." He spun away from her. Stalked toward the desk. He pushed aside the plate of croissants that she'd carefully prepared and grabbed a black laptop. "I didn't have one at our safe house. Was gonna have a secure computer brought in tomorrow, but I can use Kane's right now. He always has the best tech, and I know his password." He tapped on the keyboard. Plugged the USB drive in place.

Esme knew she had to stop him. But how? Inspiration

came in only one way. "It's a sex tape!" She lunged forward. "Do you really want to watch Jorlan fuck me?"

Wrong words. Oh, so wrong. But they'd been desperate words.

His head lifted. His blue eyes blazed. And his face could only be described as savage. "No, I don't." Cold and deadly. "And that's not what I'm going to see, is it?"

"He wouldn't give it back." She inched closer. *Once you start a lie, carry it through until the end.* "I asked him to give it back, but he was blackmailing me. So I had to get the video on my own. He didn't upload it to the cloud or anything like that. He just kept that single copy in his safe. The robbery at his house provided the perfect distraction that I needed in order to retrieve the drive."

"Did you send those thieves to his place? Did you stage the entire scene?"

Not the entire scene, no.

"You must have, right? And that's how you knew the guns they carried weren't loaded?"

Her heart squeezed. "You figured that part out?"

"I'm figuring *you* out. You were way too cool about having a gun shoved at you. You either have a serious death wish or you knew the weapons weren't loaded."

She didn't have a death wish. She did have a good ability to know her prey. "I didn't send the thieves there. I just knew what types of hits they liked. I simply made sure I was in the right place at the wrong time." She inched forward a bit more. Esme stretched out her hand. "Believe me when I say that you don't want to see what's on the drive." At the very least, she needed to see it first. Without Tyler breathing down her neck.

And...*so I can protect him.*

"Jorlan is a dead man."

She flinched.

"If he's fucking you on the video, he's dead."

Do not cry. "Again, you are so not heroic. My image of you grows more tarnished by the second."

He grabbed her. She didn't even have time to cry out. In one fast move, he'd wrapped his hands around her waist and lifted her onto the desk. He held her there, with her legs dangling off the edge, with his body between her spread thighs, and with his powerful hands curled around her.

"Sweetheart," he leaned in ever closer, "why do you persist in thinking heroes are always good?"

"I—"

He kissed her. A hot, angry, brutal kiss. Deep and driving. Possessive and commanding. His tongue took her mouth. He took her. The kiss branded and owned and demanded a response.

She should shove him away. She should bite his lip and tell the jerk to leave her alone. She should—

He pulled away. "I can taste your tears."

Dammit. *No.*

His fingers rose and with a tenderness that shattered something in her, he lightly brushed the teardrops away from her cheeks. "I don't like it when you cry. Not the fake tears and especially not the real ones." His lips thinned. "The real ones are the worst."

She nodded. They were.

"Let's try this again." His mouth came back to hers. Not brutal with intensity this time. Soft. Caressing. Asking. Stirring.

Longing.

Her eyelids fell closed. Her hands rose to press to his shoulders even as her mouth opened wider because she yearned for him when she knew that she shouldn't. But this could be the last chance she had to taste him.

A final kiss.

"There's nothing final about us."

Oh, no. She'd whispered those words against his mouth.

His hand closed around hers. Her right hand—she'd been sneaking it toward the USB drive and the laptop while they kissed. "Cute, sweetheart, but not happening."

Her eyes opened.

His eyes gleamed down at her. "For the record, I'm not leaving you. Even if you are on a video fucking him. Though I will rip him apart. Count on it. I'll make him bleed and beg, and I'll enjoy every second of that time."

Her breath choked out. "Aren't you the bloodthirsty one?"

"Yes."

Just that. A firm yes.

His fingers were still curled around her wrist. "Did you think you were going to distract me so you could swipe the drive?"

It had been worth a shot. "You were the one who put me on the desk and started kissing me. I was just using the proximity to my advantage."

His thumb slid along her inner wrist. Right over the rushing pulse. "And what would you have done if you had gotten your silken hand on the drive?"

"Tried to destroy it before you could stop me." In her mind—after securing the drive in her fast fingers—she'd envisioned herself rolling across the desk. Slamming the drive into an open drawer. Hopefully smashing it into lots of little pieces.

"You truly don't want me to see what's on the drive?"

She truly didn't. "If you see it, then there will be no saving you." *Us*.

A line appeared between his brows. "Why would you want to save me?"

"Because you saved me once upon a time. And whether you believe me or not, I did think that you'd get out of this whole protection detail business with me in one piece. Then you could go about your life. But if you see that drive —if you see what I think is on it—then there will be no going back for you." Absolute brutal honesty. She had nothing else to give him.

"You're protecting *me?*"

"Feels weird, yes? To me, too."

His fingers slid along her inner wrist once more. Her pulse skittered.

"Don't look at what's on the drive." A plea from her. No, more than that. "I'm *begging* you. Some things in this world can't be unseen."

"Are *you* on the drive?"

"My world is on that drive."

His gaze searched hers.

"There's a reason Jorlan had the drive hidden in his personal safe. It was his protection. Without it, he's vulnerable, and he knows it. That's why he is going to try so hard to get it back. Jorlan doesn't want me. He wants what's on the drive."

"He has a backup. Surely. If the contents are that important, there are other copies. There have to be."

Mocking laughter escaped her. "You don't put things like this on the cloud for any hacker to stumble upon. You put them in your safest space, and you make sure the drive doesn't get stolen. But then, unfortunately for you, a master thief just walks herself across a narrow ledge and takes what her greedy heart wants."

"Your heart isn't greedy." Certainty.

Not when it came to Tyler, it wasn't. The man was her weakness, and she knew it. She'd tried to show him how she really felt in a thousand ways. But...some dreams just never came true. "Don't watch what's on the drive. Please."

He shook his head. "I have to watch, and then, you know I'll have to turn over the drive to Gray and his people."

Begging hadn't helped before, either. It wouldn't help now. "I haven't seen the footage. I could be wrong about everything. Nothing at all could be on that drive."

Doubt covered his face. "You want me to believe that you risked your life for nothing?"

"I was on the second story at Jorlan's place. I know how to fall and how to get back up." Breezy words. As if a body-shattering fall meant nothing. "Maybe I would have gotten some broken bones, but I wouldn't have died."

He let go of her wrist. With slow but determined steps, he moved behind the desk and sat down in the chair. Tyler tugged the laptop toward him.

The baseball hat had fallen off his head. She stared at the cap as it rested against the floor.

"Don't you want to see what you stole, Esme?"

Her big goal. Getting that drive. But now she wasn't moving toward it.

"What did you intend to do with the contents of this drive?" Tyler asked.

She pushed off the desk. For a minute, her knees wobbled. Odd. They'd never done that before. Not even when she walked across a slippery ledge as light rain dusted down on her at Jorlan's party. Esme pulled in a breath, made sure her mask was in place, then she turned for Tyler. "I intended to get my vengeance, of course."

A furrow appeared between his brows.

"Isn't that the end game for all villains? To get vengeance? Wreak destruction? Those two items were at the top of my wicked to-do list."

"Esme, why in the hell can't you be honest with me?"

I have been. You just don't know it. "You're not honest with me. You steal things from me in the middle of the night. The sex is great, but everything else between us is just pretend." Utter honesty from her.

She saw the hit in his eyes.

"Don't watch," she implored him again.

But his fingers were tapping across the keyboard. So much for her pleas. There was nothing else she could do. Esme's steps were even slower than his had been. She moved to stand right behind him. One of her hands went to his shoulder. An instinctive movement.

"Three video files," Tyler said.

That was one more file than her intel had indicated. She'd just thought two would be on the drive.

He opened the first file. A grainy image filled the screen. She sucked in a breath when she saw the old café in Paris. She'd gone there so often. It had been their meeting place. And, sure enough, there he was.

Louis Turner. Of course, that probably hadn't been his real name. He'd been a CIA operative. She'd known that he was working undercover. Known that he was working *her*. Only fair, really, since her job had been to report back on him. To talk about the questions he asked her. To share any suspicions he might have.

Louis sat at a table with another man. Casually dressed,

with silver at his temples, the man wore a pair of wire-framed glasses.

"That's Thaddeus Caldwell," Tyler muttered. "He's Gray's boss at the FBI. But he doesn't wear glasses these days, and he's got more silver in his hair."

Her spine stiffened. Her hand remained on Tyler's shoulder.

"Who the hell is he talking to?" He'd paused the footage to study the screen.

"It looks different, doesn't it?" Esme mused. "When the walls are still up and the ceiling hasn't collapsed and there isn't ash and fire and hell everywhere, the café seems different? Such a beautiful place, once upon a time. I loved going there. I was the one who told him about it."

Tyler tensed beneath her touch. His head swung so he could look back at her.

But she kept peering at the image. It wasn't every day that a dead man stared back at you.

"I mentioned him to you before. He was the someone who I said could have caused a great deal of trouble in the international world."

"Because he had proof of a weapons and drug trade. Proof that he wanted in the right hands."

The proof had never made it to those hands.

"I knew him as Louis Turner." Her voice softened as she spoke his name.

"Fuck. Were you in love with him?"

Had she been? "He was using me. I was using him."

"That's not a yes or no answer."

"Sometimes there isn't a yes or no answer." Things could be more complicated. "You need more shades of gray in your world."

He started the video again. "Who the hell is recording this?"

"Probably the Feds. Or the CIA. Or—"

Louis's voice stopped her. "*I'm telling you, she doesn't know.*"

"Fucking clear feed," Tyler rasped. "Someone sure had perfect audio."

"It's because he's wired." She swallowed. "I knew he was wired on some of our talks. It only made sense that he was wired that day, too." The day the world burned.

Tyler tilted his head. "So is Thaddeus the one he was giving the intel to? The bastard is right there—Louis could give it to him at any time—"

"*Esme isn't guilty,*" Louis said at that moment. He spoke in perfect English.

In the video, Thaddeus shook his head. "All signs say that she's guilty as sin. We just can't get anything to stick to her. Just like it can't stick to her father."

Her father.

There it was. The ugly suspicion. Big and bold and breaking her heart.

"I want the proof you've gathered," Thaddeus ordered. "This operation has been compromised. *You're* compromised. We need to get the hell out of Paris before it's too late."

Louis glanced around the café. "I'll bring everything I have to you tonight."

"You were supposed to give it to me *now*."

"It's not safe now. I'll rendezvous with you later. Okay? Now, look, you need to go. You shouldn't even be here. We can't be seen together."

"You're planning another meeting with her, aren't you?

You are compromised." Thaddeus stood up. "If I know it, others will, too."

"I'm in control."

"The hell you are." Thaddeus spun away. He marched for the exit.

Esme sucked in a sharp breath. Her heart stopped.

Louis remained at the table. His fingers drummed on the top. There was a faint vibration of sound. The softest peal right before Louis pulled out his phone and looked down at his screen. A moment later...

The whole café exploded.

Tyler cursed.

She realized she'd dug her fingers into his shoulder. Too hard.

"Esme..."

She couldn't seem to relax her grip. "He was there."

"Thaddeus? Yeah, but he got clear before the blast."

"*He was there.*"

Tyler had closed the file.

"Open it again," she ordered, voice frantic. "Play it again."

He did. He reopened the file. He played it again. She heard Louis's voice, and the past washed over her once more. They'd been using each other. Love? No, not love. But something that might have been close if they'd had a chance. And there it was...right after Thaddeus left.

A moment that would change everything. An image that would seal her fate. And Tyler's.

"Stop."

Tyler froze the screen. She stared at the man on the far-left side of the image. Caught for the briefest of seconds. His profile was so familiar to her. Even the old, black flat cap he wore. The cap her mother had tried in vain to replace so many times.

I would know him anywhere. How could she not? "That's my father. He was there that day." She could barely breathe, much less speak, so the words trembled as they spilled out. "I was told..." She'd paid so much money. Worked in the darkness so long to obtain the intel. "I was told that the man who'd really pulled the strings was in the café right before the blast. Jorlan had proof. He had power because of his proof." It hurt so much to have her suspicions confirmed. "*He was there.*"

Her father walked out. She hadn't seen him at the café when she arrived because he'd gone out through the back door. She could see him rushing that way.

She'd come in the front door. "I saw Louis looking down at his phone. I called his name. I don't think he ever heard me."

Tyler's index finger tapped. The video played once more. Louis looked down at his phone.

The world exploded.

Chapter Sixteen

In that instant, Tyler absolutely hated himself. He could feel Esme's pain like a living, breathing beast in the room. He closed the file. Stared at the screen and tried to figure out how the hell to comfort her. But what comfort could he give?

She'd watched the video, and now Esme thought her father had killed the man she loved.

Esme loved him.

It had been in her voice. A softness. A wistfulness. He'd heard it and hated it.

Tyler released his clenched jaw. "You can't jump to conclusions. There was no proof that your father planned the bombing in that video. He could have just been getting a coffee or something."

"He doesn't just get coffee. He has people for that." Wooden. "He didn't know I was going to be in the café that day. I-I wasn't supposed to be. I told him about all the other times I was meeting Louis, but not that day. Not that time."

Tyler stood up and slowly turned to face her. He needed to hold her because her pain was wrecking something inside of him, but he was almost afraid to touch her. "Esme."

"Louis believed my father was a monster. He told me that on day one. I told him that he was wrong. He had to be, didn't he? Louis was using me in order to try and get intel on my father. I was using him so that I could tell my father everything the CIA and the Feds were thinking. All of their nasty plots." Soft, bitter laughter. "Not like Jorlan's party was the first time a big, joint task force was at work in my life. I've certainly seen the play before."

"You thought your father was innocent."

Her eyes seemed even darker. "I thought he wasn't a monster. There's a difference between being innocent and not being the devil himself. I knew my father wasn't a saint. I just didn't think he was the man who wanted the whole world to burn."

The café had burned.

"There isn't proof in that video," Tyler had to say the words.

"There are two more videos left to play."

Shit. "I am a bastard." He'd done this. She'd begged, and he'd still sent her straight to hell by playing the first video.

She gazed at him. He expected to see tears in her eyes. There weren't any. But there were plenty of shadows.

"I can watch," he told her, his voice more gruff than normal. "You don't have to see what's there."

"It's not me who will be hurt by the next video."

What?

"I saw the date on it."

Curious, he turned back.

"You had a really nice life growing up, didn't you?" Esme's tone was guarded. "A mom who loved you. A father who came to every football game. A great house. Plenty of money. Maybe a little too much money?"

"My grandfather was wealthy," Tyler said. He chose his words with care. He'd always needed to be careful when he talked about his grandfather. A lesson he'd been taught as a child. "Dad didn't want anything to do with the cash, but it kept coming. My grandfather always sent it." Until he'd died, and then Tyler had inherited everything. Good and bad.

"Sometimes, it's hard to cut ties," she murmured. "Even when you know a final cut is for the best."

He realized that he didn't want to watch the second video. It was going to be bad.

Except he'd learned long ago that you couldn't hide from bad things in this world. No matter how hard you tried. So Tyler opened the file. It was a long-distance shot of a car. A sleek, black ride that was driving along a curving road.

He knew that road.

And that car.

No, fuck me, no.

The car dipped into the curve.

And exploded.

Her hand was on his shoulder again because he'd sank back into the desk chair.

"What the fuck...?" Tyler snarled as his hands clenched into fists. He wanted to pound those fists into the computer and beat it into bits. "What the fuck does my parents' death have to do with the café in Paris?"

That car, that road...

"I believe the same bomber was at work in both instances. Or at least, the same individual who *hired* the bombers."

He shook his head. "You *told* me that terrorists were caught for the Paris café bombing."

"Yes, they were caught. They were charged. They confessed. They were tied to three other bombings in Europe. But, sometimes, things are not as they appear. I've warned you about that so many times." She squeezed his shoulder. "I am sorry."

And again, he shot out of the chair. He rounded on her as fury and confusion poured through his veins. "Those are my parents in that car! I know that car—I rode in it all the time! And that's the road near our house in Texas. My parents were in the fucking car that I just watched *explode*."

Now, he could see the tears swimming in her eyes. "I begged you not to watch. I'm sorry."

She was sorry. *She* was sorry? He was the one who'd demanded they watch. He was the one who'd made her see the man she loved die.

She was sorry.

He shoved the chair out of the way. The damn chair separated them. And Tyler pulled her into his arms even as the chair crashed onto the floor. He held her far too tightly. He should not. He should not hold her this way.

"Don't." Soft. From Esme. Her hands fluttered over his arms, and she didn't hold him back. "Tyler, don't you see? You can't touch me. You can't want me. You can't—*I'm sorry.*" Broken. Whispered. "It was him. I don't know why he did it. *But it was him.* He did this, and you can't want me. You can't ever love me. You can't—" The words ended as she tried to jerk away from him.

He didn't let her go. He wasn't letting her go. But his head lifted and he stared down at the horror and pain on her face. And he understood the bleakness in her eyes. "You think your father killed my family."

"I didn't. I swear, I didn't think it was going to be him." A tear slid down her cheek. "Not until I saw him in the first video."

"How did you know about this fucking drive? How did you know it would be in the safe that night?" Rage vibrated in each word. "How did you know my family's murder would be on the drive?" Because she'd known the second video would hurt him. She'd said as much. So she'd *known* the murder was on there? What could hurt more than his family's murder? *Nothing*.

"I heard Jorlan mention the drive's location. I was somewhere I shouldn't be." A ghost of a smile came and went on her face. The dimples barely flashed. "As I so often am. He said the drive was his security. That it would keep the predators at bay. He was untouchable as long as he possessed it. I'd already paid...informants to learn that there was an important recording of the café explosion."

He waited. There had to be more.

"When I was researching you, I learned about what happened to your parents. The way they'd died made me suspicious. I-I picked up a few more details from some very dangerous individuals that made me realize the two bombings might be connected." She swallowed. "Then you put the drive in the computer, and I saw the date listed next to the second video."

She'd known the date of his parents' death.

"I saw two bombings." The rage wanted to swamp him, but Tyler wouldn't let it. He spoke through clenched teeth. "But I didn't see a damn thing that told me your father was guilty." She seemed so very certain. *Why?* "What do *you* know about your father that makes you think he's evil?"

"I don't want him to be evil. I want to be wrong. But he

was in the café. It blew up after he left. My father knew that Louis was working to bring him down."

My parents. My parents. He shoved the rage back and tried to focus. Things weren't adding up for him. "Why the hell did Louis think your father was guilty?" There were too many missing pieces.

"Because, like me, my father is also often in places where he should not be. Consider it a family trait."

She thinks her father killed my parents. "Your father wasn't the only person in that first video. Thaddeus Caldwell was there, too. And the hitman who recently came after you—that hitman just died while in federal custody." A pause as his mind sorted through possibilities. "Do you think your father could have gotten inside a federal facility and had someone killed?" *Or was it Thaddeus doing the dirty work?*

"I think my father can get in and out of just about any place."

He needed to watch the third video.

But in his mind, Tyler kept seeing the footage of his parents' car. Exploding.

Just like the café exploded.

"I didn't want you to see them die. I'm so sorry, Tyler."

"How did you know they were on the video?" His hands wrapped tightly around her arms. "How the hell could you have known that?"

"Jorlan doesn't like you," she breathed. "You fought him in boarding school. Punched him out in front of everyone. He acted as if he got over it. He didn't. He never forgets or forgives a slight." The delicate column of her throat moved. "That's why he won't stop until he finds me. It's not the seven million on my head that worried me so much. It was him. He scares me."

"*How the fuck do you know so much?*" About Jorlan. About the CIA. The Feds. *Me*. Hell, she'd even known Kane.

"I know because information is my business. I don't just steal pretty jewels. I can buy jewels. You can't buy information. You have to trade for it. Barter. Work deals that you would rather forget."

Is that why she steals? She is working her deals? There was so much he felt like she was not telling him.

"I try, but, believe me, I don't know everything. It's impossible to know everything in this world. Hell, I didn't even know about Clay, not until we got here, and I realized you had a close bond with him. I mean, I retrieved intel on some of your old Marine buddies—like Kane—but I could hardly pull up classified information on *everyone* you knew. I'm good, but I'm not all-knowing. Despite my best efforts." An exhale. "I try," she repeated again, sounding almost defeated.

Rage pulsed inside of him. "How the fuck did you know that my parents would be on the USB drive?" That was the million dollar question for him.

"Jorlan bragged to one of his men once that he had something you wanted. Very badly. I do know you, you see. Made it a point to know you after you saved my life. You were my specialty. My focus." A soft exhale. "I know the one thing you want is what you never got. Despite your best efforts."

His heartbeat thundered in his ears.

"You wanted justice for your parents. You woke up one morning, and your whole life was gone. Wiped away. The cops didn't even fully investigate, did they? They just gave you a story about faulty wiring."

A story he'd never believed.

"No one was caught. No one was punished. Justice—it's the only thing you want. Jorlan knew it. He was going to use it as a bargaining tool with you. Only I took his bargaining chip away."

He could not wrap his head around all this no matter how hard he tried. It was too much. "Your bombing. My parents' death. What the hell is on the third video?" He had to see it. Tyler let her go. The chair was on the floor. He kicked it aside more. Then he clicked on that third file. He could barely breathe as he waited to see what would appear.

Louis's face appeared. A close-up shot. Louis glanced over his shoulder. Then back at the camera. "This is my insurance," he stated gruffly. "In case things get as bad as I suspect they will. No one can be trusted. Not at the Bureau. Not at the CIA. I won't turn over jack shit to them. If I do, they'll destroy you. I don't want that." He acted as if he was talking directly to someone. *They'll destroy you.* He exhaled and spoke straight into the camera. "It all has to vanish. Disappear. I have a plan, but...shit, in case something goes wrong—this is all I can leave behind. You'll find it. You will search here. You know me better than anyone." His gaze sharpened. "*You* know me, Esme."

Esme. Louis was talking into the camera, talking straight to Esme. And she was finally hearing his message.

"You found this video, didn't you?" Louis asked. "*You know me.*"

As he peered into the man's hazel's eyes and saw the intense emotion on his face, Tyler felt jealousy rise. *He loved Esme.* Great. Savage jealousy, lethal fury—just the combo Tyler needed as he fought to hold onto the razor-thin edge of his control.

"Your father is dirty, Esme," Louis said in the video. "It's not just about some hobby where he steals for a high. *It's bad.* Up to his eyes bad. You won't believe that because you love him. But it's true. His enemies vanish. He makes them disappear." His gaze jerked to the left, then back to the camera. "You knew I was working to take him down. I knew you were protecting him. You fed him intel. He led me on a long chase, but I figured out the truth in the end. It started so long ago. A lifetime ago. And he has connections, Esme. More than you can guess. Even the people pretending to be after him? They're really on his side."

Tyler's attention sharpened. *People like Thaddeus Caldwell?*

"They're scared of him," Louis continued quickly. "I can't trust them. Thaddeus—hell, there is no way I'd ever tell him what I've learned. Why is a Fed so involved in all this? It's CIA business, but he's here...*because he owes your father*. So many people owe him."

Hell.

"Where your father goes, destruction follows." Louis's gaze implored the camera—no, it implored the woman who he knew would one day watch his video. "Pull up stories. Look at the attacks. *Bombings.* That's what he does. He destroys. The people who cross him? He puts hits on them. A bomb that takes them out—and any collateral damage that might be nearby."

Esme had been collateral damage in Paris. Only her father hadn't realized the truth until too late.

Louis ran a shaking hand over his face. "I started putting the pieces together because of an attack in Texas years ago."

Sonofabitch.

"Hell, you would have been a kid back then. But he did it. I *know* your father did it. He was in Houston at the time, and the man he took out? It was a guy who tried to testify against your dad. This man went to the Feds in Houston. He made a mistake, and he went to Thaddeus. The guy had intel to use so he could bring down the house of cards. Only the next thing that happened was that the poor bastard and his wife got blown to hell in their Lincoln."

My parents.

"Now Thaddeus is here in Paris. He's involved in a CIA operation when he shouldn't be. He's pushing me to hand over what I know. To tell him everything." A quick, negative shake of Louis's head. "I will not trust him. I won't make that mistake."

The mistake my father made? Tyler shook his head.

"Your father likes to watch the explosions. He's always close. *Do the work, Esme.* Look into his travels. Pull up attacks that occurred when he was in different parts of the damn world. You'll see that I'm right." A sigh. A sad one. "I'm right. I'm sorry. He's evil, and I want to help you but if you found this...Hell, if you found this..." His lips pressed into a line. Silence. Then, "You have a really great smile, Esme. Did I ever tell you that? It lights up the whole freaking room."

The video stopped.

Tyler could not move. He felt frozen to the spot.

The silence stretched until—"I didn't find the video after the bombing." Esme's muted voice. "I was in the hospital for so long. I-I wasn't supposed to be in the café."

"Your father wouldn't have set the explosion if he'd known you were there." His hands fisted and released. Fisted.

"By the time I was released, all of Louis's belongings were long gone. I have no idea how Jorlan got hold of Louis's message."

"There could be more copies." Of everything. Somewhere—

"Do you hate me?" Low.

"What?" He was still staring at the screen and feeling dazed and shocked and angry and as if he'd just lost his parents all the hell over again. The wound was as fresh and raw as ever.

"I'm so sorry that you lost your parents. I just, I—"

She touched him. He flinched.

Her hand immediately pulled back. "I understand."

No, she didn't. He didn't understand the emotions ripping him apart.

"I'm going back to the safe house," she told him. "You do—you do whatever it is that you must with those files. But, ah, I'm not so sure I'd be handing them to Thaddeus Caldwell." Her steps shuffled away from him. She went straight to the door. He should stop her. Call out to her. Say something.

My parents. The Lincoln. The fire.

"I'll help you lock him away," Esme quietly promised. "I'll help you get your justice."

He looked up at her. Her face was far too pale and tense and sad. *Stark.* That was how Esme looked. All of her beautiful, glowing brilliance was gone.

You have a really great smile, Esme. Did I ever tell you that? It lights up the whole freaking room.

Esme unlocked the door. Stepped out. The door closed behind her with a soft click.

Tyler swallowed. He unclenched his right fist and reached for the laptop. His fingers were shaking as he closed the files and pocketed the USB drive.

The door swung open. Tyler's head immediately whipped up. *Esme?*

No. Not Esme.

Kane. A glowering Kane.

"Uh, not to tell you how to do your business..." Kane began. Then he stopped. "Who the hell stole your puppy?"

"What?"

"You look like someone just stole your best friend." Kane glowered. "Stop that shit. I'm right here."

Tyler shook his head.

"I'm right here," Kane repeated. "You're right here. But the woman you're supposed to be protecting? She's walking out of the house. Alone. Not to tell you how to do your business...*but this ain't it.*"

No, it wasn't. And he needed to get past the shock and grief and rage and go after what fucking mattered. He rushed for the door. Shoved Kane back.

"That's more like it," Kane praised.

Tyler ignored him. He bolted out of the house. Bounded down the steps. Esme was in front of him, walking with her head down and her shoulders hunched, and she looked so sad and broken that it made his heart shatter all over again.

He didn't know what in the hell he was supposed to do with Esme. But letting her go? Not an option. No matter how fucked up and tangled their pasts might be. "Esme."

Her shoulders stiffened. But her steps didn't slow. If anything, they sped up.

So did his. "Esme!"

She took off—running away from him.

Oh, the fuck, no. He chased after her, but, surprisingly, Esme was super fast. Only maybe he shouldn't have been surprised by that discovery. How could he predict anything about her?

She beat him to the house. Rushed inside first. She'd

had the key, after all. But he caught her just steps past the entranceway. His hands flew out to curl around her, and he hauled her back against him. "*Esme.*"

"I don't want to hurt you!" Esme cried out. "That was the last thing I wanted. It couldn't be him, don't you see that? *It couldn't.* Because it wasn't before. He didn't do it. It was her. Everyone was wrong, but he took the suspicion. He took it all those years and covered for her. He was good. No one ever knew. Just me. I knew what he was doing. *I knew.*"

Tears were on her cheeks. "I hate your tears." One hand rose to cup her cheeks. To swipe away the tears.

"You hate me," she breathed.

He shook his head.

"You do. How could you not? If he killed them...if my father ordered the hit, *how could you not hate me?*" The darkness of her eyes was almost painful to see. No, it wasn't the dark that was painful. It was the pain in her stare.

And, suddenly, Tyler felt as if he was truly seeing Esme for the first time. Not blinding bravado. Not some brilliant mask that hid a thief or a criminal. He saw Esme. Beautiful. Broken. Trying to hold herself together and fix the world around her. Trying to *protect.*

"You wanted to watch the video before me," he said, understanding *her* now. "And you were going to deliver my parents' killer to me, weren't you?" She'd known so much more than she revealed. *Tricky Esme.*

"It was going to be a thank you for your help. You can't protect me without some kind of payment." Her lower lip wouldn't stop trembling. "But it's all wrong. He wasn't supposed to..." Her words trailed away.

"Who did you think was going to be on the USB drive, Esme? Who was going to be guilty?"

"One of the Feds. Someone in power. Someone I could take down."

"Thaddeus." He had been on the video. And Louis had thought the guy was dirty. But...*I don't fucking know Louis. I don't know a damn thing about the man except that he was in love with Esme.*

Tyler's Esme.

"Louis said it was my father. Someone killed Louis to stop him from talking. *My father* did it. He was right there. He was so furious with me after the bombing, so angry every time he visited me in the hospital. As if it was all my fault. *When he'd done it.*" Her words came so fast and held so much pain. "And now everything I ever wanted is *gone.* I'll never have it. I'll never have what I want—"

"What did you want?" Tyler demanded. If another tear slid down her cheek, he would lose his mind.

Another tear slid down her cheek. "You."

He shook his head. No way had she said what he thought. And his mind was utterly lost. Mind, heart, everything. Lost to *her*.

"I wanted you, Tyler. I wanted the good guy, for once. I wanted someone like you to care about someone like me. But you can't. You won't. Because someone like me—I wreck your world. I wreck you." A hard shake of her head. "This is over. The protection detail is done. I don't care what price is on me. I have to get away from you." She broke free and rushed for the stairs.

She didn't even get up the first step before he had Esme in his arms. He pulled her against him, her back to his chest, even as his arms looped around her. His mouth went to her ear, and he swore, "You won't ever get away."

"Tyler..."

"I can't let you get away. Because you're what I want."

He would be wrecked without her. He spun her in his arms. His mouth crashed onto hers. He didn't want to think about the past. Death and cold graves. A world that had shattered and never been put together right again.

He didn't want to think of two black coffins, side by side in a rainy cemetery.

He didn't want to think of a café that had exploded in Paris. A woman too still and bloody in his arms.

Esme wasn't the villain. She was *not* his villain. But she damn well might be his everything. His feelings weren't rational when it came to her, and he didn't care. Fuck rational. Fuck normal. Fuck *good.*

Esme was his.

His to protect.

His to keep.

His to take.

His mouth plundered hers, and he could taste the salt of her tears. *I hate Esme's tears.* The only thing about her that he hated. Did he want to rip her father apart? Hell, yes.

But he didn't want to hurt Esme. Never, ever did he want to hurt his Esme.

Her mouth was open beneath his desperate lips. Her tongue met his with a wild greed. Her hands stroked over him even as he pulled her ever closer to his body.

Screw this. Need more. He grabbed her hips and lifted her up. Her legs automatically wrapped around his waist. The thick length of his cock pressed against the crotch of her jeans. She rode him through the fabric. Up and down, arching. Pushing.

Moaning softly for him.

He needed to fuck her. Right then. Right there. Fuck her deep and hard and let the rest of the madness that was life and death fall away from them both. Tyler tore his mouth from hers and began climbing the stairs, with her legs still wrapped around his waist.

"What are you doing?" A surprised cry as she clutched him tighter. "You'll kill us both!"

"Hold on, baby." He had her, always. He could carry her up the stairs any day of the week.

She held him tighter. Kept her legs wrapped around him.

"It's hot the way you're so strong, Tyler," she whispered. "*Je veux te baiser*."

"It's hot when you speak French. Drives me insane." No, he was already insane. Had been, since the moment he first saw her at Jorlan's party.

He reached the landing. Turned for her bedroom. Didn't lower her. His cock wanted *in* her. He wanted in. They needed condoms. If it hadn't been for the condoms, he would have fucked her on the stairs.

I will fuck her on the stairs. In the bed. On the floor. Against the wall. Anywhere and everywhere until Esme understands that we aren't pretend. We aren't ending. I won't let go.

He hit the light switch with one hand. His mouth went back for Esme's—

Wrong.

He stiffened. His head whipped back up.

"Tyler?" Uncertainty. "Did you...did I do something wrong?"

He lowered Esme to her feet. His gaze swept the room. The room that had been completely *trashed*.

She sucked in a sharp breath when she saw the destruction.

"We're getting the hell out of here." Right then. No

alarms had blared. The security sensors hadn't picked up any intruders and sent an alert to his phone.

But someone got inside. Someone could still be inside.

He bent and pulled out the gun that had been strapped to his ankle. "Esme, stay behind me."

"I need a gun! This is a point I meant to bring up to you much, much sooner, but I need a gun."

His right hand held his gun. His left reached for her. "Stay behind me." He'd been so distracted when he entered the house. Fucking amateur mistake. Someone could have been downstairs, and he'd been so locked and *obsessed* with Esme that he hadn't even checked his surroundings.

He had to get her out. Her safety was priority one. He'd take her to Kane, then come back and search every inch of the house. But first, he had to get her out.

The hunters found her. Too fast. But, if the Feds had been involved...

Gray could have told his boss where we were. Even though I ordered Gray to keep the location private. Tyler had tried to go completely off everyone's radar, but he hadn't done the job well enough.

Someone was searching in the bedroom.

Looking for...the USB drive?

They were at the bottom of the stairs now. He stilled and swept his gaze around the lower level of the house. He didn't see anyone. The house felt too damn still. And the hair at the nape of his neck had risen. His instincts were screaming.

Get out.

Get out.

He whirled around.

Esme's eyes were wide. Scared. "Tyler?"

He grabbed her and threw her over his shoulder, then

he ran for the door. He had Esme secured over his shoulder, and the gun gripped in one hand.

"Tyler, what in the hell are you doing?" Esme cried out.

He yanked open the front door. Rushed out with her calling his name. He bounded off the porch steps. He hurtled forward.

And then he was flying—because the house behind him had just exploded. A thunderous detonation that blasted and destroyed and sent him and Esme hurtling through the air before they both slammed into the unforgiving earth.

Chapter Seventeen

"TYLER!"

His eyes cracked open.

Kane glared down at him. "Don't you freaking ever scare me like that again, you understand?" Kane gripped his shoulders and shook him. *Hard.* "Fuck. Thought you were dead!"

His ears were ringing. His body aching. And fear nearly choked him as Tyler shot upright.

"No, dammit! The EMTs need to check you for spinal injuries."

And some men in EMT uniforms were rushing toward him.

No time for that.

Kane began, "You can't just get up—"

Tyler just got the hell up.

"Or I guess you can," Kane muttered. "Out cold one minute, charging like a bull the next. Whatever. Do you." He slapped a hand on Tyler's arm. "Just glad you're not dead."

"Esme." His eyes were on the house. The still burning

remnants of the safe house. Chunks of wood and debris were scattered all over the yard. Windows had shattered.

Firefighters were battling the blaze. An ambulance waited about twenty feet away. Clay's patrol car sat near the edge of the sidewalk, with its driver side door hanging open.

Tyler frowned at the chaos. How the hell long had he been out? And where was Esme? "Esme!"

"She's all right." Kane stepped in front of him. "Breathe. Don't lose your mind. The woman is alive."

But he didn't *see* her.

"You got her out. I heard her telling Clay how you carried her out right before the house blew." A shake of Kane's head. "What tipped you off? How the hell did you know what was happening?"

"The bedroom was trashed." His hands had fisted. "Someone searched the house while we were at your place. Didn't care about the mess left behind—that told me the guy must've had a plan in place." *Where is Esme?* His chest was far too tight. His heartbeat too fast.

"A plan as in...he was gonna blow up the house and everyone inside? Except you got out before he could?"

Barely. He felt blood trickling down his side. He'd *barely* gotten out.

"You probably have a concussion. You were out cold when I first came across you and Esme. Checked your pulse to make sure you were still in the land of the living—spoiler alert, you were—then I got your lady to safety STAT before coming back for you."

He grabbed Kane's shirtfront. "*Esme.*"

"Right. Esme. She was holding tight to you and screaming your name. Only like I said, you were out cold." Kane frowned down at the fists that were wrinkling his shirt. "Wanna take a breath? And ease that grip? I promise, she's fine. She's in the back of the ambulance. Figured you wouldn't want her standing out in the open, considering it seems like this location has been seriously compromised. So I got her to safety then came back to you."

Tyler let him go and lunged for the ambulance.

"Had to drag her–kicking and screaming–for the ambulance," Kane's voice followed him. "She did not want to leave your side."

Tyler reached the ambulance. He yanked open the back door and–

"I want *out of here!*" Esme yelled. She jerked on her right wrist. A wrist that was cuffed. One handcuff was around her delicate wrist. Another was around the metal edge of the gurney beneath her.

"What in the hell is happening?" Tyler demanded. Why was Esme cuffed?

Esme's head whipped toward him. The golden hoops on her ears bounced with her quick movements. Relief–wild joy–flashed across her face. "Tyler!"

He jumped into the back of the ambulance. "Get the cuffs *off* her!" Tyler barked at the young EMT who stared with wide eyes.

"But...the sheriff said she had to stay put–"

Tyler grabbed Esme. He pulled her close. As close as he could get her in the back of the freaking ambulance and with her cuffed.

"Sir, you're bleeding pretty badly." Worry filled the EMTs voice. "The side of your shirt is soaked with blood."

Esme's scent wrapped around Tyler. The ache in his chest eased. She was safe.

"I am going to kick Kane's ass," she promised. "He wouldn't let me stay with you. You were unconscious, and I was so afraid."

He eased back so he could stare down at her.

"You're supposed to be bulletproof," she said. "You can't get hurt."

Anyone could be hurt.

"You're bulletproof to me," she added. "My superman."

Fuck, he wanted to kiss her. He wanted to haul her out of that ambulance and get her as far away from the rest of the world as possible.

But she was still cuffed.

"Tyler!"

Clay's voice.

Tyler looked over and saw Clay standing near the open rear door of the ambulance.

"Tyler, we need to talk," Clay informed him. "Now."

"Give me the key to her cuffs." A deliberate pause. "*Now.*"

"No."

What? Tyler pressed a kiss to Esme's cheek. "Be right back." Then he let her go and jumped from the ambulance. He ignored the twinge in his side and the blood that was making his shirt stick to him. Tyler stood toe to toe with Clay even as the wind blew the scent of ash toward him. "*Give me the key to her cuffs.*"

Clay's hands were on his hips. "I think she needs to be brought into custody."

"Are you insane right now?" Tyler reached for Clay.

Then Tyler swayed. For just a moment, the whole world seemed to sway.

Clay grabbed him. "You have a concussion, jackass," he groused. "You can't protect yourself right now, much less her." Then he raised his voice. "EMT! Check him out!" He maintained his grip on Tyler. "The reason she's cuffed? It's because I'm trying to keep her safe. Trying to keep her out of the open and attempting to keep her alive."

The world swirled around Tyler once more. He reached up and touched the back of his head.

Blood.

Dammit.

"I'll protect her," Clay swore. "You need to get your head examined. Literally, man." The faint lines around his eyes tightened. "You could have died in that house," he said, voice grim. "Is she worth it?"

Click.

Tyler frowned. Then glanced to the left. Esme was there. And she'd...wait, had she just cuffed herself to him?

He blinked.

Her killer smile flashed. "Did I ever mention that I once dated a world-renowned escape artist? He taught me a few tricks." She winked.

Tyler could feel the cold metal of the cuff against his skin.

"No? I didn't mention it? I mean, you think you know your wife." Her chin angled up. "And yet she still manages to surprise you."

She had one cuff around her wrist. The other locked around his. Linking them.

"You're going to the hospital, darling," she told him. "And I am one hundred percent staying at your side."

Hell, yes, she was. Because when it came to Esme's safety, he didn't trust anyone else. His head turned toward the sheriff.

And he caught the white-hot glare that Clay was firing at her.

"Where I go," Tyler announced, and he made sure his

voice brooked no argument, "my wife goes. You got a problem with that, Sheriff?" *If so, too damn bad.*

But Clay just grimly shook his head. "No problem."

* * *

"I STAYED OVERNIGHT," Tyler snapped. "I took all their damn tests. This is absolute bullshit."

"You're a grumpy patient." Esme nodded as she yawned and sat in the chair near the hospital bed. During the night, she'd slept off and on as she pretzeled herself in the chair because no way was she leaving Tyler.

He needed her.

I need him.

Tyler had been knocked out by the force of the blast. Did he even know *why* he'd been knocked out? Probably not. They'd been hurtling through the air. She'd been over his shoulder. Because of the way the blast had sent them flying, when they landed, she *should* have been on the bottom. Esme knew she should have been the one who took the brunt of the impact. Her head *should* have been the one that slammed into the ground right before Tyler's body came crashing down on her.

Only things hadn't happened that way. Because even as they tumbled toward the unforgiving earth, Tyler had twisted his body. Twisted them both. He'd cushioned her. In the end, she'd landed on top of him. His body had slammed into the ground. His head had made a sickening thud as it connected.

His arms had been around her one moment. In the next instant, they'd fallen away as his whole body went limp. She'd been absolutely terrified.

Kane had told her that her screams had been even

louder than the blast. Probably an exaggeration, but she'd been screaming her head off so, maybe.

Tyler hadn't been moving. She hadn't been able to get him to wake up. And when she'd touched the back of his head, his blood had coated her fingers.

In that one, terrifying instant, Esme had come to some very important conclusions. Conclusion one? *I'll protect you from here on out.* Because her priorities had shifted.

That tended to happen when the man you loved nearly died saving your life.

The man I love.

She was still fully adjusting to that truth. She'd dreamed of him for so long. Painted him as the perfect hero in her mind as she followed his exploits from a distance. Honestly? She'd been afraid that she built him up to be larger than life.

Then his life had nearly drained away right in front of her.

"Esme?"

She blinked. One of her hands was twined with his. She'd hauled the chair closer to the bed during the night, scraping it across the floor. Her legs were tucked under her, and a scratchy blanket that one of the night nurses had brought in covered her body.

"Why do I feel like you just went a million miles away from me?" Tyler asked.

"I didn't go anywhere." Her fingers squeezed his. "Still right here."

His thumb stroked over her knuckles. "You didn't have to stay the night."

"You're here. Where else would I go?"

"With Kane."

Her brows climbed.

"You could have gone with him. He would have kept you safe until I got clear from this damn place."

Ah, back to growling. Someone was as bad of a patient as he was a morning person.

Which reminded her...

She hadn't done one single good thing that day. And it wasn't even *early* morning. Closer to ten. No...her gaze darted to the clock. Eleven. The doctor was supposed to be in soon and hopefully, they'd be getting out of that hospital.

"We both know Kane did offer me a place to stay," Esme said. Such a nice way of phrasing things. Kane had tried to force her into leaving with him. There had been no offer. He'd picked her up and tried to carry her out of the hospital room while Tyler glowered.

So she'd kicked Kane in the shin and threatened to scream until every security guard in the place came running.

Kane had seen the wisdom in letting her remain at her husband's side.

"I politely declined," Esme reminded Tyler as she unfolded her legs and stretched slowly.

He released her hand. "Would have been safer for you to go with him. I could have met up with you later."

Her fingers curled, then flexed. "Yes, but if that had happened, who would have protected *you?*"

He sent her a frown. "I don't think the bomb was meant for me."

"Shh." She pushed the covers aside and hopped to her feet. Esme stood by the side of his bed. Actually, she gave a bit of thought to climbing into that bed with him. *I was too worried. No way was I letting you go.* "You aren't supposed to mention the b-word." A shake of her head. "As far as everyone in town is concerned, there was a gas line leak at an old house. A terrible situation, but luckily, the two newlyweds escaped with only minor injuries."

"That story will only last so long. A house can't just explode without an investigation following the blast."

Yes, she knew that. "Clay is stalling." Though she still had not forgiven the jerk for the cuffs. "He's controlling the investigation for now. By the time he loses that control, I figure you and I will be out of Asylum. Clearly, it's not a safe place for us any longer."

"Clearly." His stare was unblinking. "You still have the drive?"

She nodded. He'd given it to her right before the hospital staff had stripped him down.

"Keep it on you, Esme." Low. "Because some bastard searched the house for it, and when he couldn't find it, he blew up the whole place. I'm not even sure we were his main target. I think he was trying to make sure the drive vanished."

"Pretty sure that when someone leaves a bomb," a bare whisper from her, "in your home, that means you're the main target, but thanks so much for trying to sugarcoat things for me."

His eyes narrowed.

She swallowed. Her hand rose and pressed to his jaw. The light stubble teased her palm. "You...you contacted Grayson yesterday. You told him everything was fine here."

"Yes."

"Not to call you a liar to your face, but everything is not fine here. Things are on fire here."

"I don't trust his boss. Not for one minute."

"Do you trust Grayson?"

"He's been my friend for a long time." His head turned. His mouth pressed to her palm. Right in the center. A soft kiss that made her shiver. "Someone compromised our location. If Gray is reporting straight to his boss, then I can't tell him what's happening."

"The Feds are after us, my father is..." Esme stopped. Exhaled.

He kissed her palm again. Over her hand, his eyes met hers.

"How can you do that?" Esme asked as a pang shot through her. "How can you still stand to touch me knowing what he did?" The guilt ate her up.

He slowly lowered her hand but didn't let go. "Baby, I'm gonna do more than touch you. I'm fucking you at the earliest opportunity."

She sucked in a breath. Well, that had certainly been blunt. And reassuring. *He still wants me. Tyler isn't turning away in disgust even though our past is twisted and dark and bloody.* He wasn't telling her to get the hell out of his life.

He was saying he wanted to fuck her. At the earliest opportunity.

Very promising.

She would also, in fact, like to fuck him at the earliest opportunity.

"I want more details about the bombings," Tyler informed her quietly. "I want to know how your father connected with my parents. I want to know why they were targeted. I'm not going to take some stranger's word on a two-minute confession that Jorlan had in his possession. I don't trust anything coming from Jorlan. I will dig for the truth on my own."

"And if the truth is exactly what Louis said?" She was far too conscious of each heartbeat that passed as she waited for his answer.

"You aren't your dad. You aren't paying for his sins."

"They were your parents." He couldn't just get over this. "You should hate me."

"Thought I told you already, hate is the last thing I feel. It will *always* be the last thing I feel where you are concerned."

"What do you feel?" And she held her breath as she waited for Tyler to reply.

Chapter Eighteen

A SHARP KNOCK SOUNDED AT THE DOOR BEFORE TYLER could answer Esme's stark question. A moment later, the door swung open. The doctor poked her head inside. "Who is ready to bust out of this place?" Vanessa Raye asked with a wide smile.

Me.

But Esme just sent the doctor a weak smile. Vanessa had come in earlier to check on Tyler, and now, this *should* be the visit that officially released him from care.

Dressed in green scrubs and wearing sneakers, Vanessa bustled toward the bed. "How is the patient?"

Tyler growled.

"Fantastic." Vanessa nodded as she checked his chart. "So, let's just run through a quick review, then you can ditch the hospital gown and get out of here."

"I don't know." Esme cast a quick glance over the thin gown that stretched across Tyler's shoulders. "I kinda like it."

He growled again.

"It's even better from the back," she murmured.

His head turned toward her.

She winked. "Got a killer view."

"Ahem." From Vanessa. The doctor put down the chart. "Tell me your name," she told Tyler.

Esme tensed. Right. Doing a memory check with concussion patients was standard, she knew that. But considering that she and Tyler were lying about their names...

"Tyler Hollow," he said with no hesitation. He still gripped her hand.

Vanessa nodded. She pointed to Esme. "And who is she?"

"My wife."

"Where did you two meet?"

Oh, damn. Did we ever cover that part of the story?

"At a friend's party," he replied easily. "I looked up, spotted Esme, and knew that she was the only thing I'd ever want to see again for the rest of my life."

Her heartbeat kicked up.

"That is so romantic." A sigh from Vanessa. Then she winced. "I'm so sorry that your new life in Asylum has been, um, difficult so far."

A house exploding qualified as a bit more than just difficult.

When Esme glanced over at the doctor, she found Vanessa's stare on her. "First, you are nearly run over helping my daughter..."

Esme shook her head. "I'm just glad she is okay."

"Then your house—all of your belongings—are gone in a flash." A sympathetic shake of Vanessa's head. "The town is going to help you. Know that."

"Ah, say again?" Why would the town help her? They didn't even know her.

"Clothing and food have already been donated. And my dad has a house out on Bayview Road that you guys can use when you leave the hospital. He's already said that you can stay there as long as you want."

Helpless and confused, Esme looked at Tyler, then back at the doctor. "That's—that's too much. We couldn't possibly take a *house!*"

"You saved his granddaughter's life. You can stay in a house that is just sitting there." Vanessa's mouth tightened. "Please, let us do this. It's our way of trying to pay you back for what you did for Kady Jo."

Tyler's fingers squeezed Esme's. "We appreciate your help. Everyone's help. Thank you. But our housing needs have already been taken care of."

They had?

A half-smile tilted Tyler's lips. "You probably noticed the guy standing outside our hospital room."

Vanessa glanced over her shoulder toward the door. "Pretty hard to miss Kane."

"Oh, good, you know him already," Tyler noted.

Esme didn't speak. She had no idea where Tyler was going with this chat so...she just waited. And watched.

"I've seen him in town a few times," Vanessa returned.

"He's already offered us a place to crash for the next few days."

Vanessa crinkled her brow. "He stayed the night here."

Yes, guarding me. Way to keep a low-profile, Kane.

"But, you knew him before, didn't you?" Vanessa motioned toward Tyler. "Clay mentioned that you were all in the Marines together, so you are old friends."

"Right. Friends worry about friends." An easy response from Tyler. "We appreciate the offer from you and your dad, but we're covered. Thank you, though."

"Thank you," Esme echoed. When was the last time someone had tried to help her this way? And a whole *town* was helping? That was just...overwhelming.

She didn't know how to respond.

"You're still getting the clothes and food," Vanessa warned. "And anything else you need, just say the word." She cleared her throat. "Now, let's finish up this exam because I know you are ready to leave this place in the dust."

Vanessa meant the hospital. But Esme knew that, soon enough, they'd be leaving the entire town of Asylum. Too bad. She could have liked the place quite a bit.

If someone hadn't blown up her home.

Vanessa quickly finished up the exam, and then told Tyler, "You're clear to go. Be warned that you may experience some headaches and nausea." She rattled off the medicines he could and could not take. "But if you lose consciousness, if you have seizures or signs of confusion, you come back to me right away, got it? You seek immediate medical help. And no heavy lifting. Zero, understand?"

"Got it."

"Clay has been handling your paperwork." Vanessa fiddled with the stethoscope around her neck. "He told me that when you had the all clear, he'd have a ride waiting for you out back."

"Thanks, doc."

She nodded but her stare had shifted to Esme. "Thank you," the doctor said. "That little girl happens to be my world. You ever need me for anything, you just say the word."

"I'm just glad I was there to help." And she was. "She's a beautiful child. I know you're proud of her."

Vanessa nodded. "Very proud." A soft exhale. "Take care of the patient, would you?"

"I'll do my best."

Vanessa marched from the room.

"Really didn't need to stay here overnight," Tyler murmured. "Overkill."

He'd argued that point before. She'd just argued back. "We were in a secure facility. A very public place. And your buddy Kane was at the door. Considering you were unconscious after the blast, I didn't want to take chances." *And you needed medical care.* The concussion hadn't been his only injury. Blood had soaked Tyler's shirt.

"You can get out of handcuffs."

That was a conversational change.

He was also sliding from the bed. Turning his back on her and giving Esme one killer view of his ass.

Damn. Her hand rose and tugged on her right hoop earring.

He yanked off the hospital gown. Balled it up. Tossed it onto the bed.

Double damn.

She just watched him dress. It was almost as much fun as watching him undress. Kane had brought in fresh clothes for him—and for her—the previous night. She'd been able to change right away, but Tyler had been stuck in his hospital gown.

"Esme."

Le sigh. All of his clothes were back in place. "Yes?"

He faced her. "You can get out of handcuffs."

"Yes, I can." Something that had mightily pissed off Clay.

His eyebrows lowered. "But when I cuffed you at Jorlan's, you didn't escape."

"Why show the world my skills?" A flippant response. She was so very good at those. And she was also very good at ditching cuffs. Something that came in handy in certain circumstances.

He crossed to stand right in front of her. "You didn't want to get away from me." Tyler spoke with utter certainty.

So why deny the obvious? "True."

"Because you had a master plan in place."

That master plan had been blown to hell. Literally.

"You stayed with me," Tyler noted.

"We're a package deal." She wished that she could read all of the emotions swirling in his eyes.

"With that blast, you relived one of the worst moments of your life."

The faint smile on her face bled away.

"I know the explosion reminded you of Paris." Gruff.

Yes.

"But you didn't cry. You didn't crack at all. You stayed strong and you held *my* hand all night long."

A lump seemed to choke her, so she swallowed it down. Mostly. "I cried plenty. You just didn't see because you happened to be unconscious and sprawled on the ground at the time."

He leaned forward, and his mouth pressed to hers. A soft, tender kiss. Maybe the softest, tenderest kiss she'd ever had in her life. And just what was she supposed to do with that?

"You chose me," he said.

She had.

"I choose you, Esme."

What did that mean?

But the door was opening. Again. Could no one respect

privacy? Even as she frowned, Kane was there, looking all big and bold and a bit too knowing as he quirked a brow at them. "Doc just told me it's time to blow this joint."

She glared at his choice of words.

"Yeah, sorry." He had the grace to wince. "I have a shitty sense of humor sometimes." He held the door open. "I also hate hospitals and don't want to stay here another minute. Tyler has the all clear. Let's get moving. *Now*."

And they did. They rushed through the hospital. Went out the back and found Clay waiting for them as he stood beside a Jeep.

His stare swept over Tyler. "You look like death walking, my friend."

"Thanks, man."

"Sure you should be moving?" Clay seemed uncertain. "I can take care of Esme for you. Maybe you need to stay here longer."

"I'm done. We're leaving." He held tightly to Esme's hand.

"You're the boss." Low, from Clay. He and Kane jumped in the front of the Jeep. Esme and Tyler slid into the back.

"The local fire investigator is trying to nose around the house," Clay explained as they took off. "I'm stalling as best I can. The way that place ignited and the blast trajectory..." A long whistle. "I'd say we've got a professional in town."

"You would know," Tyler said flatly.

She cast him a frown.

The Jeep accelerated.

"Clay is a demolition expert." Tyler's gaze was on the back of Clay's head. "Trained by Uncle Sam to get the job done."

He was a *what?* Talk about information she would have enjoyed knowing much, much sooner.

"I don't do that anymore." A quick retort from Clay. "You know I can't...*fuck.*" He jerked the wheel to the right. The Jeep flew off the road and came to a jarring stop.

The seatbelt pulled hard against Esme. "Hey!" Esme snapped. "There is a man with a concussion back here! Watch that crap!"

"I like her," Kane said to no one and everyone. "I really do. I didn't, not at first. But she's grown on me."

Clay whipped around and his narrow-eyed stare went straight to Tyler. "You think it was me? Is that the BS you're saying to me right now? When I am *helping* you?"

Esme did not speak. Tyler wasn't saying that, was he? No way did he suspect his friend.

Except, Tyler wasn't making a denial.

Clay gaped at him. "You really think I'd blow up my own damn house? With you in it?"

Tyler gazed steadily at him. "Questions have to be asked."

"Fuck. *Fuck.*" Clay slammed a hand into the steering wheel. "You don't trust me. After everything we've been through together? I'm the one you doubt? And not the criminal right next to you?"

"No need for name calling," Esme said primly.

"The house was wired to explode." No emotion filled Tyler's voice.

A shiver slid over Esme. There was a lethal air about him. One moment, he'd seemed normal, almost at ease. Then as soon as they'd gotten away from the eyes at the hospital and into the Jeep—everything changed in a blink.

He was waiting for this moment.

Kane was also now staring at Clay. And his profile appeared cold. Savage.

They both suspect Clay? Why hadn't they told her about their suspicions?

"The house is in a million pieces." Tyler never took his focus off Clay. "And it just so happens there is an expert on explosives right here."

That was when she realized...

Kane had a gun in his hand. He'd pulled it out and aimed it at the sheriff.

"What is happening?" Esme demanded in a voice that squeaked. When had they planned this? While she'd slept in the uncomfortable chair?

"I came to that same conclusion myself," Kane announced. "Figured we'd have a very serious chat as soon as we were all alone."

This counted as a chat?

Clay's focus whipped to the gun. "You're pointing a weapon at a sheriff." A pause. "*At your friend.*"

"Yeah, I am. I'm a crazy bastard like that," Kane informed him without even missing a beat. "You had access to the house. You would have known how to bypass the security system because you set it up. And you would have known exactly how to rig the bomb. So from where I sit—from where Tyler sits—you look guilty as sin."

This could not be happening. Esme touched Tyler's arm. "You honestly think one of your best friends would do this to you?"

"Seven million dollars is on your head, Esme. I think anyone would kill for that." He leaned forward.

"This is bullshit!" Clay cried out. "*I'm helping!* I wasn't even there, all right? I was...hell, I was with Vanessa. She was at my place. Comes by every morning after she drops off her kid at daycare. I have a freaking alibi! Call her. She'll tell you. *I didn't do this shit.*"

"We will call her," Kane promised. "But right now, I'm gonna need you to get out of the vehicle."

Clay gaped. "You are not serious. It's *my* Jeep."

"And we're borrowing it. See, Tyler and Esme need to vanish. I don't think *you* need to know where they're going. Not right now. Not with the gambling debts you've piled up. You always did like to get in games that were way above your head. Remember that time in Monte Carlo? Had to drag you out of that casino."

Esme's stomach knotted.

"You tried to take Esme away from the scene," Tyler charged. "You cuffed her."

"I was trying to protect her! What the hell? This is insanity! You can't doubt *me!*"

"It might be insanity," Tyler agreed. "And I'll apologize like hell later if I'm wrong. And I'll say it was the concussion talking, and I'll be really, really sorry for being an asshole, but Esme's life is on the line, and I'm gonna need you to get out of the Jeep."

Esme held her breath.

Clay got out of the Jeep. He stood near the driver's side door with his hands at his sides.

Esme was far too conscious of the gun in his holster.

"You're making a mistake," Clay told them. He seemed both angry and sad.

Kane slid into the driver's seat. "I pulled your phone records. You've been calling the Feds."

Clay blanched. "What? When did you do that?" He raked a hand through his hair. "Look, dammit. *One Fed.* I called one Fed! I used to report to him on classified operations back in the day. Dammit, I owed him! He buried the work I did before. He helped me put that life behind me. *I owed him,*" Clay repeated, almost desperately, "and he just wanted me to check in and let him know that Esme was safe and secure. Such a simple job. And it's Grayson's damn boss! Of course, we can trust him."

Grayson's boss...*Thaddeus?* Esme leaned forward and poked on Kane's shoulder. "We should drive away now. Very swiftly. Drive away. Now."

"Thanks for confirming a suspicion," Kane told the other man. "FYI, when the hell would I have actually had time to pull phone records?"

Clay blinked. "You...lied to me?"

"Back up, man," Kane ordered. "Don't want to drive over your foot, but I will."

Clay jumped back.

And the Jeep hauled ass away.

* * *

THIS WASN'T HAPPENING. Clay watched in utter disbelief as the Jeep rushed down the road. Dust flew into the air after the vehicle. *His* vehicle.

He whipped out his phone. Two seconds later... "They *know,*" he snarled.

"What?" The voice in his ear was confused. And worried.

"They know I've been talking to you." Because he'd walked straight into a stupid trap. Of course, Kane hadn't pulled phone records. He should have never bought that BS. "Look, they are going to disappear. Into the wind. Kane is helping them. Tyler thinks he can trust him."

"Kane Harte can't be trusted by anyone. You know that."

Yeah, I do. The man wasn't called Heartless Harte for nothing. *And he just pulled a gun on me.* "They'll be gone as fast as possible. What in the hell am I supposed to do?"

"I've gotten word that a top hunter is in Asylum."

Oh, you've gotten word? Like...now you've gotten word? "This news would have helped yesterday."

A grunt. "Don't know if he was there yesterday. Could have been."

Total bullshit. "They just left the hospital."

"Then he will probably have eyes on them already. Your friends need to be very, very careful."

His friends had just turned on him. They thought he was out to get them.

"Word is that Tyler Barrett now has a bounty on *his* head."

Fuck.

"And that Esme Laurent is to be brought in alive."

Alive. "Since when?" He'd thought the bounty was for her death. Clay yanked at his too tight collar.

Instead of getting an answer, he was told, "Tyler Barrett is a dead man. He just doesn't know it."

No, no, dammit. This couldn't happen. "I'm trying to help them!"

"Then you should probably try harder."

Chapter Nineteen

"End of the road," Kane announced an hour later. He braked the ride outside of a no-tell motel. "At least for me." He turned around. "I'll take the Jeep back. Clear out my things from Asylum and meet up with you later."

Tyler saw Esme peering at the motel.

"Lucky number seven is all yours." Kane waved toward the small office. "It's an old-fashioned place. You actually get to use a real key to get inside. Get it from the guy in the little admin office—his name's Roger—and you'll find all the supplies you need waiting in your room."

"Uh..." Esme cleared her throat. "How did you arrange all of this? And when?"

"I know people." An easy response that was, Tyler knew, a massive understatement. Kane's connections were legendary. Sometimes, for the wrong reasons. "This will be a safe place for you to cool down a bit. Regroup. I'll check Clay's story with Vanessa, and then we can figure out what our next move will be."

Tyler shoved open his door and climbed out. Esme

scooted over, and he helped her exit, then kept a hand on her waist.

"There is one more thing you need to know." Kane's voice had turned halting. His mirrored sunglasses hid his gaze. "Might be better if you and I just talk for a moment, Tyler."

He didn't let Esme go. "Say whatever it is in front of her."

"Oh, so you're trusting her now?"

He was doing more than that.

"Fine. Got a tip last night while you were all sprawled out in the hospital bed."

"I wasn't sprawled—"

"There's a bounty on your head, man." Serious. Hard. "Why do you think I pulled a gun on someone I've known for years? *You are in danger*. You saved my life—twice—so I owe you, and I always will. I would walk into the fire with you a dozen times. Hell, I did once before already, remember? And I'd do it again. People know that you're the one standing between Esme and death. So they're gunning for you now. Without you, she'll fall."

The hell she would. "I have no intention of letting Esme fall."

"Figured you'd say something like that. Considering the way you just kept saying her name over and over after you came awake following that blast." A considering pause. "I don't think it's Clay. I can still see his face after that nightmare in Paris. He'd set the devices on our missions before, but never seen the wreckage left after an explosion. People died that day, and it changed him. He got out after that. Stopped his work with the government. Came back to his Asylum." His jaw tightened. "I just don't see him wiring a house to kill one of his best friends."

Esme edged forward. "Yet you pointed a gun at him."

"Because *my* job is to protect Tyler. And you. That is the job of a best fucking friend, and I hold the title with Tyler for a reason." His fingers drummed on the steering wheel. "There's a motorcycle behind your room. The keys to it are in your nightstand drawer. After you get changed and you eat some of the food, hit the road. There are two burner phones you can use in the bags you'll find waiting in your room. We'll plan a meetup."

"A motorcycle, too?" Esme whistled. "I am impressed and frightened by your skills."

"Same, lady, same." He waved them back. "You know that warning I gave Clay about his feet? Watch yourselves."

Tyler hauled Esme back right before Kane drove away.

"He's a really good best fucking friend," she murmured.

Yeah, he was.

Tyler curled an arm around Esme's shoulders and led her to the small office. Sure enough, Roger was waiting. He barely glanced their way before tossing them the key.

"Friendly fellow," Esme commented.

"You don't make friends in places like this one." You worked hard to forget faces. A short walk, and they were standing in front of lucky motel room number seven. He put the key in the lock, opened the door, and stared at the paradise that waited for them.

No way could he not wince. This place had to be far, far below Esme's normal standards.

"Please tell me that bed vibrates." Esme rushed across the room and hopped on the bed. She spread-eagled and frowned. "After the hell of that hospital chair, I could use a vibrating bed."

One eyebrow rose. "You usually have to start the vibration."

Her head turned toward him. A frown pulled at her brows. She had—quite obviously—not spent a lot of time in no-tell motels.

Despite everything, a smile tugged at his lips. "Sweetheart, that bed won't vibrate on its own." *But I can sure as hell help.*

She pushed up onto one elbow and studied him. "You didn't tell me that you suspected Clay."

A very sore spot for him. "I don't like thinking that one of my friends might betray me."

"But seven million dollars can buy a lot of things." A delicate pause. "Including a new friend?"

Maybe. "He knows ballistics. He knew the house, inside and out. But I just..." Tyler turned away from the sight of Esme on the bed—such a tempting sight when he needed to stay focused—and made his way to the small table near the left wall. Two bags were on that table. He opened them. Saw the weapons inside. Two guns. Three knives. Nice. Clothing—for him and Esme. Two burner phones.

Sometimes, Kane's skills and connections *were* scary. Even to him.

"You just didn't want to admit you might have been wrong to trust him? Is that why you didn't tell me sooner?"

He put one of the guns down on the table. "I didn't want a friend to have tried to kill me." His head turned, and, once more, his eyes were on her.

She remained on the bed.

Way too sexy. "Esme..." Where to start?

"I should go shower. I'm pretty stiff from that hospital chair."

The chair she'd stayed in all night so she could be close to him.

"I'd tell you to join me, but I know you're supposed to be careful with those stitches of yours."

He'd almost forgotten them. Turned out he'd cut open his side and his arm during the blast. He barely felt the pull of the stitches. His attention was centered somewhere else.

Esme had swung her legs to the side of the bed. But she hadn't stood yet. Her bedroom eyes were completely on him. "Where are we going next?"

He knew where he wanted to go.

In her.

Yeah, but he was trying to hold the hell back. Danger stalked them. He shouldn't be jumping the woman at the first opportunity. Even though that was very, very much what he wanted.

"Get some rest," he said. "You didn't sleep much last night. You grab a few hours of sleep, and I'll make arrangements."

She nodded. But, again, didn't move. "Are we going to hide somewhere else?"

"Not like I'm planning to just turn you over to the bad guys."

Her head tilted forward. The dark curtain of her hair hid her face, and then, she rose. Came right to him. Her hand lifted and pressed to his chest. Right over the heart that raced for her. "I think that is exactly what you should do."

What the fuck? Tyler could only shake his head. He must have heard wrong. Was the concussion impacting his hearing now?

"Running and hiding didn't work so well for us the first time. Did we even make it forty-eight hours? Seventy-two?" Her lips pulled down. "Our safe house exploded. We almost exploded with it. Now you've turned away from an old friend because you suspect him. In a short time, I've pretty much destroyed your life."

No, she hadn't. "I'm not just going to give you up." He would never do that.

"Not even if it winds up saving your life? Because Kane said a target is on you now. How much is the going rate for a U.S. Marshal's life? Or rather, his death?"

He didn't know.

"Trade me," Esme urged him, and she appeared completely serious. "Save yourself. It's the smart thing to do." Then she walked away. The woman actually dropped that bombshell BS on him and headed toward the bathroom like it was absolutely nothing. She paused by the open bags. Trailed her fingers over them. Grabbed a change of clothes.

Kept moving. Like nothing had happened.

Totally no big deal. Just a little matter of her dying so he could live.

The hell that would happen.

The bathroom door closed behind her. The shower thundered on. His gaze remained locked on the door.

Had those been tears gathering in her eyes before she marched away? Jaw locking, he headed right for the door. His fingers curled around the knob and twisted. Nothing happened.

She'd locked the door.

"Esme."

"I'm showering."

"Open the door."

"I'm showering."

His gaze bored into the wood. "I've finally figured you out," he muttered. Then, louder, for her, he said, "I'm going to kick the door in if you don't open it. So...make sure you step back, would you, sweetheart?"

"You would not dare!"

A breath and a prayer seemed to be holding the old door in place. Probably wouldn't even take a kick. "Move back," he commanded. He waited. Gave her time, then he rammed his shoulder into the door.

It flew open. He'd been right. No kicking needed.

And, sonofabitch, those *were* tears on her cheeks.

"You have an issue with bathrooms and barging in on people." A shudder swept over her. "You need to work on that. It's weird."

His hands fisted. No way was she going to distract him. "You ran away so I wouldn't see you cry."

Her right hand swiped over her cheek. "I have no idea what you're talking about."

"When you lie, your voice gets extra haughty. You better watch that tell in the future."

She stopped mid-swipe. "I can't believe you broke down the door! Seriously, what is it with you and bathrooms?"

"The door needed breaking." He motioned toward the pile of clothes she'd taken into the bathroom. "I'm guessing a burner phone is currently hidden under there? Did you tuck it under the shirt when you realized I was coming in after you?"

Her hand fell. "I have no idea what you mean." She frowned. "I have *no* idea what you mean." She clearly had tried to change up her tone. Less haughty. Kinda cute.

But she knew exactly what he meant. "The tears are a problem for me. A big one. I hate for you to cry. Didn't we cover that?"

"Well, you didn't have to come in after me. Why can't a woman cry in peace?"

"Because your tears break me apart, when I see them and when I don't. From now on, no more crying."

"You can't *order* someone not to cry and just make it magically happen."

Really? He was pretty sure he just had given the order. And it would happen. But, fine, for now... "I'll just kick the ass of the next person to make you cry. Fair enough?"

"Tyler..."

He reached out and lifted up the shirt. Sure enough, a burner phone was right there. "Who were you gonna call, sweetheart?"

Her hands went to her hips. "You know so much, tell me."

"Your father."

She didn't deny it.

"You were going to call him. Offer to meet him."

Again, no denial.

So he kept going. "I figure you were probably going to seduce me at some point."

"You wish."

Yes, he did. Fervently. "You were going to give me mind-blowing sex. And then you thought I might fall asleep afterwards. While I slept, you were going to sneak away and meet your father because you believe you can convince him to call off the hit on my life. You think *he* is the one who put out the hit. Both on you...and on me."

"Why would he put out a hit on me? I'm his daughter."

"Because you were in federal custody. He was afraid you'd tell the wrong information to the wrong people. People not on his payroll. So the hit was placed, and a killer came calling for you. But I was there. I stopped him."

"I do appreciate that."

I will always be there. "You still have the drive." He'd given it to her at the hospital. Not like there had been a lot of places to hide it when he'd had to don the hospital gown.

"I might."

He waited.

"I *do*."

"You're going to give him the drive, and, in exchange, you think he'll cancel the hit on me."

"That's a whole lot of suspicion pouring from you."

"That's a whole lot of zero denial coming from *you*, sweetheart."

Her hands dropped from her hips. Her shoulders squared. "Let me make sure I'm following along properly."

"All right." He waited.

"You think I'm the evil villainess who is about to seduce you. Then leave you."

"Never said you were evil. I'll punch out the next bastard who does."

Her lashes swept down to conceal her gaze. "I don't think you can actually have sex so soon after a concussion so my plan—if that was my plan—it's flawed."

Cute. "Esme..."

Her lashes lifted.

"Sweetheart." He smiled at her. "It will take one hell of a lot more than a concussion and some stitches to stop me from fucking you."

"You say the most romantic things."

He eliminated the space between them and towered over her. All traces of humor were gone. "How's this for romantic? You try to sacrifice yourself to protect me, and I'll fuck you so long and hard that you won't walk for a week."

She bit her lower lip as she seemed to consider his words. "We need to work on your romance."

"You didn't call anyone."

"You didn't exactly give me the chance." An exhale.

"How'd you know I took the phone? I thought my technique was flawless."

"You palmed it perfectly, but, sweetheart..."

She'd been staring at his neck. He waited until she had to look up and meet his eyes. He didn't like the way she kept avoiding his gaze. As if she had something to hide. As if she was afraid to see him.

Only when that beautiful darkness was locked on him did Tyler finish, "I know you now. Inside and out."

"Tyler...*I want you safe.*"

"I will be." His hands reached out and curled around her waist. He lifted her up against him. "But you will never sacrifice yourself for me. That's not how this works between us."

Her hands grabbed his shoulders. "Your stitches—"

"Told you they wouldn't stop me." He took her mouth. Thrust his tongue inside and felt the control he'd been trying to hold fracture. "Nothing is gonna stop me when it comes to you."

A low moan pulled from her.

Thought I wasn't gonna get her out of the house in time. Thought I was gonna lose her. Another explosion. Her gorgeous eyes closed. Her body limp.

In truth, he hadn't needed the freaking hospital or even the stitches. He would have survived just fine. Not like he hadn't stitched himself up before. But he'd wanted to make absolutely sure Esme was safe. So he'd gone in the ambulance—with her—and when he'd been at the hospital, he'd ordered her checked out, too. Then, because the place had good security, he'd kept them in the room overnight. He'd known that Kane was working to get a new place set up for them. A new identity. An escape path.

And, sure enough, Kane had delivered.

But Esme hadn't realized Tyler was staying in the hospital for her safety. She'd been worried about him. Holding him tight all night.

He'd been so very wrong about her. She wasn't some heartless villain. In fact, he thought her heart might just be too big. Esme wanted to save the world. She just pretended that she was trying to wreck it.

He carried her to the bed. Lowered her down. When she was settled, he eased back and stared at her.

The minutes ticked past.

"Uh, Tyler?" Her hair trailed over her shoulders as she stared at him. "Something wrong?"

"I'd kill for you."

She blinked.

"Not because of the job. Not because I've been assigned to protect you. But because it's you." He wanted her to understand this. "You're not a job. You're Esme. My Esme."

Her smile came then. The smile that drove him wild. Slow and pure, it flashed her dimples and made the sparks of gold shine in the darkness of her eyes.

"I want to be gentle," he told her.

She nodded. "Because of your injuries. I promise, I will be so careful with you."

"No, sweetheart, I want to be gentle because it's you. But..." He grabbed the hem of his shirt and yanked it up. He sent that shirt flying and didn't give a damn about his stitches. "I don't know if I can be...*because it's you.* I want you more than I have ever wanted anything in this world."

She tossed her shirt aside, too. Her black bra teased and tempted. "Then come take me."

He was trying to warn her. Tyler knew he was walking on a razor's edge of desire.

"But if you pop those stitches, I will be very angry with

you." She reached for his hand. Brought it to her mouth. "Very angry." She nipped his palm.

Lust shot through his body and straight to his already straining dick. He kicked off his shoes and tumbled her back onto the bed. Her hands reached eagerly for him. He kissed her and he tasted his Esme, and he wanted so much more. He wanted to take and take and have her screaming his name.

But the walls in that motel had to be paper thin. And the sounds Esme made?

Mine.

Just as Esme herself was...

Mine.

He yanked the bra away and feasted on her breasts. Those tight nipples drove him into a frenzy. He licked. Sucked. Had his turn to lightly bite with his teeth.

She jolted beneath him. "Tyler!"

"Shh." A rough order. "Don't want any bastards next door to hear."

Her breath panted out.

He licked her nipple again.

"Ty...ler!"

He loved it when she moaned his name that way.

Chapter Twenty

Tyler was sliding his way down her body. He didn't want her to cry out. She knew the walls had to be stupid thin in the motel. Not like she wanted whoever their neighbors were to hear her yelling in ecstasy but...

He'd stripped her completely.

Her breath shuddered out.

Tyler shoved her thighs apart even more.

She bit her lower lip and whimpered as she looked down at him. *This isn't going to work. I'm not going to be able to stay silent.*

He put his mouth on her.

Her body bucked against him. A hard jolt because his mouth felt so insanely good. "Tyler!" A quick pant. "Tyler, I can't—"

His head lifted. "I'm tasting you until you come."

She nearly came right then and there. With those eyes of his blazing at her and with him between her spread legs...

He went back to her. His tongue licked right along her clit. Over and over. Then he thrust his wicked tongue inside of her.

Esme threw her hand over her mouth to try and muffle her own cries. Her hips were twisting and surging against him, and he was relentless. He tasted her with a stark passion. A possession that seemed to mark her very soul, and there was no stopping him. He took her with his mouth again and again.

Her body was trembling. *Too close. Can't stop.* The explosion built and built and—

He pulled away from her.

She was right on the edge. Shaking and shuddering and she just needed a little bit more to go over. She needed *him.*

He yanked her hand away from her mouth. His mouth crashed onto hers. He swallowed her gasps and moans even as she felt his dick push at the entrance to her body. Long, thick, hard. And behind his jeans, dammit! The jeans were in the way.

She arched against him. Her hands grabbed for his hips as she pulled him toward her. She rode him through the jeans, but it wasn't enough. She was going mad. Her body too taut and tense as she remained trapped on the edge.

Then one strong hand worked between their bodies. He strummed her clit while he kissed her. "Got to keep that mouth of yours busy," he rumbled against her lips. "So you don't scream. Though, baby, I do love it when you scream for me."

One long finger worked inside of her. A second followed.

His lips pressed hard to hers. Her whole body had gone stiff. *So close. Push me over the edge. Make me come. Push me.*

But he...

He pulled away.

The sound of her heaving breaths was far too loud. "Torture." She licked her lips.

He stood on the side of the bed.

"You're torturing me, Tyler." Not cool.

"Never." He ditched his jeans and boxers. His dick shoved toward her. "Just giving you something for that mouth."

Her eyes widened.

"Scoot over, sweetheart."

She scooted.

He sprawled out beside her.

"You get on top," he ordered.

Okay. She started to—

"Other way. I want you on my face, and I want my dick in your mouth."

She almost melted. How could she get any wetter for him?

She crawled on him, as directed, her movements a little uncertain as the mattress squeaked. And then her fingers reached for the long, thick length of his dick. She stroked him first. She pumped him. He felt so good in her hand—

"*Tyler!*"

He'd grabbed her hips in a fierce grip and hauled her onto his face. His tongue plunged right into her core, and she squeezed her eyes shut as the torrent of wild sensation slammed through her.

So good.

Too good.

So close.

Her mouth had opened because she was about to cry out, and she hurriedly closed her lips over the head of his cock.

He was licking her and thrusting his tongue against her,

and she took as much of him into her mouth as she could. Her mouth was just as frantic on him as his was on her. His grip was unbreakable as he held her against him. The feelings pouring through her were too intense. Overwhelming. There was no control. No way for her to stop and—

"Baby, get the fuck *on* me."

His hands—careful—pulled her up and around. She straddled him. Dazed, her breath rushed out. His dick pushed at the entrance to her body. All she had to do was lift her hips, and she could take him inside.

All she wanted to do was lift her hips.

"Condom," he bit out. "In my jeans...back pocket."

She stared at him. When had he gotten a condom? At the hospital? Her heart raced so hard it shook her chest. "I'm protected. Clean bill of health."

"I've never gone bare with anyone."

Her breath shuddered. Did that mean he didn't want to go bare right then?

"Only you. *Take me the fuck inside.*"

Her knees pushed into the mattress. She rose up, and then when she came down, Esme took him inside. He filled every single inch of her, and she couldn't catch her breath, much less cry out. So intense. So powerful.

She sank down on him, then his steely grip around her waist lifted her up.

Down.

Up.

Her hands flattened on his powerful chest.

One of his hands left her waist. Rubbed her too sensitive clit even as his hips began to lift and shove in a rhythm too powerful to control. He heaved her up and down, the bed squeaked more, and, the people next door must hear them.

I don't care.

Pleasure poured through her. A thunderous eruption that rocked every cell in her body. She would have screamed, but Tyler shot up at that moment. His mouth claimed hers. She came as he kissed her, and she felt him jetting into her at the same time. The release went on and on. Her inner muscles squeezed him as tightly as she could. He rolled with her on the bed. Put her beneath him. Just kept thrusting.

One climax ended.

Did another begin?

Because he got hard again. Stayed hard? She was dazed and desperate. Her body too sensitive and ready, and he just kept thrusting.

He caught her legs. Shoved them over his shoulders.

Kept thrusting.

She was coming. Still? Again?

Coming.

His gaze bored into hers.

He thrust and thrust.

Every single part of her felt marked by him.

Owned.

Did he feel the same way?

Sweat slickened his body.

His eyes never looked away from her.

And as pleasure broke again—impossibly, again—she stared into his eyes, and she didn't scream, but she whispered her deepest, darkest secret, "*Je t'aime.*"

I love you. She gave him that confession right before he slammed deep and came inside of her.

* * *

KANE SAW the swirl of lights heading straight toward him. His hands tightened on the steering wheel of the Jeep. He knew trouble when it was rushing dead-on for him.

Especially because, as the swirl of those lights got closer, he saw that they were attached to a very familiar sheriff's patrol car.

He kept driving.

Right until the moment the patrol car swerved into the middle of the road, blocking both lanes, blocking *his* path because tall trees were on either side of the old two-lane highway and going around the other vehicle wasn't an option. Even as Kane slammed on the brakes, Clay was jumping out of the patrol car. Only Clay wasn't alone. He had one of his junior deputies with him.

The deputy instantly pointed his gun at Kane.

Just freaking fantastic.

Clay rushed toward the driver's side of the Jeep. He had his gun up, too. "Out of the vehicle!" Clay snarled. "And keep your hands where I can see them!"

Nodding, Kane climbed out of the vehicle. He kept his hands up and wasn't the least bit surprised when the deputy barreled forward to pat him down. And to take Kane's gun.

"He's clear now," the deputy said. Young, maybe only around twenty-one or twenty-two. With bright red hair. Nervous hands.

Kane never liked twitchy hands. They tended to accidentally fire weapons.

"Cuff him." Clay kept his weapon pointed at Kane. Dead center on his chest. *Now is that a friendly thing to do?*

"You're mad." Kane nodded. "I did expect you to be a little pissed, considering how we parted ways."

"*Cuff. Him.*"

The deputy grabbed Kane's arms. Cuffed Kane's hands behind his back.

"Good." A grunt from Clay. "Now you take the Jeep back to town, Deputy Griffin."

The deputy hesitated. "Aren't we supposed to read him his rights?"

Yes, that was the typical way these sorts of situations should go.

"The jackass stole my Jeep! We caught him red-handed."

The deputy still appeared uncertain. Maybe Kane could work with that uncertainty. "I borrowed it." A careful clarification. "I was on my way to bring it back." A shrug. "Friends let friends borrow their cars in emergencies."

"Friends don't pull fucking guns on friends!"

The deputy swallowed. His eyes could not get much bigger in size.

"Take the Jeep back to town," Clay commanded him once more. "I'll be right behind you with the prisoner."

"Uh, shouldn't I help you get him in the patrol car, at least?"

Kane's shoulders stiffened.

"Yes." Clay smiled at him. "Let's put the prisoner in the back of my patrol car."

"You're holding a grudge." Kane nodded. "I can respect that. I tend to be pretty vengeful myself." Understatement of the century.

The kid deputy started shoving Kane toward the back of the patrol car. The indignity.

And there seemed to be no way out of the situation.

Fuck. They pushed him in the rear of the vehicle, behind the ancient cage because Asylum's patrol cars were as old as dirt, and then the deputy slammed the door, sealing Kane inside.

Through the window, he watched as the deputy took the Jeep and drove it back toward Asylum. Clay stood in the middle of the road as the deputy vanished. When the deputy was no longer visible, Clay pulled out his phone and made a quick call.

Kane's eyes narrowed. He couldn't make out Clay's low words. The conversation was short. Straight to the point.

Then Clay was headed for the patrol car. He climbed into the front seat. Cranked the car and got them out of the middle of the road. He didn't drive far, though. Just turned the car...

Not in the direction of Asylum.

Instead, Clay began driving the patrol car...*the way I just came.*

"Never would have thought that you'd pull a gun on me," Clay said. "Doesn't friendship mean anything to you?"

It meant plenty. With people who were *actually* real friends. "You're going the wrong way."

"Friends don't do that stuff. Friends look out for each other. They *help* each other."

Sure. "Would it *help* if I said that I was coming back to apologize?"

"You were coming to check my alibi."

That, too. He pulled against the handcuffs. Esme had sure shimmied out of her cuffs fast enough at the blast site. If only he'd gotten her to show him exactly how she pulled off that trick. "Can't we talk about this?"

"*You pulled a gun on me.*"

"Not like I was gonna fire."

"You think I'm guilty." Anger seethed in his words.

Kane's head turned as he watched the trees pass in a

blur because Clay was driving far too fast. "Want to explain to me how you're *not* guilty?"

"I'm helping a friend. Don't you get that? I'm trying to protect Tyler. To save his life."

Tread carefully. But Kane had never really been the careful type. He was more of a bulldozer. "You have no alibi, do you?"

No answer.

Hell. "Who did you just call on the phone, Clay?"

"Tyler is going to be all right. I made sure of it. He'll be clear. She was the problem."

His eyes closed. "You went back to gambling, didn't you? Hard." Gambling had always been Clay's addiction of choice. No matter how much help they'd given him, Clay had gone back to the games again and again. He'd never seemed to get that some games could completely screw your world to hell and back.

"You don't know what my life is like! Don't you judge me."

"Did Vanessa find out? Did she dump you because she couldn't handle what you were doing?" He'd picked up whispers of gossip about them in town. About how Clay kept wanting to make things official, but Vanessa was delaying.

"Vanessa doesn't know. Leave her out of this."

Clay slowed a bit—finally—but just so he could turn the vehicle. To the right. The tires still screeched. Kane tensed. *How had Clay known to take this path?*

"I'm a sheriff, dumbass. You think I didn't have my own car secured? That I couldn't track it every moment? I could see exactly where you took my ride. I knew when you stopped long enough to let Tyler and Esme out. I know where they are."

Kane strained against the cuffs. "You already gave up their location." That had been what the short and sweet phone call was about.

"We're going to be met at their motel. Esme will be taken into custody."

"Custody?" What bullshit! "She's already in the custody of a U.S. Marshal! She's in Tyler's custody!" He twisted and strained and couldn't get out of the freaking cuffs.

"Tyler is compromised. I could see it when he looked at her. She has him under her spell."

"She isn't a fucking witch!"

"He will do whatever she says. Believe any lies she tells him." Clay's voice deepened. "I can't let her spread those lies. I was just doing what I was supposed to do."

Kane stopped struggling. "When?"

"Everything will be all right. Tyler's safety has been guaranteed. It's just Esme who needs to vanish."

"*When* were you doing what you were supposed to do? Now? You're following orders now? Or did you do something in the past?"

No response.

"You did," Kane charged. "You've been on the take for a long time, haven't you?"

"I was following orders. Just like you. When our team had a mission, we completed that mission. Collateral damage happens."

Ice poured through his veins. "You were in Paris." The day that haunted Kane.

"We were all in Paris."

"You didn't run into the café with us." He remembered this. At the time, he'd just thought that Clay had been shell-shocked because Clay had never seen a detonation up close.

He just made things explode from a distance. But the things that were supposed to explode? Not people. Munitions stockpiles. Stolen vehicles. Even a tank once. They had never, ever sent Clay out with a target on a person. Those hadn't been the type of orders they received.

Unless Clay had been getting different orders.

A heavy stillness stole over Kane. "You blew up that café, didn't you?"

"There was a CIA double-agent inside. If he'd gotten away, a lot of people would have died."

He surged toward the cage. "People *did* die that day! And you didn't help! You stayed outside while I ran in with Tyler. You *watched!*"

"I had to make sure he didn't get out. Louis Turner was a very dangerous man. I was supposed to watch the front to make sure he didn't get out—*and he never came out the front!*"

I'm staring at a very dangerous man. "Who did you talk to on the phone? Who did you call, Clay?"

No response.

"Your boss? The same person who told you to blow that café to hell and back?"

"I didn't set that bomb in Paris—" Clay stopped. "You don't understand."

Then make me understand.

Clay made another turn. The SOB knew exactly where to go. "I came home after Paris. I was promised that my past would be erased. No one would ever know...But there are some things you can't forget. I would see that scene in my head, over and over."

"Yet you just tried to blow up one of your closest friends! You tried to kill Tyler, so don't give me that BS and act like you're some traumatized victim!"

Clay slammed on the brakes. The patrol car screeched to a halt. He whipped around and glared through the old cage. "I was trying to get the evidence back."

What evidence?

"I couldn't find it. I didn't have time to search longer, so I blew up the safe house." He snapped his fingers. "Evidence destroyed, just like that. And I made sure Tyler got out of the house. I waited until I saw him running on the porch before I detonated. I knew he'd come busting out of the home as soon as he saw the wreckage I'd left during my search. He was never in danger. Never. I wouldn't kill a friend."

But you would kill plenty of other people, wouldn't you? "What about Esme? Would you kill her?"

"I won't be the one who pulls the trigger." Clay turned back around to face the front of the vehicle.

No, you just plan to deliver her to the highest bidder. "Seven million dollars can buy a whole lot of things, can't it?"

Clay was driving again. "Yes. It can even buy a person a brand-new life."

And, in the process, it could absolutely destroy someone else's life. "Hey, Clay?"

"Yeah?"

"Hate to break this to you, but we're not fucking friends anymore."

A low laugh. "Figured that out...right when you pointed a gun at me."

Chapter Twenty-One

JE T'AIME. TYLER'S HEART SLOWLY STOPPED ITS FIERCE thundering. His eyes opened.

Just as Esme attempted to sneak from the bed.

Precious.

His arm flew out and curled around her. He tugged her back toward him. "Thought we agreed that the technique of seducing me into oblivion wasn't going to work."

Her hand trailed lightly across his chest. "Were you using the technique on me or was I using it on you? I'm a bit confused."

"You just said you loved me."

He felt the shiver that skated over her.

She blinked. "Plenty of people say things in the heat of the moment that they don't mean."

"You're not plenty of people. You're my Esme."

"Tyler." She pressed her lips together. Then, "I thought you didn't speak French."

"That why you said it in French? Because you didn't think I'd understand your words?"

Her lashes swept down. "I said it in French because I

was at my most basic, my most bare, in that instant. The words tumbled out." She looked up at him. "They don't have to mean anything."

They meant everything. "Who was he protecting?"

"I don't—"

"Before our safe house was blown to pieces, you told me that you thought your father was good. That he'd been protecting someone. Only you never told me who he'd protected." But Tyler had an idea.

She studied him. "You think because I say that I love you—you think now I'll tell you every secret I have?"

He thought she trusted him, and he would never destroy her trust. It was too precious. "You just told me your biggest secret. I don't think you say that you love people very often." Quite the opposite. "I think you guard your heart at all costs. You didn't even tell Louis, did you?"

"I didn't love Louis."

His eyes narrowed.

"He didn't trust me, not completely, and I never trusted him. I never told him—" She broke off. "My mother."

"What?"

"I never told Louis what he was trying to discover. He thought my father was this horrible master thief. That my father had been working in the business of darkness for years. But it wasn't my father. It was my mother." She rolled away from him and pulled the sheet with her. Esme stood beside the bed, and she wrapped the sheet around her body, toga-style. She looked sexy and beautiful with her hair disheveled, and he wanted nothing more than to pull her back against him.

But his job had been to uncover all her secrets.

She was handing those secrets to him on a silver platter.

He climbed from the bed and hauled on his jeans. Then he waited.

"The Fox has been at work far longer than you and your friends in law enforcement probably realize. At first, she started just by lifting a few jewels from unsuspecting friends. But that was too easy, and she liked a challenge." Esme walked toward the window. The sheet trailed after her as she peeked outside. After a moment, she turned back to Tyler. "She was always striving for more. Always wanting more. She had the perfect cover. A world-renowned opera singer. She could travel the world, and no one would so much as blink an eye. Who would suspect her? She was so lovely, so kind, so talented." A soft laugh. "She was actually all of those things, but my mother also enjoyed playing very dangerous games."

"When did your father find out?"

"When I was about five. He caught her in the act. That was when he made the decision to cover for her. To begin pulling suspicion onto himself. He didn't care what gossip followed him, as long as she was safe." She crept forward. The edge of the sheet rustled near her feet. "I don't think my father loved anything in this world as much as he loved her. After she died, he just wasn't the same person. It was like I lost them both that night."

He wanted to pull Esme into his arms. *I will not lose you, Esme.*

"She died the night before my sixteenth birthday. We were supposed to have this big, elaborate party at my father's estate. But I didn't want a party." Her lips lifted as if to smile, only they immediately curled down. No dimples ever flashed. "I wanted to just spend time with them. I wanted to get away from all the people and all the fake masks that everyone seemed to wear all the time around me.

My mother insisted on the party. She made up the guest list. She invited people I didn't even know and then when everyone was sleeping, she made her way across the sloping roof and toward the balcony of a room that was occupied by a very, very influential British businessman. A businessman and a spy. She wasn't going there to have some sort of clandestine affair. She was going to steal secrets that he possessed. Only she slipped. She fell. I found her the next morning and..." She looked at the floor as if the thread-bare carpet held all the mysteries of the world. "My father had it all covered up. A tragic accident while she was horseback riding. That was the story. She'd gone out for a late-night ride, and the horse bucked, and we didn't know until the next day, and it was all so very sad. Heartbreaking." Her shoulders slumped. "You know, I think that might be when I became afraid of heights, too. Or maybe that's when I became afraid of everything."

He had to cross to her. "Esme."

She didn't look up. Still seemingly focused on the carpet.

His hand reached out and curled under her chin. He forced her to look at him. "Esme."

There were no tears in her eyes, but plenty of sadness stared back at him. "I tried to make it right. The things I went on to take? Most of them had been stolen from their real owners. Often by her. I tried to fix everything that was broken, but sometimes, you can't do that. No matter how hard you try."

No, sometimes, you couldn't.

"I thought my father was innocent. He always protected her—*because he loved her*. People will do some insane things for love in this world."

Yes. They would.

"I never thought he was evil. Not until Louis came calling. Whispering all his stories into my ear. But I still did not want to believe him. Louis thought that my father was the Fox. He wasn't. First, my mother was. She was the Fox."

"Then it was you."

A nod. "Yes." The sheet slithered.

"You told your father everything that Louis said."

"I did. I was my father's spy, and then Louis died. I nearly died. And now, I've finally found the video that showed me that my father was there the whole time."

His thumb brushed over her lower lip.

"My big confession." She backed up a step.

His hand fell.

"You have everything you wanted, don't you? I've told you the secrets your friend Grayson wanted so badly. You should call him now. Tell him to come get you. Your work is done."

"You trust Gray? You trust his boss?" Because Tyler didn't trust Thaddeus. Not for a second.

"It's not about trust. I think you need real answers about your family. You deserve them. The only way to get those answers is to have Thaddeus and my father questioned."

That wasn't the only way. "Jorlan knows what happened. He's the one who had the damn drive."

"He won't talk. Not unless he's made to talk. It would take quite a lot to make someone like him break."

"Yes, well, your father isn't going to suddenly confess to all his sins. Neither will Thaddeus." She had to understand that. Unless... "Esme." His eyes narrowed on her. "You changed your masterplan, didn't you?" Fuck. *I should have anticipated this.*

"I really do love you."

He wanted to haul her against him and never let go.

"I don't expect you to love me back. That would be asking too much."

Why the hell would it be too much?

"Our worlds shouldn't have collided, but they did. First in Paris, by chance. Then now. But this time, it wasn't by chance. It was because I staged things. I'm good at that. Setting the stage. One of my specialties."

"What have you done?" He whirled away. Finished dressing. Grabbed a gun. Checked it. Shoved it into the back waistband of his jeans.

Esme dropped the sheet. Completely nude, she walked across the room and also reached for fresh clothing. "I haven't *done* anything. Not yet. No need to panic. But a new master plan must be created." She put on a bra. Panties.

For a moment, he just stared at her. The faint line on her stomach haunted him. The scar that would always remind him of how close he'd come to losing Esme, before he'd gotten the chance to know her. "Esme."

Esme tugged on a shirt and jeans. She slid sneakers on her small feet. A soft exhale escaped her as she stared at him. "There's a hit on you," Esme told him. "I have to protect you."

"Sweetheart, my job is to protect *you*." How many times did he have to remind her of that important fact?

"Your side is bleeding." Concern shadowed her face. "I think we tore your stitches."

"Screw the stitches. Screw everything but—"

A car door slammed outside.

Screw everything but you. You are what matters to me.

Automatically, though, he hurried toward the lone window at the front of their room. When he looked out, shock rolled through him. "Get a gun," he ordered her.

"Finally!" He heard the rush of her feet as she hurried across the room. "I've been wanting one of my own for ages."

His eyes were on the familiar figure outside. "You didn't text anyone."

"What? No, I didn't get a chance before you came bursting in the bathroom."

He watched the figure head toward the office. "Esme, we need to work on that new masterplan of yours. Now."

"Tyler?"

He looked over his shoulder at her. "Thaddeus Caldwell just pulled up at our motel."

She shook her head. "H-he can't be here." A stutter when Esme never stuttered. "Only Kane knows where we are."

Kane who'd dropped them off so quickly and left in a flash.

Esme rushed toward Tyler. "He was there in Paris with you. He saved people, just like you did. He's your friend."

"I want you to listen carefully to my instructions." No way would Thaddeus come alone.

She gripped the gun in her hand.

"Crawl out the bathroom window."

"What?" Her voice cracked.

"You're small enough to fit through the window. I want you to go out the bathroom window. You're going to take a burner phone with you. You're going to take the key to the motorcycle. You'll get on the motorcycle, and you'll haul ass away from here." A sudden thought struck him. "You do know how to drive a motorcycle, don't you?"

"Of course, I do. It's me." But she waved that point away. "I'm not leaving you, Tyler. There is no way I'm running away while you stay behind. You and I both think the guy out there is dirty! Either he's working with my father or he's pulling some seriously shady business on his own."

He hauled her close. Kissed her. "You promised that you'd follow my orders without question." He let her go.

"If I did, I lied." She grabbed his shirtfront and hauled him right back to her. She kissed him. Hard. "I do that. I'm a liar. Spoiler."

"Don't talk that way about the woman I love. No one calls her names, ever."

Her eyes went very wide. "You didn't say that."

"Yes, sweetheart, I did." He pulled away from her and grabbed the key to the motorcycle. Then he shoved the key into her hand. She'd tucked the gun into the front of her jeans. *Please know how to use that gun, Esme.* His fingers closed around hers as he forced her to grip the motorcycle key.

"No, I mean...*you didn't say that now*. Now, as in, when you're telling me to leave you. When some dirty FBI guy is outside. You can't do this to me *now*. You can't say you love me now."

He wanted to kiss her. But if he kissed her again, he wouldn't stop. And she had to get to safety. "I'll tell you again later," he promised. "First, get the hell out of here."

She did not move.

"Esme, *go*."

"I won't leave you to face the wolves on your own."

"I am the wolf, baby. I'll take care of the danger and then come right after you."

"How will you find me?" Then, instantly, "No, not happening. I will not leave you."

The motel room door shook as a hard fist slammed into its surface. "I know you're in there!" Thaddeus called.

They were running out of time. "Esme, *go*. That's an order. Get the hell out of here. Thaddeus did not come alone. He'll have backup appearing soon. I will keep them distracted. *Go*."

"Is this truly what you think of me? That I'll just save my own ass and leave you to fight alone?"

Tyler didn't answer. He did pick her up and carry her into the bathroom. "I am the wolf," he said again. Then he hauled the broken door shut and went off to face the Fed at the door.

Chapter Twenty-Two

Tyler swung open the motel room door. He was highly conscious of the gun nestled against his lower back. "Thaddeus Caldwell. To what do I owe this unexpected surprise?" *Other than the fact that you are probably here to kill me, you conniving sonofabitch.*

Thaddeus glanced over his shoulder, then he peered back at Tyler. "You're compromised."

Clearly. He had a dirty Fed standing in front of him. "How did you find me?"

"Doesn't matter."

Oh, but it did.

"What matters is that we need to get you and Esme Laurent out of here, now." He stood on his toes and strained to see over Tyler. "Get her and let's go."

Yeah, no. "How did you find me?"

"Gray, all right? He told me your location."

Impossible. Seeing as how Gray didn't know the location. But Tyler nodded. "I see."

"You and Esme trusted the wrong people."

"I'm not sure Esme trusts anyone." *Except me.* He

would always go to great lengths to guard her trust. No way would he ever allow Esme to lose faith in him.

"You were sold out, Tyler. I'm here to transport you. It's a major favor I'm doing for her father." Sweat dotted Thaddeus's brow. "She's told you about him, hasn't she? You got her secrets? You know that her father is the real mastermind?"

"She's told me her secrets." He still stood in the doorway. Esme should be gone by now. Right? *Be gone, Esme.*

"Let me inside," Thaddeus urged him. "I can't be spotted. And FYI, that jerk at the front desk was too eager to give up your room number. Fifty bucks was all it took."

Was it really? Tyler stepped back. A wave of his hand directed the other man inside. When Thaddeus crossed the threshold, Tyler closed the door after him. Then Tyler put his back to that door and watched Thaddeus.

First, Thaddeus peered at the wrecked bed. Then he looked over at the bags. And finally, his gaze flew to the broken bathroom door. His attention remained on that door. "Is she in there?"

"Why are you doing favors for her father?"

Thaddeus took a step toward the bathroom. "He's a bad man." Bitter laughter. "Serious understatement. He's been pulling strings and working crimes for years." Another step. "You know..." A sigh. "I hate to be the one to tell you, but I think her father killed yours."

He remained in position near the door. "You don't say."

Those bored words caught Thaddeus's attention. He stopped creeping toward the bathroom door and swung his attention to Tyler. "You don't seem surprised."

"I've spent the last..." What was it now? "Seventy-two? Ninety-six hours? Whatever—I've spent the last few days with Esme. At this point, I can tell you that it takes a lot to surprise me."

"She told you what he did. And yet you still are protecting her."

"Seems that way."

Thaddeus whipped out his gun and pointed it straight at Tyler. "Then you are an idiot."

"I'm not the Fed who has been in bed with a criminal so, are you really one to judge?"

Thaddeus cast a disgusted glance at the wrecked bed. "Want to try that again? Looks like I just interrupted your latest screw with a criminal."

Tyler did not take his gaze off his prey. "Here's the thing. No one is gonna be calling Esme any names. Never again."

Thaddeus laughed. "You dumb fucker. I'm about to load bullets into your chest. You're hardly in the position to be giving orders."

There was a silencer on the gun. Figured. Not like Thaddeus would want attention drawn to his crimes.

"You won't be around to stop me from doing whatever the hell I want with Esme." Thaddeus's smile still lingered. "She's hiding in the bathroom, isn't she?"

"Why don't you go see for yourself?"

But Thaddeus didn't take the bait. "Better idea." More laughter. Then, "Esme!" Thaddeus raised his voice. "Esme, come out here now or I will shoot your boyfriend in the next five seconds!"

She couldn't come out. She was long gone. *Be gone, Esme.*

"Five..."

Tyler stared at Thaddeus. "I'm curious. Did *you* order

the blast at that café in Paris? Did you do it because Louis Turner knew you were as guilty as they come?"

"How the hell do you know Louis?" Thaddeus shook his head. "Four!"

"Funny thing. Louis left a video that I recently had the pleasure of viewing. Actually, I saw a couple of videos."

"Three!" But the color had bled from Thaddeus's face.

"You were in one of them," Tyler disclosed. "Maybe you want to see them? Because I still have the footage." No, he didn't. Esme did. But he was buying himself some time.

"Two." The gun shook in Thaddeus's hands. "I knew that Jorlan had lost his ace in the hole. When he came to the FBI office, all shaken and demanding to see Esme, I knew then." He nodded. "Thanks for the confirmation. I'll be sure to eliminate him next."

Thaddeus was going to fire. Tyler knew it.

"One–"

Tyler yanked out his own weapon. He brought it up and around in a flash.

But Esme had just launched out of the bathroom. She slammed her body into Thaddeus's back. They both hurtled to the floor. Thaddeus fired his weapon, and the bullet went wild, blasting through the window and shattering glass.

Thaddeus tried to bring his weapon around and fire at Esme. She was pounding his head–with her gun–and he was snarling and screaming.

"Enough." Tyler lunged across the room and pressed his gun to Thaddeus's temple. "You stop fighting right now, or I will blast a hole in your head."

Thaddeus stopped fighting.

Esme slammed the butt of her gun against the FBI boss one more time.

"Sweetheart," Tyler said softly. "Come stand beside me."

She did. But she glared at Thaddeus the whole time.

Tyler kept his weapon on the Fed. Shoved against his temple. "Are you hurt at all?" he asked Esme.

"I broke a nail."

His jaw tightened as he studied the dirty Fed. "That really pisses me off, Thaddeus. She broke a nail."

"*Fuck. You.*"

"How did you find us?" Tyler demanded. He'd asked that question too many times. If he didn't get an answer, he just might have to pull the trigger.

Thaddeus smirked. Like he had some big secret.

"Did my father send you to kill me?" Esme asked.

Thaddeus's gaze cut to her. "That what you think? Girl, your father is the only thing that has been keeping you alive! *I'm* the one who put out the hit on you. Me. Because I suspected you had that cursed drive the minute you were arrested at Jorlan's. Louis always said there was more to you than met the eye. That lying sonofabitch was right, for once. I knew I had to take you out because—while I might have been able to control and predict Jorlan's moves—I couldn't control you." He shoved his hands down on the floor and started to rise.

Tyler simply slammed his foot into the man's spine and pushed him right back down. He also kept the gun at Thaddeus's temple. "I'm going to ask you some questions. You'll respond honestly, or I'll get twitchy with the trigger."

"Uh, Tyler?" Esme tugged on his shirt. "You said he wouldn't be coming alone."

"I also said for you to get that sweet ass of yours out of the motel." She hadn't.

"You don't leave the people you love behind," she noted in her quiet, husky voice.

Shit. His heart squeezed. "Esme." He loved her so much. Even if the woman couldn't follow orders for shit. Thaddeus had been correct—there was no controlling or predicting Esme. "Check the window for me, sweetheart. There *will* be backup coming." But maybe they'd have time to get real answers before that backup arrived.

She darted away.

He felt the tension pouring through his body. Time for the truth. "You know what my grandfather did." No BS. No pussyfooting around. The stark truth.

Thaddeus pressed his head harder to Tyler's gun. "Are you like him?" Thaddeus seemed curious. "Or are you like your old man? Weak. Useless."

"I don't see anyone outside!" Esme called.

"Does she know?" Thaddeus asked. He seemed genuinely curious. "Does she know that your grandfather—your whole family—is as bloody and twisted as they come? Your grandfather *was* the mob, and no matter how hard your dad tried, he couldn't wash that blood away from his hands. You hear that, Esme? You picked the wrong protector!"

"No." Her fierce denial. "Tyler is good. It's *my* family that is twisted. It's *my* father who killed his—"

Rolling laughter from Thaddeus tore through her words. "That what you believe? And why? Probably because dear *Louis* told you? And, of course, you believed him." More laughter. "I fed him that BS. Always good to have a fall guy at the ready, and your father has long been due for a fall."

"Who killed my parents?" Tyler bit out.

"Your grandfather, you bastard. Your grandfather killed your parents. Your family tree is full of blood and betrayal. You're twisted to the core." He sent a mock sympathetic look toward Esme. "You thought you were getting a hero, but you just got one of the most twisted sonsofbitches out there! His grandfather ordered Tyler's dad's killing. He ordered the death of his own son! Tyler's family is a pit of vipers, and you can't trust a single one of them."

Tyler shook his head. "I'm not like him."

"Like who?" Thaddeus showed no fear. Just rage as his stare flickered to Tyler. "Your spineless father? The one who ran away from New York and tried to start a whole brand new life in Texas? The same prick who later *came to me* wanting to turn over evidence because he was so scared that his world was going to implode? Or do you mean that you're not like your grandfather? The man who didn't even hesitate when I told him what was going down. The minute he knew your father was selling him out, he told me to take care of the problem. *And I did!*"

Tyler's teeth ground together. "You're confessing to killing my father?"

"You should've been in the car with your parents. Every freaking one of you should have been wiped out!" Spittle flew from his mouth. He heaved out a shuddering breath. "Your grandfather couldn't handle the shit that had gone down. Said he'd never meant for things to go so far. That I was just supposed to *threaten* his son. Didn't the bastard get that the time for threats had long passed? It was a time for action. But your grandfather couldn't live with himself after the funeral. The weak prick put a gun in his own mouth."

Tyler had known that his grandfather took his own life. He'd thought the suicide was due to grief not to—not to—

Killing my father. My mother. Ordering the hits on their lives. Tyler started to squeeze the—

"Tyler!"

Esme's voice. His Esme.

"Tyler, a sheriff's car just pulled up! It's Clay!"

Thaddeus laughed. "I lied to you about Grayson. Clay is the one who tipped me off. I was already in the area, and it was so easy to get here when he gave me your location. He was texting me GPS coordinates for the Jeep you stole—he did that the entire time you were supposedly running to safety. I was on your trail, every moment. He even called me a bit ago to let me know that he'd be coming to seal the deal here with me."

Clay.

"Here's something else for you to spin around in that head if yours. If you kill me, Grayson is a dead man." Again, Thaddeus just pressed his head to the gun, as if daring Tyler to shoot. "He didn't reveal jack shit to me. Not even after the torture. He's still alive. For the moment. But if I go out, if you pull that trigger, you may as well be killing Grayson yourself!"

"*Clay is coming toward the door. Oh, no! He saw the bullet hole in the window. What do I do?*" Esme's frantic voice.

"Answer the door," Thaddeus directed her. "Invite him to join the party."

But they didn't need to invite him to the party. Because the door was suddenly flying open. Clay had kicked it in. The motel had walls and doors that were way too thin and weak. Clay burst in—gun up—but he staggered to a stop when he saw Tyler with his weapon pressed against Thaddeus's temple.

"What in the hell is happening here?" Clay bellowed.

"Behind you!" Thaddeus yelled. "She's hiding—"

Esme had already launched her body at Clay. But he spun, and his weapon stopped her cold. "This is where it ends for you," Clay told her, voice flat. "Sorry, but there's a lot of money sitting on that pretty head."

"No!" Tyler yelled. He lifted his weapon away from Thaddeus. Instantly, the Fed was on his feet. "Don't shoot her, *don't!*"

Clay kept his attention on Esme, but he told Tyler, "Drop your weapon."

Tyler dropped his weapon. No hesitation. Not when Esme's life was on the line.

"Now walk out of here." Clay cast him a quick glance. "Don't look back. I made a deal, man. You'll get to go free. I just have to take care of her."

The fuck that was happening.

"Walk out," Clay urged again. His gaze pleaded with Tyler to follow his order. "Thaddeus and I will handle Esme."

Tyler's gaze swung to land on Esme's face.

"You're my friend," Clay said. "Killing you was never part of the deal. You get to go free. *It's just her*."

Did Esme still have her gun? Tyler thought that she did. Her right hand was hidden behind her jeans.

"Go," Esme told Tyler. She even sent him a smile. "Don't look back, Tyler. Promise me that you won't."

"You don't leave the ones you love behind," he reminded her. Then his gaze slid back to Clay.

"*Walk out!*" Spittle flew from Clay's mouth.

Tyler didn't move.

"What in the hell is going on over here?" A disgruntled male voice. One that might have been a little drunk. "You assholes need to keep the volume down!" A man in a stained, white shirt lumbered toward the open motel room door. "I'm trying to—" His eyes widened as he took in the scene that waited for him. "Fuck!" He turned and ran.

"Stop him!" Thaddeus blasted. "Dammit, Clay, you are screwing up everything! You didn't even destroy the damn drive. *Tyler* saw it. He isn't leaving! He's *dying*!"

Tyler cut a glance behind him at the Fed.

Thaddeus had Tyler's gun in his hand. From this close, there was no way he'd miss when the bastard fired at him—and Tyler knew that Thaddeus was firing. He could see the deadly intent in the other man's eyes.

Tyler wanted to tell Esme that he loved her. Wanted to tell her that he'd started to make dreams for them. For the first time in a very long while, he'd dreamed.

But that sonofabitch is about to fire at me.

"Don't shoot Tyler! Don't hurt him!" Clay yelled. "Tyler, fuck, hit the deck!"

Tyler dropped.

Guns blasted. Not silenced gunfire. Thunderous blasts. Immediately, his gaze went to Esme. Her eyes were wide and horrified, but she wasn't hurt.

Clay…was.

Red bloomed on his stomach, darkening the brown of his sheriff's uniform. He weaved and looked down at himself. "Shouldn't it…hurt more?" Clay crashed onto the floor.

Tyler rolled and looked up. Red spilled from dead center on Thaddeus's chest. He'd dropped the gun and had slapped both hands over the wound. Blood poured from between his fingers.

Tyler grabbed the gun and leapt to his feet. "You bastard!"

Thaddeus hit his knees.

"You killed my father?" Rage had the whole room turning a blood red. "My mom? *You* were behind the bombing in Paris? You did it all?"

"H-help...me."

"Fucking help *yourself*."

Thaddeus crashed in front of him. Tyler whirled as his attention flew to Esme. "*Esme!*"

She had her hands on Clay's chest. "I can't stop it! Tyler, call for help! Tyler, please—"

"*He's not calling anyone*."

Too slowly, Tyler's head swung toward the open motel room door. Who the hell else was coming to the room? More backup for Thaddeus?

A man stood in the doorway. Big, wearing a mask on the lower portion of his face. His icy blue eyes glinted. "The dead can't call." Then the man fired the gun in his hand.

The impact of the bullet slammed into Tyler. It shoved him back, and he hit the wall near the bathroom. His head thudded hard into the wall, the same freaking spot on the back of his head where he'd been hit after the blast. His body began to slump. The room to dim. He saw Esme. She was screaming and lunging for him, but the man in the doorway wrapped his arm around her and hauled her up against him.

Then that bastard looked over at Tyler. He looked...

And he put the gun barrel over the mask—in the spot that would cover his lips. *Shhh*.

Esme broke away from the masked man.

Snarling, the masked man pointed the gun and fired.

Bam. It seemed like a hammer drove right into Tyler's chest, right over his heart.

Esme was still screaming and fighting when the masked man hauled her out of the motel room

* * *

The gunfire and the screams maddened Kane. He'd been slamming his feet into the rear window of the patrol car, but the stupid thing wouldn't break. His friends were inside the motel—they'd better not be *dying*—and he was trapped inside the cop car.

Kane lunged upright and peered out of the window just as some dick in black came running out with Esme locked in his arms. Esme was scratching and headbutting him and the prick wasn't letting her go. "Esme!" Kane roared. "Esme!"

Her head whipped toward the patrol car. "*Tyler!*" Her desperate cry. Then she slammed her head back against her attacker.

He didn't let her go.

But his mask did fall.

Kane's eyes widened. The bastard met his stare for just a moment, then he was rushing away with Esme. He threw her into the back of a van. The vehicle screeched away.

"*Esme!*"

The window hadn't broken. Time to try something else. He twisted and heaved and slammed his feet into the old cage that separated him from the front seat. The thing looked freaking ancient. It had to give.

His feet drove into it again. The metal shuddered.

It had to give.

He hit it again. Again. The metal screeched and buckled.

He drove his feet into it another time. The metal busted loose. Hell, yes. Like a snake, he slithered his way into the front, shoving the metal with his shoulders now. Keys waited near the dashboard. Including a key for the cuffs. He had the cuffs off in five seconds, and then he was running for motel room number seven.

Lucky seven.

The other people staying at the motel had all ducked for cover and gone into hiding when the gunfire started. He was the only one heading toward the violence. And when he entered that room...

Fuck me.

He staggered to a stop.

Clay was on the floor with a pool of blood beneath him.

Thaddeus Caldwell—an FBI bastard he'd encountered more than a few times over the years—sprawled motionless near the open bathroom doorway. And Tyler...

Tyler was...

Groaning.

And rising. Tyler's hands went to his chest.

Kane raced to him. He didn't see any sign of blood on his friend. "Tyler!"

"He...shot me."

Who had? Lots of options were currently spinning through Kane's head.

"Rubber bullets. That SOB." Tyler took a lunging step forward. "He *has* her."

Kane blocked his path. "I know exactly which *he* you mean. But we have to call for help, man."

Clay let out a ragged groan.

"Clay will die without help. We need *backup,*" Kane snarled. "And we need it now." They couldn't handle what was coming on their own. No way.

When that mask had fallen outside, he'd seen the face

of the man who'd hauled Esme out of there. It had been a face that he knew.

A face of a man they'd called a friend.

Kane's gaze darted to Clay. Sometimes, your friends could really let you down.

His stare flickered back to an enraged Tyler.

And sometimes, your friends could be absolutely lethal sonsofbitches who terrorized the whole world.

Chapter Twenty-Three

"You look like you want to rip me apart."

Esme didn't speak to her captor. Her hands were cuffed—his mistake—and her feet were bound with thick rope. They'd been traveling for hours. The jackass had drugged her. He'd stopped their van shortly after leaving the motel—mostly because he had to, she'd jumped out the back—and he'd jabbed her with a needle. The next thing she knew, she'd woken beside him in a completely different ride.

How long had she been out?

Where the hell were they going? She'd been trying to keep an eye out for road signs, but he seemed determined to only travel on snaking back roads with zero signage.

Where is he taking me? And how can I kill him?

"It's really not personal, you know." He spoke easily. As if he often chatted with women who were cuffed in the seat next to him. "Just a job."

"I will..." Her throat felt too dry. Raw. "Cut you into pieces at my first opportunity. *Je promets.*" *I promise.*

He laughed.

She didn't.

Her control was razor thin. She kept seeing this jerk shoot Tyler. Not just once. Twice. Once when Tyler had already been down. She'd needed to get to him, but the monster currently driving the car had taken her away.

"There was a bounty on his head. My employer wanted your U.S. Marshal dead. He had to get shot."

She didn't cry. There was no room for tears when rage fueled her. Esme would allow no grief.

Kane had been in the patrol car at the motel. He must have gotten out. Kane would have gotten free and rushed to help Tyler. Tyler could still be alive. No, no, he *had* to be alive. She wouldn't even consider any other option. Any other option would lead straight to madness for her.

"Sure looked like a whole lot of violence went down in that motel room." His eyes were on the road again.

Her eyes were on him. Memorizing every feature. Square jaw. Sharp nose. Slight scar cutting just under his lower lip. Frigid blue, soulless eyes. A tattoo of a snake along his left wrist.

Oh, he was a snake, all right.

"Not that I'm complaining," he added, all conversational-like. "Provided the perfect distraction for me. Doubt I would have been able to sneak up on your boyfriend if he hadn't been busy with the two bodies in the room."

"I am going to make your death hurt." Another promise.

Soft laughter. "You're kinda cute when you're plotting murder."

She'd already plotted his death a dozen times.

"When did you and the marshal hook up? Did you always plan to use him and did he know just how bloodthirsty you are?"

Tyler knew everything about her. Just as she knew so

much about him. Thaddeus hadn't been making dramatic revelations to her. She'd known already that Tyler's grandfather had been involved with the mob. But Tyler had no blood on his hands. *And I didn't know his own grandfather had ordered the hit on Tyler's parents.* That part had been news. She'd wanted to rush to Tyler and comfort him. Instead, she'd been dragged away from the man she loved. "Who hired you?"

"Your ex." An easy answer. "I'm taking you to him now."

Jorlan. She sucked in a breath.

"He wanted me to kill the marshal. That was step one. Step two is bringing you to him. He wants a personal chat with you. Said you were to be brought in alive." His hold tightened on the wheel. "Of course, I did promise to kill you as soon as he was done with that fun talk he wanted to have...so, there's that."

A lump choked her.

"Want to hear some music?" Her soon-to-be-killer turned on the radio. "I hate silence, don't you?"

"Yes." *Tyler, be alive.*

Be. Alive.

Esme went back to plotting the murder of the man beside her.

* * *

"He's dead. Absolutely fucking dead." Tyler paced in the hospital. He wasn't talking about Clay. Clay would live. The docs were working on him now. Thaddeus hadn't survived the ambulance ride, and Tyler couldn't give a shit about that traitorous SOB.

All of his focus was on Esme. And on the man who'd taken her.

A man that Tyler knew. Too well.

What game are you playing? Why are you screwing with my Esme?

And where the hell was Gray? He'd tried to make contact, but Gray appeared to have disappeared. *What did Thaddeus do to him?*

Kane stood at his side, a solid, immovable object. Kane had gotten help at the motel. Contacted authorities who weren't freaking as dirty as they came.

But he hadn't gotten Esme. She is gone.

And all Tyler could do was wait on the phone call that had damn well better come.

"*Where is my daughter?*"

His head whipped to the right. Three men marched toward him. Two of the guys he instantly pegged as security. They had that tough-as-nails, I'll-break-you-in-a-flash look about them. Tyler ignored them because it was the third man that mattered.

The man with Esme's eyes. Etienne Laurent.

He'd figured her father would show up, sooner or later. Turned out, it was sooner.

Etienne strode straight to Tyler. His goons covered his left and right sides. The light hit her father's dark hair, with silver gleaming near his temples. His face was hard with intent, and rage shone in the darkness of his eyes as he squared off with Tyler. Only darkness. No faint traces of gold. His eyes weren't *exactly* like Esme's.

"You had one job, Marshal Barrett. Just one."

"He's had a really long day, buddy," Kane began angrily.

Tyler waved him away. He could handle this. Besides, Etienne deserved his rage. "I'm getting her back."

Etienne swept him with a judging glare. "Why would she choose someone like you? All you will do is disappoint her."

"I'm getting her back," he said again. It was a vow.

"But will you get her back alive? Or will my Esme come home in pieces?"

Tyler could have sworn his heart stopped.

"You have no clue how to find her, do you? She was taken while you watched."

While she screamed for me.

Pain nearly blinded him.

"You looked at her and saw a villain. You never knew her." Disgust tightened Etienne's face. "*I* will get my daughter back, and I will make sure she never sees you again." He whirled from Tyler.

"She starts each day trying to do something good." The words were pulled from him.

Etienne had begun to storm away, but he stilled.

"She wakes up so happy—the brightest morning person you have ever seen—and she tries to do good."

Etienne glanced back. Tyler could have sworn the other man's lower lip trembled. "Esme's mother taught her that. Her mother..." He swiped a hand over his face. "She wanted Esme to be different than she was. Better than us both." His hand fell. "Esme was always the best thing in our world." His head turned away. He started to march away once more.

"She's the best thing in my world," Tyler said. He made sure his voice carried. Esme had thought this man was a killer, but it hadn't been him. "You tried to protect her, didn't you? Because you knew Esme was in danger. All the way back in Paris, you knew."

Etienne whirled and was back in front of Tyler in a blink. "That bastard Louis was using her! Lying to her about me. He was working with Thaddeus, and that piece of scum was always trying to blackmail his way into my life. I was not going to let them use my Esme. I told her to stay away from Louis. Not to meet him anymore because the game was too dangerous. I *saw* Louis with Thaddeus that day in the café. I knew trouble was coming." He straightened. "I just didn't realize how close it was. Not until my daughter was pulled from the rubble."

I pulled her out.

"You think you know Esme?" A hard, negative shake of Etienne's head. "You have no clue who she truly is."

"She bakes the best chocolate chip croissants in the world."

Etienne's stare sharpened on Tyler.

"And when she lies, her voice gets all arrogant. Haughty. That's how I know she's pretending. Because the real Esme isn't like that. The real Esme is warm and caring. She's the kind of woman who will risk her life to save a child. She's the kind of woman who will fight like hell for someone she loves." He remembered her flying out of the motel bathroom and attacking Thaddeus. "She can't follow orders for shit. And she always hides when she sheds real tears. But that's stopping. Because she's not going to cry any longer." *But she'd been crying when she was taken away from me.*

Etienne watched him with glacial eyes of black ice. "You made my daughter cry?" Anger. Nope. More like rage.

Tyler got it. He'd want to kick the ass of any man who made *his* daughter cry. *I'm going to find Esme. We're going to have a future together. And if any fool ever makes our daughter cry, I will destroy him.* "Maybe you should go ahead and take a swing at me." He motioned to the two silent goons. "Or let them do it. I deserve a punch." More than that because Esme had been taken.

Etienne rubbed a hand over the bridge of his nose, as if considering something, then he said, "Esme loves silence."

Tyler could feel Kane watching them. "She hates it. Comes from all that time when she couldn't hear a thing."

Etienne's hand fell. "Why in the hell would she choose you?"

"Because she mistakenly thinks I'm some kind of hero."

"Esme doesn't like heroes. Mostly because she doesn't believe they actually exist."

"I pulled her from the café in Paris."

Etienne backed up a step.

"She mistakenly thinks I'm a hero," he said again. "But I'm about to show her that I will do things no hero will ever do."

"Uh, Tyler..." Kane edged closer. "Public place. We should probably not be saying—"

"I am going to find the man who ordered Esme's abduction—the same man who put a hit on my life—and I am going to kill the bastard. There will be no escape for him."

Kane coughed. Then, for the nurses who were side-eyeing them, he blustered, "Nothing to see here! Just a little theater work!"

Etienne rolled back his shoulders. "You know that Thaddeus put a hit on my daughter."

"Yes. The original one. But I'm pretty sure Jorlan Rodgers is the prick we can blame for what happened at the motel. He's the one behind her abduction."

"Jorlan?" Surprise flickered in Etienne's eyes. "Jorlan wants to marry my daughter. He's been obsessed with her for years."

"He's a twisted monster, and his obsession is over." Because Jorlan was about to be over.

"If you know he's responsible, then why are you here?" Etienne gestured to the hospital.

He was there because Jorlan was in the wind and no one could find him. But Tyler had an ace in the hole. A very unlikely ace. An ace that he did intend to beat the hell out of later, but an ace nonetheless. "I'm waiting for a—"

A phone vibrated.

Not his phone. Tyler didn't have a damn phone at the moment.

Kane's phone.

Kane glanced down at the screen, then he handed the device to Tyler. They both knew this ace in the hole.

Ace. Asshole. Same thing.

Tyler read the text. His breath shuddered out. "Any chance you happen to have a private plane I could borrow? It would really speed up the rescue process for your daughter."

"*You know where she is?*"

He did now. He and Kane had just gotten the message they'd been waiting for. An old friend—and sometimes enemy—had sent the information he needed. "The thing about me..." Tyler shoved the phone back at Kane. "I have friends in all sorts of places."

Etienne pointed toward the operating room. "Like your *friend* Clay Banks?"

"Clay fired the shot that took out Thaddeus. He saved my life."

Etienne did not respond to that news.

"Yeah, this talk is fun and all, but I'm getting to Esme. Come on, Kane." He brushed past Etienne and his goons.

"Your friend Clay did not set the bomb in Paris," Etienne revealed.

That stopped him. For just a moment. This time, Tyler was the one who looked back. "How the hell do you know that?"

Etienne smiled. It was not Esme's brilliant smile. It was cold and calculating and deadly. He crooked his finger at Tyler.

Tyler edged back to him.

"My daughter was nearly killed in that bombing. The person I love most in this world." Etienne's hand gripped Tyler's shoulder. "You truly think I did not immediately use every resource I have to uncover the real mastermind?"

He thought Esme's father might just be one dangerous bastard.

"Louis Turner was not the man he appeared to be. He wanted to take his betrayals and make them all disappear. He thought the best way to do that was by staging a very public death."

What. The. Hell?

"He'd been trained. The gentleman had quite the background in detonations. Not that most people would know that. The CIA and the FBI hid his real past. But I discovered the truth. That man even worked for the bomb squad once upon a time, under a different name. In a different life."

"You trade in secrets," Tyler murmured.

"Just like my daughter."

I need Esme.

"Louis realized that Thaddeus intended to eliminate him. What Thaddeus *didn't* know was that Louis was one step ahead. Louis was a tricky sonofabitch. Wearing wires with everyone. Always making videos. Trading secrets left and right. When Louis realized he was a target, he simply eliminated the bomber that Thaddeus had hired in Paris... and then Louis finished the job."

Tyler's stomach knotted. "So he never intended to turn information over to the *right hands*."

"There was nothing *right* about Louis." Bitter laughter. "Louis knew that Thaddeus was waiting for an explosion, so he gave the bastard one. Louis knew exactly where to put the bomb and exactly where he should be positioned, so that he would escape injury." His voice lowered even more as he asked, "How was it fair that he got to escape injury when my daughter was driven into a world of silence? She had to undergo multiple surgeries for her face and for the injuries to her body. She had to suffer while that monster thought he could just slip away? No, not on my watch."

Tyler understood that Louis Turner was truly dead. Now. He might have slipped from the wreckage of that café, but he hadn't started a new life anywhere. "She never knew."

"I don't always like to shatter my daughter's illusions."

"Louis left a video saying you were guilty as hell. Basically pointing the finger at you for the bombing. And for the murder of my parents."

Etienne's brows rose. "I know nothing about your parents."

"Yeah, turns out, Thaddeus Caldwell killed them." He couldn't touch on that pain. Not now. He had to focus on Esme. "Jorlan got hold of that video."

"Jorlan gets hold of many things he shouldn't, it would seem."

He won't keep Esme. "Why did Louis leave the video calling you out?"

"Because my Esme had to make a choice. He wanted her to choose between him and me. She chose me. Over and over again. She did not truly love him. He hated that. I suspect that, in the end, it made him hate *her*. So he did one last thing to try and wreck her." His hand released Tyler. "I do not think she would choose me...over you."

"She won't ever have to do that. I would never make her do something like that. I want Esme happy. I want the people she loves in her life." Questions slammed through his head. "What about the ones convicted of the Paris bombing? Esme said they confessed."

"Not all confessions are true. Those individuals set other bombs. They killed other people." Anger twisted in his words. "And they made deals with Thaddeus and his international cronies. Deals that we will never fully unravel." Etienne inclined his head. "I have a private plane at the small airport thirty minutes away. Take it. And any weapons that you need. They will be waiting inside the hangar."

"Thank you."

"You will find Esme. You will take out any threats to her."

Hell, yes, he would.

"And you will love my daughter for the rest of her life?"

"I'll love her until I take my last breath."

"Then go save the day, *hero*. My daughter is waiting on you."

She wasn't going to get a hero.

She was going to get the bastard who would tear apart anyone who dared to hurt her.

Tyler headed for the elevator. Kane was right at his side.

And before those elevator doors closed, Kane said, "Your future father-in-law is slightly scary. I think I could like him."

"Kane..."

"Who are we going to kill first?"

"Jorlan Rodgers. The hitman he hired has to deliver Esme directly to him. And we're going to be there for the exchange." He couldn't wait to see Jorlan's face when a dead man interrupted his private meeting.

Surprise, surprise, asshole. I'm still breathing, and I'm here to send you straight to hell.

Chapter Twenty-Four

THE BASEMENT WAS DARK AND HOT AND SHE COULD hear things scurrying on the floor near her feet. "Great ambiance you have," Esme told her captor as he pushed her forward. He'd cut the ropes from her ankles right before they'd entered this old monstrosity of a house. The better for her not to fall on her face as she took mincing steps due to the restriction of the ropes.

Now just her hands were still secured—cuffed. In front of her. His mistake, of course. And she was just waiting for the right moment to surprise him with her skills.

The problem was that he currently had a gun shoved into the base of her spine. The same gun he'd used on Tyler?

She stumbled.

Do not think about him. Not yet. Tyler is safe. Kane got him out and got him to a hospital. Tyler is safe. Alive.

"The dungeon décor is top-notch," she complimented. "I can tell the owner of the place really went all-in on the horror vibe."

"You always talk, don't you?" he groused back. "Lady,

can't you be quiet for like, two minutes? Really don't want to drug you again."

She really didn't want to be drugged again.

A big door swung open up ahead. The groan of its hinges seemed far too loud. A groan and screech.

Then...

"*Bonjour, Esme.*"

Of course, it would be him. She'd known this meeting would be coming. It was actually one of the reasons she hadn't tried to get away sooner. She'd wanted to stand toe to toe with this particular monster.

He'd put a hit on Tyler. That would not be forgotten or forgiven. Ever.

Jorlan strolled out with a wide grin on his face.

"The overdramatic scene, the roaches on the floor, the rats scattering about." She ticked off each item with an impatient tap of her foot. "Doesn't take a psychic to feel your stench all over this place."

He lost his big grin. Jorlan raced straight up to her and pulled back his hand to slap her in the face.

She braced for the hit.

Only it never came. Because the big, bad hitman who'd dragged her all the way to this hellhole stopped Jorlan before he could strike her. "Not part of the deal," he gritted out.

"Are you insane?" Jorlan roared at him.

"Maybe." A pause. "Probably. Depends on who you ask, I guess."

Jorlan jerked away from him.

"You don't get her—not even to rough her up—until I get my payment," the hitman said. "Payment for her kidnapping and for the murder of U.S. Marshal Tyler Barrett. I'm sure his death made the news."

His death. His death. Those words echoed sickeningly in her ears.

Jorlan laughed. "He died, and so did Thaddeus Caldwell. Talk about eliminating two problems at once. That Fed bastard was always trying to push his way into my business."

His death.

Nausea rose within her. "I'm going to be sick." Esme leaned forward. The curtain of her hair flew around her. With the hair covering her, she grabbed for the hoop earring she wore in her right ear. Long ago, she'd learned that nearly any earring would work for this trick. But the hoops were particularly good because the thin gold was so malleable. She'd been wearing the hoops when she got out of her cuffs the last time, too. She just needed to twist the material just right...

The hitman hauled her back upright. Her hair flew back over her shoulder and—hopefully—disguised the fact that she was now minus one earring. She palmed it in her hand.

"Do *not* throw up right now," the hitman warned. His gaze almost seemed worried as he studied her face. Aw. A hitman with a heart. Fun to know.

"He's not dead," Esme declared.

The hitman's gaze sharpened on her. Had he noticed the missing earring?

"You're lying to Jorlan." *Sow discontent. Get them to turn on each other.* That was what she needed to do.

"Uh, lady..." The hitman's eyelashes flickered. "Watch yourself."

"No, you watch *yourself.* Tyler isn't dead." She surged toward Jorlan. "This jerk is lying to you. I was there. I saw it all with my own eyes. Tyler isn't dead. This clown is just trying to get a payday without actually turning in the work."

Suspicion flashed on Jorlan's face.

She was going to need a whole lot more than suspicion to get this show rolling. "Are you seriously going to be conned by this hack, Jorlan? Come on, you're better than this. Why on earth would you think you could trust this guy?"

Jorlan backed up a step. "You were friends with Tyler."

Wait. Who had been friends with Tyler? The hitman?

"Friends turned enemies." Jorlan nodded. "That is why I hired you in the first place." His hand went behind his back. "I knew you were aware of Tyler's inner circle. I knew you'd be able to track him better because you knew who he'd turn to for help."

The hitman stepped forward and positioned his body so that he was partially in front of Esme.

Perfect.

She began working with her earring on the cuffs while the two men were squaring off. *What is up with that bit about friends turned enemies?*

"I did track him," the hitman threw out. "Followed him to Asylum. Got a visual on him at the hospital, and I was on his tail all the way to that rathole of a motel. I took him out, and I brought her here. I did exactly as *you* ordered, Jorlan. Now pay up. You ordered her kidnapping, and you ordered the murder of U.S. Marshal Tyler Barrett. Transfer the money to my account right the hell now, or I will take her out and leave her on the doorstep of the nearest police station."

Oh, she actually liked that idea. *Snick.* The cuffs opened. Or at least, one cuff opened.

She could have sworn that the hitman's shoulders stiffened. Had he heard the telling sound?

"I'll transfer the money." A grudging agreement from Jorlan. "You did what I hired you to do. Come with me. My computer is inside. We'll take care of our business, and then you can leave."

Surely the hitman wasn't going to believe that line? "You're dead," Esme informed him, probably a bit too gleefully. "You were dead the minute you walked in here. There is no way Jorlan ever lets you walk out."

Now he did glance back at her. "Worried, are you? That's sweet."

You shot Tyler. "He could slice the skin from your body, and I wouldn't be worried." She did need the two men to fight soon so that she could have the chance to get to whatever computer was inside, grab some evidence, then burn the world down around Jorlan. She needed—

"Help!" A sharp, desperate cry. A cry that came from the room behind Jorlan. "*Help!*"

Her head craned around the hitman. Jorlan was smiling. Again. A terrible sign.

"Didn't I mention that I had company?" Jorlan scratched his jaw. "No? Sorry. I do. A certain upright FBI agent wouldn't give up Tyler and Esme's location, so Thaddeus sent him my way. The guy thought I could work my magic on him. Turns out, Grayson Stone can withstand a surprising amount of pain."

Esme shook her head. "What have you done?"

"*You're torturing an FBI agent?*" A snarl from the hitman. He raced forward. A wild, desperate move. The kind of move that Esme had hoped he would make.

The hitman rushed right past Jorlan, apparently intending to find the FBI agent—an odd move for a hitman

—so he didn't see when Jorlan slowly spun after him and raised his gun. Esme realized that Jorlan was going to fire and shoot the hitman in the back.

She should give zero fucks. But....

Friends turned enemies.

Something nagged at her.

And...

The hitman bellowed, "*Grayson!*" Bellowed with real worry.

Oh, dammit.

This time, someone else was working a scheme. *The hitman isn't what he appears to be.* So she had to try and save the day. As usual. She swung out with the loose cuff on her wrist, and Esme rammed it into Jorlan's head even as she screamed. "*He's got a gun!*"

The hitman spun around.

She hit again. The cuff slammed into Jorlan's temple. Jorlan staggered back. The gun fell from his fingers and clattered to the floor. She hit him once more. Harder. And again. The metal cuff slashed into his skin, and blood flew onto the slimy brick wall near him. "Get Grayson and get out!"

She heard the thud of steps. She'd better not be wrong about that hitman guy.

But Tyler can't be dead. He can't have killed Tyler. So the scene had to have all been wrong and...*You're smart if you believe absolutely nothing that you hear and only about half of what your eyes can see...*How could she have forgotten her own words to live by?

If she believed half of what she'd seen...

Tyler had been shot.

But not killed.

The stage had been set. A scene played out. *Tyler isn't dead.*

Jorlan caught her hand. He jerked her toward him, and their bodies pressed together. "Esme," he said with a kind of feverish delight. "You won't get away."

"Jorlan," she said with disgust and hate. "That hitman just recorded everything you said." He'd deliberately gotten a confession, so that must mean he'd been wired. "You're going to jail. You'll be behind bars for the rest of your miserable life."

His eyes widened. He looked over to the left.

She turned her head to peer in that direction, too. The hitman had a bleeding and limp Grayson thrown over one shoulder. "That strike you as someone who is the bad guy?" she taunted.

Wrong thing to say.

Jorlan spun her around so that her back was to him. One arm locked brutally around her throat. He began to squeeze.

"Stop!" A roar from Jorlan. "Or I will snap her neck!"

The hitman froze. Horror filled his eyes.

"I will break her neck right here and now," Jorlan vowed. "Drop the Fed! Drop any weapons you have! Get on your knees or I will kill her!"

"The fuck you will."

Her head whipped to the right. Oh. Oh, those were the sweetest, most beautiful words she'd ever heard in her entire life. Because those words were spoken by Tyler.

Tyler was rushing toward her and Jorlan. Surging straight for them like a seriously pissed-off avenging angel. His blue eyes burned, his face was locked into savage lines, and he gripped a gun in his hand even as he closed in on his prey.

I knew he wasn't dead.

Kane was right behind him. Covering his six, as his friend liked to do.

"You're dead!" Jorlan snarled.

"No. But you're about to be." Tyler stopped about two feet away. "You think I'm gonna miss from this close of a distance?"

Jorlan's hold tightened on her. He'd threatened to break her neck, but it felt more like he was strangling her. She couldn't pull in a breath. Her hands rose to claw at his painful grip.

"I think you won't do a damn thing!" Jorlan thundered back. "Not while I have *her*. You fool! You fell for her, didn't you? You think you get to rush in and take her now? *No.* This isn't the way I go out. This isn't—"

Clawing at the arm around her neck wasn't working. Esme was afraid she might pass out at any moment. So, new tactic. She went for his eyes. Her hand flew up and her curled fingers and sharp nails went straight for his eyes.

He screamed, and his hold loosened. Dizzy, dazed, she fell to the floor. From the corner of her eye, she saw the glint of metal. A blade? Jorlan had pulled out a blade from who the hell knew where, and he was slashing it down toward her. Aiming for her face.

Tyler fired. Two quick shots. She heard the blasts echo around her. They thundered and then there was silence.

She sucked in a breath. Another. Her heart raced, and she couldn't hear *anything*. Overwhelming silence. Because of the thunder of the gun?

Jorlan had fallen beside her. His blood had splattered onto her.

She stared at him.

Two shots.

One to the heart.

One to the head.

Jorlan would never get up again.

Hands reached for her. Gentle, careful hands. Her head turned from the sight of Jorlan's dead body. Tyler had crouched in front of her. His lips were moving—

"*Esme.* Esme, tell me that you're all right."

She touched his face. Such a perfect face. "I knew you weren't dead."

His mouth took hers. He kissed her with a bittersweet desperation.

"I need help over here!" A bellow from the hitman. "Gray is losing a ton of blood. He needs an ambulance!"

"On it!" Kane's shout.

Tyler pulled away from her. Esme saw Kane running to help carry Grayson.

"Ambulance is outside," Kane assured him. "So are about half a dozen cops. Let's go."

Cops. An ambulance. Esme started to rise, but Tyler caught her in his arms and lifted her against his chest.

"I am one hundred percent capable of walking." She looked down at Jorlan again as Tyler began to carry her out of that horrible place. Esme shuddered at the sight of all the blood and what was quite possibly brain matter. Esme turned her face away and curled an arm around Tyler's neck. "But you may carry me." He could do anything. Just... *never make me fear that way again. Never make me be so afraid that I won't see you again.* "You should have told me what you had planned. Keeping schemes secret is not cool." Mentally, she vowed to never keep a scheme from him again.

He was walking through the grim corridor that led back to safety. "Wouldn't have kept it from you. I didn't know what was happening. Not until the rubber bullets slammed into me. My head hit the wall. Fucking concussion. Got knocked out for a few moments."

Her hand feathered over the back of his head.

"Kane saw Ronan without his mask and realized what was going down. The SOB has been undercover for so long. Hell, I *never* expected for Ronan to be at that motel."

Undercover, as a hitman. *Ronan*.

"Former Marine turned gun for hire." Tyler tightened his hold on her. "We publicly cut ties years ago because of the cases he was working. And when I realized he'd taken you..." His mouth pressed against her temple. "I knew he'd send me and Kane a message as soon as he could. He might seem like the devil," Tyler rasped, "but he's—"

"Really on the side of the good guys?" Esme finished.

Tyler was climbing the stairs now and still carrying her.

"Not sure we're one hundred percent good." They reached the landing. Tyler stared down at her. The harsh overhead light glared onto them. "I just killed a man."

"You were saving me." He'd killed for her.

"He was dead before I entered the room. He was dead the minute he ordered you taken *from* me."

"You say the most romantic things. Truly." She wanted him to kiss her. She wanted him to hold her. To take her away from everyone and everything and...

They were outside. Sure enough, half a dozen patrol cars were also there. So was an ambulance. Kane and, uh, Ronan, were carrying Grayson toward the ambulance. Cops seemed to be swarming.

She and Tyler couldn't disappear. There would be questions to answer. Statements to give. The press to avoid.

"How's this for romantic?" He still held her. Wasn't

even out of breath. As if carrying her had been nothing at all.

Esme peered up at him.

"Sometimes, you meet someone," Tyler told her, voice gruff and shredding at the edges, "and you know right away that the person is trouble."

She swallowed. Her throat felt raw. And maybe those words made her feel raw. *He still thinks I'm trouble?* Not that he was wrong. Case in point...*just look around.*

His hold tightened around her. "The kind of trouble that you have been looking for your whole life."

Where was he going with this?

"You meet someone, and you know the person is going to change *everything* for you."

Okay, his words seemed promising.

"You meet someone, and you know right away that nothing will ever be the same again. Your world can't be the same, because the woman you just met is gonna change everything. She's going to change you. You will love her more than you've ever loved anything."

She couldn't stop her smile.

"You will fight for her. You will kill for her. You will *live* for her. Because nothing matters to you as much as she does."

He truly could say the most romantic things.

"And when she smiles at you, you get lost."

Esme had to ask, "Are you—are you lost in me?"

"I'm lost without you, Esme. And I never, ever want to be lost again."

The blue lights from the patrol cars were flashing in a bright swirl. She ignored the lights. And the cops. And everything but Tyler. "You won't be," she promised him. She'd found her hero. Esme did not intend to let him go.

"You're my non-negotiable," he told her. "Forever."

He kissed her and all of the terrible fear, the pain, the grief that had nearly smothered her since she'd left the motel—it finally vanished. There was no room for anything but happiness. Hope.

And love.

Sometimes, maybe the good guy did fall for the bad girl.

Sometimes, you meet someone...and you know right away that the person is trouble.

Sometimes, you could also meet someone and know you were staring at your forever.

Tyler was her forever. "*Je t'aime*," she told him. "*Je t'aime.*"

I love you.

Epilogue

"I have something for you."

Esme sent a slow, seductive grin Tyler's way. She was currently sitting on the edge of Grayson's desk in the FBI office while they waited for Grayson to come and give them a final report, but if Tyler was in the mood to play, she could certainly enjoy some fun with him.

He bent down on one knee before her.

She lost her grin. "What are you doing?"

He opened his hand. "Thought you might like this back."

Her ruby ring—her grandmother's ruby ring—lay nestled in his palm. "Tyler!"

"And, uh, I was also thinking...maybe you'd like to... date me?"

She took the ring. Slid it back onto her finger.

"After we dated a while, we could—"

"Tyler." She cut through his words by sighing his name. "You married me first, and now you want to date me?" A pretend marriage, granted, but it could not be forgotten.

He was still on one knee. "I actually want to marry you. For real this time."

Wild hope flared inside of Esme.

"But I'm trying not to rush you. The Feds and the CIA have just completely cleared your name."

They probably shouldn't have *completely* cleared her name because she had been guilty of some crimes. *A few*. Maybe more than a few. But the people in charge had been overeager to make amends, especially since one of their own —Thaddeus Caldwell—had been as dirty as sin. The joint task force had gotten to work on Esme's behalf. They'd erased all references to her being the Fox from the dark web. They'd also put out a trail of breadcrumbs that indicated the deceased Thaddeus had actually been the Fox.

After all, you couldn't put a bounty on a person who was already dead.

Esme was free and clear. She'd agreed to provide more information to Grayson and his team. Because she was helpful like that.

Grayson had been patched up at the hospital. He'd been pissed as hell at Thaddeus, and with Grayson's testimony—plus the recorded evidence that Ronan had gotten because, yes, he had been wired—Esme and Tyler were both being celebrated for bringing down some very dangerous individuals.

Esme wasn't exactly sure which government agency Ronan had really been working for while he played the role of a hired killer. Though it was certainly a role he'd played well.

At the first opportunity, Ronan had apologized for drugging her. And for not contacting Tyler sooner. It seemed Ronan had waited a while on contacting Tyler because he'd needed to be absolutely sure Jorlan would be alone for their meeting. Once the location had been secured and Jorlan's presence guaranteed, *then* Ronan had texted Kane and Tyler.

Apparently, Ronan hadn't trusted Esme not to blow his cover, so he hadn't told her that she wasn't in danger from him. She had no idea where he would have gotten the idea that she was not the most trustworthy woman on the planet.

Ronan had also not realized that Tyler had been briefly knocked out after he'd fired his shots—he hadn't known about Tyler's concussion. He'd thought Tyler would leap right up to help Clay.

Ronan's apologies had seemed genuine.

Tyler had punched him in response. Twice.

Then they'd gone for drinks. Men could be such asses sometimes.

And, other times, they could be amazing. She admired her ring. She had missed that ring.

But back to what Tyler was saying. The very important things he was saying.

"I think your father may even semi-like me," Tyler told her.

Her father did semi-like him. The father who was not the villain she'd feared. *Like father, like daughter.* Their appearances had been designed to deceive.

"I will be a good husband to you, I swear it. I'll work on my morning mood. I'll try not to be an asshole first thing in the day."

Her hand—with the ruby ring in place—pressed to his cheek.

"I'll try to be a man good enough for you," he told her with his eyes all serious as if he could ever be anything but good in her mind. "And I will work to prove, every single day, that you are the most important person in my life."

"You are too good for me." When would he get that?

"No." An instant denial. "Esme, you are my *everything*."

Sometimes, she couldn't quite believe it. This man loved her. She could see the love when he looked at her. Feel it when he touched her. They'd endured so much, and now, they had the chance to truly be happy.

Clay had survived his surgery. He hadn't been behind the bombing in Paris. Instead, Thaddeus had been the culprit there. Clay *had* set the bomb at the safe house, though. The Feds were in talks with him, as he was being held behind bars. Some sort of deal would probably be made with him, though she didn't know what yet. She *did* know that Tyler and Kane were not in a forgiving mood when it came to the sheriff. Not that she blamed them one bit.

"So, Esme, will you date me? Then, when you're ready, will you marry me?"

She thought they could skip ahead to the important part. "I'm ready right now."

His eyes widened. He also rose to his feet. Towered over her. "Now?"

"I've been half in love with you since Paris. And I am completely and irrevocably in love with you now. You are the man I want. When I think of my future, you're what I see. Only you, Tyler."

"I will make you happy," he vowed.

"I already am."

His hand curled under her chin. He leaned in slowly. His lips feathered over hers.

The door flew open. "I've got the last reports. This case

is closed and you can—*seriously? In my office?*" Grayson's voice rose a very high notch. "Get a room, man."

Tyler lifted his head. His smile warmed her heart. "We're gonna get a marriage license."

"What?" Grayson's shock was clear. "Is this another mission? You two going undercover?"

"No, it's not a mission. It's for real."

"Forever," Esme affirmed.

"Feel like coming to my wedding?" Tyler asked Grayson.

Grayson hurried across the room and slapped a hand on Tyler's shoulder. "Hell, yes, hell, yes!"

* * *

"You're sure about him?" Her father stood with Esme before the closed church doors. She could hear the music playing from inside. But they didn't enter, not yet. "If you're not sure, we can leave right now."

Of course, he would have a quick getaway available for them. Typical.

But Esme shook her head even as she patted his arm. "He's the one for me."

"You love him?"

"With all that I am." With every scheming part of herself. Every hopeful part, too.

Her father inclined his head. His guards—always present—opened the doors for them. Her eyes went straight for the man at the end of the decorated aisle. Tyler.

She walked forward. Her feet brushed over the rose petals that had been left behind by Kady Jo. The little girl and her mother had been invited to the wedding. Esme had a soft spot for them both.

Tyler didn't wait for her to come to him. He bounded toward her. Met her halfway down the aisle.

Kissed her right there.

He was learning to not always follow the rules. She loved that about him. No, she loved everything about him.

Esme would never forget how she'd felt when she saw him rushing to the rescue in that horrid basement. The instant she'd known for certain that death hadn't taken him from her.

The world started spinning again.

Together, she and Tyler walked the rest of the way down the rose-petal-covered aisle. Then it was time for the vows. To swear that she'd love him forever.

Spoiler alert, she would.

Esme released a soft breath as they faced each other.

And that is how even a villain gets her happy ending.

All she had to do was marry a hero. One with a bit of his own dark side.

Bonus Material

Dear Reader,

Thank you for reading WHEN HE PROTECTS! I hope you enjoyed their adventures—Esme certainly kept Tyler on his toes!!

Would you like to read special bonus material for Tyler and Esme? Because even though their book is over, I just had to write a wee bit more for them...in the bonus, you can see what the holidays are like Esme and her very *real* husband, Tyler. You'll get a peek at Halloween, Thanksgiving, and Christmas for them.

To access this bonus material, you just need to fill out a quick form and sign up for my newsletter. I will immediately send you an email that gives you access to the extra material. (And if you are already a subscriber to my newsletter—don't worry, you will not be added twice! Just put your email to the form, and the bonus holiday scenes will be sent your way.)

Sign up for the bonus material: cynthiaeden.com/bonus/whp

Thank you, again! I appreciate you taking the time to read WHEN HE PROTECTS.

Best,

Cynthia Eden

Want to read Ronan's story? Then check out WHEN HE HUNTS.

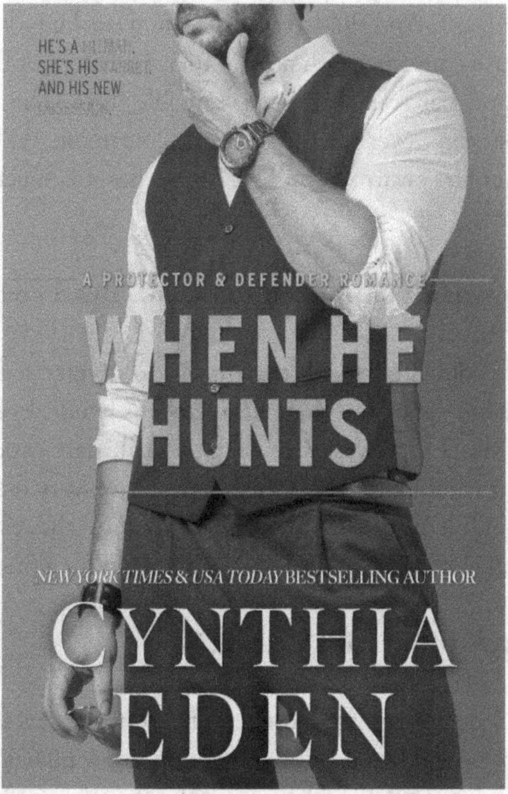

She's a dead woman walking.

Luna Black knows that she's being hunted. The price on her head is astronomical. She was in the wrong place at the wrong time, and she saw some very dangerous people doing some very, very bad things. Now she needs to reach the Feds, stat, *and* get a new identity and a new life. Because her old life? Definitely *over*.

It's not personal. She's just a job.

Ronan Walker lives in the shadows. His job? Simple—to deliver death. And the latest hit has him tracking down the very elusive and unpredictable Luna. But he's not the only hitman on her trail. Luna has valuable intel. The kind of intel that can never see the light of a courtroom. When the other hunters swarm in on her, Ronan has no choice but to intervene.

Death wasn't supposed to be so...dead sexy.

After he defeated the group trying to abduct her, Luna expected to die by the gorgeous stranger's hands. Even as he kissed her, Luna was sure that the tall, dark, and fierce predator would kill her. Only...she woke up, very much *still* alive, and handcuffed to his bed. Before she can even scream, he offers her a deal...protection, but for a price.

Is he a hitman with a heart?

No, he's not. Not even close. His heart never gets involved in a job. Ronan faked Luna's death, and now he has to keep her with him in the shadows until the Feds are ready to use her in order to bring down a massive criminal ring. The problem? He's not exactly used to sharing close quarters with anyone. Especially not someone like Luna...a woman who pushes him to the edge and makes him want to let go of the fierce control that he's kept in place for years.

On the run. Hiding in the shadows. Pretending to be a couple in love...

Sometimes, it's easy to pretend. To act like lovers. But what happens when the pretending starts to feel all too real? The longer they are together, the more Luna realizes there is so much more to Ronan than meets the eye. He protects her, he defends her from every threat, and she...just might be falling hard for the hitman who swears he can never love...

The story of her life. To fall for the man who delivers death.

Author's Note: Ronan deals with death. He's worked undercover as a hitman for years, only seeing the darkest side of life. Then he meets Luna. A woman named for the moon but who feels like sunlight in his arms. No way should he want her as badly as he does. No way should he start to think of Luna as his. But...he does. And anyone coming after Luna will find that Ronam will take "protecting and defending" her to a whole, new level. No one else will touch Luna, no one will hurt her, and he will deliver death to anyone who tries to take her from him.

The story of Mary Hill. To fall for the man who delivers death.

[illegible]

Author's Note

Thank you very, very much for reading WHEN HE PROTECTS. I appreciate you taking the time to read Tyler and Esme's story! This was such a fun book to write. Esme took me along on her journey, and I just held on for the ride! And Tyler...I do love a fiercely protective hero. Especially one who falls so hard and loses his heart so completely!

If you have time, please consider leaving a review for WHEN HE PROTECTS. Reviews help readers to discover new books—and authors are definitely grateful for them!

If you'd like to stay updated on my releases and sales, please join my newsletter list. Did I mention that when you sign up, you get a FREE Cynthia Eden book?

By the way, I'm also active on social media. You can find me chatting away on Instagram and Facebook.

Again, thank you for reading WHEN HE PROTECTS. Thanks for enjoying romance books!

Best,

Cynthia Eden

cynthiaeden.com

More Books By Cynthia Eden

Protector & Defender Romance

- When He Protects

Ice Breaker Cold Case Romance

- Frozen In Ice (Book 1)
- Falling For The Ice Queen (Book 2)
- Ice Cold Saint (Book 3)
- Touched By Ice (Book 4)
- Trapped In Ice (Book 5)
- Forged From Ice (Book 6)
- Buried Under Ice (Book 7)
- Ice Cold Kiss (Book 8)
- Locked In Ice (Book 9)
- Savage Ice (Book 10)
- Brutal Ice (Book 11)

Wilde Ways

- Protecting Piper (Book 1)
- Guarding Gwen (Book 2)
- Before Ben (Book 3)

- The Heart You Break (Book 4)
- Fighting For Her (Book 5)
- Ghost Of A Chance (Book 6)
- Crossing The Line (Book 7)
- Counting On Cole (Book 8)
- Chase After Me (Book 9)
- Say I Do (Book 10)
- Roman Will Fall (Book 11)
- The One Who Got Away (Book 12)
- Pretend You Want Me (Book 13)
- Cross My Heart (Book 14)
- The Bodyguard Next Door (Book 15)
- Ex Marks The Perfect Spot (Book 16)
- The Thief Who Loved Me (Book 17)

The Fallen Series

- Angel Of Darkness (Book 1)
- Angel Betrayed (Book 2)
- Angel In Chains (Book 3)
- Avenging Angel (Book 4)

Wilde Ways: Gone Rogue

- How To Protect A Princess (Book 1)
- How To Heal A Heartbreak (Book 2)
- How To Con A Crime Boss (Book 3)

Night Watch Paranormal Romance

- Hunt Me Down (Book 1)
- Slay My Name (Book 2)
- Face Your Demon (Book 3)

Trouble For Hire

- No Escape From War (Book 1)

- Don't Play With Odin (Book 2)
- Jinx, You're It (Book 3)
- Remember Ramsey (Book 4)

Death and Moonlight Mystery

- Step Into My Web (Book 1)
- Save Me From The Dark (Book 2)

Phoenix Fury

- Hot Enough To Burn (Book 1)
- Slow Burn (Book 2)
- Burn It Down (Book 3)

Dark Sins

- Don't Trust A Killer (Book 1)
- Don't Love A Liar (Book 2)

Lazarus Rising

- Never Let Go (Book One)
- Keep Me Close (Book Two)
- Stay With Me (Book Three)
- Run To Me (Book Four)
- Lie Close To Me (Book Five)
- Hold On Tight (Book Six)

Bad Things

- The Devil In Disguise (Book 1)
- On The Prowl (Book 2)
- Undead Or Alive (Book 3)
- Broken Angel (Book 4)
- Heart Of Stone (Book 5)
- Tempted By Fate (Book 6)
- Wicked And Wild (Book 7)

- Saint Or Sinner (Book 8)

Bite Series

- Forbidden Bite (Bite Book 1)
- Mating Bite (Bite Book 2)

Blood and Moonlight Series

- Bite The Dust (Book 1)
- Better Off Undead (Book 2)
- Bitter Blood (Book 3)

Mine Series

- Mine To Take (Book 1)
- Mine To Keep (Book 2)
- Mine To Hold (Book 3)
- Mine To Crave (Book 4)
- Mine To Have (Book 5)
- Mine To Protect (Book 6)

Dark Obsession Series

- Watch Me (Book 1)
- Want Me (Book 2)
- Need Me (Book 3)
- Beware Of Me (Book 4)

Purgatory Series

- The Wolf Within (Book 1)
- Marked By The Vampire (Book 2)
- Charming The Beast (Book 3)
- Deal with the Devil (Book 4)

Bound Series

- Bound By Blood (Book 1)

- Bound In Darkness (Book 2)
- Bound In Sin (Book 3)
- Bound By The Night (Book 4)
- Bound in Death (Book 5)

Stand-Alone Romantic Suspense

- Waiting For Christmas
- Monster Without Mercy
- Kiss Me This Christmas
- It's A Wonderful Werewolf
- Never Cry Werewolf
- Immortal Danger
- Deck The Halls
- Come Back To Me
- Put A Spell On Me
- Never Gonna Happen
- One Hot Holiday
- Slay All Day
- Midnight Bite
- Secret Admirer
- Christmas With A Spy
- Femme Fatale
- Until Death
- Sinful Secrets
- First Taste of Darkness
- A Vampire's Christmas Carol

About the Author

Cynthia Eden loves romance books, chocolate, and going on semi-lazy adventures. She is a *New York Times*, *USA Today*, *Digital Book World*, and *IndieReader* best-seller. She writes romantic suspense, paranormal romance, and fun contemporary novels. You can find out more about her work at www.cynthiaeden.com.

If you want to stay updated on her new releases and books deals, be sure to join her newsletter group: cynthiaeden.com/newsletter. When new readers sign up for her newsletter, they are automatically given a free Cynthia Eden ebook.

www.ingramcontent.com/pod-product-compliance
Lightning Source LLC
Chambersburg PA
CBHW012141210525
27099CB00012B/473
9781965259108